Praise for Michelle Rowen

'... and a
g... roine
paired with a Brontean hero. Let us welcome this fresh voice to the genre'
Booklist

'Rowen perfectly balances suspense and wit'
Publishers Weekly

'Four stars! Fun and clever . . . this novel is bound to appeal to those who like their romance a little offbeat and definitely humorous'
Romantic Times BOOKreviews

Fanged & Fabulous

'What's a new vampire to do? Win a lot of readers with her upbeat persistence, that's for sure. You can't put *Fanged & Fabulous* down'
Charlaine Harris

'Rowen has done it again. She has written another wonderfully amusing, suspenseful story . . . It's terrific!'
Romance Reviews

'Four stars . . . An exciting, action-packed and often humorous tale . . . a great addition to Rowen's vampire series
Romantic Times BOOKreviews

Lady & the Vamp

'You can't put this book down'
Charlaine Harris

'Michelle Rowen never disappoints! I love her work'
New York Times bestselling author Gena Showalter

'I've been bitten and smitten by Michelle Rowen'
New York Times bestselling author Sherrilyn Kenyon

Also by Michelle Rowen from Gollancz:

Bitten & Smitten

Fanged & Fabulous

Lady & the Vamp

IMMORTALITY BITES

Fanged & Fabulous

Michelle Rowen

First published in Great Britain in 2010 by
Gollancz
An imprint of the Orion Publishing Group
Orion House, 5 Upper St Martin's Lane, London WC2H 9EA
An Hachette UK Company

1 3 5 7 9 10 8 6 4 2

A CIP catalogue record for this book is available
from the British Library

ISBN 978 0 575 09402 4

Printed in Great Britain by Clays Ltd, St Ives plc

The Orion Publishing Group's policy is to use papers that are
natural, renewable and recyclable products and made from wood
grown in sustainable forests. The logging and manufacturing
processes are expected to conform to the environmental regulations
of the country of origin.

www.michellerowen.com
www.orionbooks.co.uk

To Bonnie
Not fanged, but definitely fabulous

Chapter 1

Jogging is great exercise. Running for your life—even better.

At least that's what I tried to tell myself.

It was the new jogging suit that did it. I felt all *J. Lo* in my fuchsia velour (admittedly a little outdated, but happily purchased for half price) out for a quick, late-afternoon jog. Feeling good in the cold but fresh February air with my newest pair of very dark sunglasses firmly in place.

I guess I shouldn't have smiled at the cute young guy by the hot dog cart outside of my apartment building. Firstly, because, hello? I'm *taken*, thank you very much.

Secondly, because of the whole "fang" situation.

Fangs never seem to go over very well with vampire hunters.

Next thing I know, instead of getting a modest work-out—surprisingly enough, a diet of diluted blood is *not* calorie-free—I was hightailing it through a nearly deserted park with a hunter on my Reebok-clad heels.

I shot a look over my shoulder. "Leave me alone!"

"Stop running, vampire!" he hollered.

I eyed the wooden stake he had in his right hand, and then picked up my pace, darting past a couple of speed walkers who didn't bother to give us a second glance.

Almost an entire month had gone by without seeing a single hunter. A *very* good month. Enough for me to let down my guard way too much.

Not good.

"I'll catch you!" the hunter shouted from a few steps behind me. "So why don't you stop running and save me some time?"

I jumped up as we passed an overhang of evergreens and grabbed at the nearest icicle. Then I stopped abruptly and spun around to face him with the sharp piece of ice clenched in my hand.

He skidded to a halt, almost slamming right into me, and looked at me with confusion. "You stopped."

"I'm trying to be more proactive these days. Come near me and this—" I indicated my drippy weapon "—is going through your eyeball."

My heart was beating so hard and fast I thought it might burst out of my chest like the slimy creature in *Alien*. Vampire hearts beat just as hard as human hearts. I never thought they did before I became one. I used to think that vampires were undead. But they aren't. They're just another kind of alive. Heartbeat mandatory to stay that way, otherwise what difference would that famous wooden stake make?

Hunter-boy was actually kind of cute. Probably in his

early twenties, with fashionably shaggy dark hair, a thin but attractive face, and brown puppy-dog eyes. He wore a black leather jacket over . . . beige Dockers?

I could totally take him.

"Proactive?" He raised an eyebrow and shifted the stake to his other hand. The frozen air puffed out of his mouth with every breath he took.

I shivered, and it wasn't just from the temperature. "Yeah, that's acting in advance to deal with an expected difficulty. I looked it up. It means that instead of running like a chicken with my head cut off—pardon the cliché—I will confront my attacker and deal with the situation in a calm yet forceful manner."

"You're smart for a vampire," he said.

I raised my eyebrows at that. "Really?"

"A vampire who's about to die."

I tensed and curled my other hand into a fist. I'd been going to self-defense fitness classes with my best friend Amy for a couple of weeks. It was true that only a few hour-long lessons probably weren't going to earn me any major ass-kicking awards, but I felt a little more confident about my current woman-in-jeopardy situation. A *little*.

Proactive with a capital P. That's me.

Okay, now I was shivering *and* sweating. I take it back. I wasn't confident. Not in the slightest.

Hunter-boy was going to stake me. Easily.

"What's your name?" I blurted out.

"Chad."

"Seriously?"

"Yeah. Why?"

"Is that short for anything?"

"Yeah, it's short for 'I'm going to kill you now.' " He frowned. "Why are you still talking?"

He kicked the icicle out of my hand. It hit the ground next to me and shattered. I blinked at it.

I held my shaking hands up in front of me. "Look . . . Chad, just walk away now. You *do not* want to mess with me." What was I going to do to get out of this alive? To defend myself? I'd go for the groin. Always a good place to start. And end.

"Let me tell you a little something . . . " he paused expectantly and raised his eyebrows.

"Sarah," I offered, without thinking. *Stupid*.

"The only reason you're still talking, Sarah, is because I'm allowing it. I might not look it, but I've dusted over a dozen vamps, this year alone."

I swallowed hard and felt a trickle of perspiration run down my spine.

"Well, if you've killed that many," I said, even less confident now if that was possible, "you should know it's not really dust. It's more like goo."

"Whatever." He looked down at the stake, ran his thumb along the sharp tip, and then glanced over at me. "Now let's get this party started."

Hell, he looked fairly harmless what with the Dockers and all. Guess you can't judge a man by his casual, stain-resistant pants anymore.

I turned and tried to run farther into the park along the snow-covered, cobblestone path, but before I got more than a few steps, I felt his hand clamp down on my shoulder, stopping me in midflee. He spun me around, then shoved me so hard that I stumbled back and fell to the ground in a heap. I scrambled back a few feet on my butt and looked around frantically. We were all alone. Why were we all alone? Where were innocent by-standers when I needed them?

"I'll make it quick." Chad winked at me. "If you stay nice and quiet for me."

Yeah, like that was going to happen. "Are you aware that you're the bad guy?"

That stopped him, but his stony expression didn't change. "What?"

I shuffled back a little more, feeling the cold snow against my bare hands. "Vampire hunters are evil, homicidal bastards who kill for the fun of it. They're the bad guys. Vampires are completely harmless. Like adorable, pointy-toothed bunnies."

He laughed a little at that and stepped closer. "Yeah, right."

I held a hand up in front of me to stop him from getting any nearer and slowly and shakily rose to my feet.

Keep him talking, I told myself.

I tried to smile and felt my cheeks twitch nervously. "Let's talk big picture here, Chad. Do you know what you'd be doing if you murder me?"

"*Slay*, you mean."

I shook my head. "Don't try to make it sound all Hollywood. You'd be *murdering* me. Just because you think I'm a monster. But I'm not a monster. I'm just a little dentally different than you."

He studied me for a moment, his expression growing uncertain. "You drink blood, don't you?"

I made a face. It sounded so gross. "This is true. But it's provided by willing donors. There's kegs of the stuff, hopefully sanitized and homogenized or whatever they do to make it clean and disease-free."

"You're an undead creature of the night." He frowned and jabbed the stake in my general direction.

I looked up and pointed at the sky. "Sun's still up, isn't it? And I'm breathing. Heart's going all pitty-pat. Seriously, you need to read up a little on the topic. Take some notes."

Chad sighed heavily. "You're saying that everything I've been told all my life—everything I've ever believed—has all been a lie. That I haven't been doing my job as a protector of mankind by ridding it of blood-sucking monsters, I've actually been killing innocent people."

I nodded enthusiastically. "Bingo!"

He stared at me for a moment and then snorted. "You're funny. That's almost enough for me to let you live, but you know what? Not going to happen."

Bingo denied.

I tried to scramble away from him, but he grabbed my fuchsia-covered leg and pulled me back until he was completely on top of me, pinning my arms under his knees so all I could do was thrash from side to side like a wounded seal. He grabbed my face and squeezed, making my mouth open up so he could inspect my fangs. He ran a thumb over one of them.

"I usually take these from the young ones I slay. Got myself a nice necklace now."

I sank my teeth (fangs included) into his hand as deep as I could, and he pulled away with surprise and a sudden yelp of pain.

He smacked me across the side of my face. "Shouldn't have done that, vampire."

"You touch me again and my boyfriend is going to rip your lungs out," I hissed.

"Yeah?" He smirked and looked around from his position on top of me. "I don't think I see your boyfriend anywhere. Or anyone else for that matter. It's just you and me."

"He's a master vampire and he's not a big fan of hunters. Lungs? Ripped out? Do I need to repeat myself?"

That got his attention. "A master vampire? In Toronto? There's only one that I've heard of."

"That's him. Do I need to mention the ripping out of lungs again?"

His raised stake lowered slightly, and his brow furrowed. "Did you say your name was Sarah?"

"So what if I did?"

"Sarah *Dearly*?"

I struggled to get out from under him but he had me pinned too firmly. "Get off me, you bastard."

Surprisingly, he did. As if there were wires attached to his body like a marionette, he sprang to his feet and stared at me with a deep frown while I slowly got up and brushed myself off.

"Sarah Dearly," he repeated. "The master vampire's girlfriend."

I glanced at him warily. "How do you know my name?"

His eyes widened. He breathed in a deep breath of cold air and let it out slowly before he spoke again. "Everyone knows about you."

"Everyone?"

"The Slayer of Slayers." He said it under his breath and took a step backward.

"The what of the what?"

"Last month . . . the massacre at the vampire lair. You killed so many hunters . . . so many . . . " His voice trailed off and he brought a hand to his mouth.

What in the hell was he talking about?

He took another step backward and hit the thick trunk of a tall oak tree next to a park bench. "I . . . I . . . should never have . . . " His eyes shifted back and forth and I noticed the hand that held the stake was now shaking. "Please, spare me. That whole thing earlier, me acting all tough . . . that was just an act. The other hunters . . . they're so mean, and they all think I'm weak. I was just out for a hot dog and a Coke, that's all. Please, don't hurt me. I was kidding about the fang necklace! Really!"

Last month, there had been a hunter/vampire showdown at the Midnight Eclipse, my boyfriend (sounds like a silly thing to call a six-hundred-year-plus-old vampire, but that's what he was) Thierry's secret vampire bar.

It was true that the night in question was a major deal, that a lot of people got hurt, both hunter and vampire, and that I may have . . . possibly . . . *sort of* . . . had to kill a hunter named Peter, jerk that he was. But that had been pure self-defense—and something I was still feeling great gobs of greasy guilt from, even though he'd majorly deserved it. And it had been with a gun, not with my bare teeth as Chad seemed to indicate with the fearing-for-his-life expression on his now-sweaty face.

Now everyone knows my name?

The theme song from *Cheers* suddenly began to play in my head.

I took a step toward him and he fell to his knees, the stake falling to the ground. He put his hands together and began to pray in barely coherent whispers. With a trembling hand he reached inside his shirt to pull out a heavy silver cross, which he then held up to ward himself against me.

I sighed. *Let's just nip this in the bud, shall we?*

I closed the remaining distance between us, reached forward, and grabbed the cross to show him that it didn't hurt me at all. It was quite pretty, actually. And shiny. His eyes widened in fear.

Then I grabbed his shirt and pulled him up to his feet—easy to do since he was like a rag doll now—then brought him close enough that our eyeballs were only inches from each other.

"I will let you live . . . *today*," I said, calmly and dangerously. I used to aspire to become a world-famous, well-paid actress, so I just called on that questionable ability to give my words a little extra weight. "But if you or your friends come near me again, I shall bathe in your blood."

Ew. Did I just say that? How disgusting.

But it seemed to get my point across. Chad was now the one scrambling backward, nodding like a lunatic, saying, "Yes, yes, I promise," over and over again. Then he got shakily to his feet, and with a last look of fear—

the intense kind one might have just before losing total bladder control—he turned and ran from the park like the proverbial bat out of hell.

I leaned over and picked the stake up from where Chad the Vampire Slayer had dropped it and studied it for a moment. I had to go find Thierry, tell him what had happened here, and ask him what I should do about it. If anybody would know, he would. He just wasn't going to be too happy about it.

Slayer of Slayers, huh?

I threw the stake into a nearby garbage can.

That new little nickname was *so* going to come back to bite me in the ass.

I first tried calling Thierry's cell phone, but it immediately took me into voicemail, which was frustrating at the best of times. He wasn't at his townhome, either. So I'd gone back to my apartment to change, then paced back and forth impatiently until eight o'clock when I knew somebody would be at his new vampire club. It didn't open for another hour, but some of the staff would already be there setting things up.

It had only been one week since Haven opened. I didn't like the place as much as Midnight Eclipse. Instead of being hidden behind the façade of a tanning salon, the entrance to Haven was a plain-looking door located along an abandoned alleyway. No bells, no whistles. Just an ugly, three-hundred-pound vampire bouncer named Angel (unfortunately, no relation or even a passing resemblance to David Boreanaz) who sized up vamps who came a-knocking.

Typically the entrance was also monitored by Barry Jordan, the manager of the club. He was extremely short and usually dressed in a tuxedo as well as a sour and annoyed expression. The guy hated me with a passion. Can't say I was all that thrilled with him either. Unfortunately he recently married my best friend Amy, who seemed to like him just fine for some odd reason.

Barry had a really annoying habit of calling Thierry "the master," which was very Renfield, and kind of creepy. And he seemed to have a big problem with those who did not refer to him that way. Namely, *me*.

Barry wasn't at Haven tonight. It must have been his night off.

The club was small, intimate, with dark walls, ornately carved cherry wood tables and chairs. A splash of color came from the blue and teal ceramic tiled floor, which had a swirling pattern like a whirlpool. Actually it looked more like a flushing toilet, if you ask me. Modern chandeliers dripped from the ceiling, filling the club with a soft, flickering light that filled me with anything but ease. I was way too stressed out by the time I got there.

"Where's Thierry?" I blurted out as I entered the club.

George was lighting a candle on a nearby table and he looked up at me. "Do you realize how often you enter a room saying that?"

I blinked at him.

"You could come in here with a 'Hi George, how are you doing George,'" he continued. "But, *no*. It's all about Thierry."

I felt a wave of anxiety. "I need to find him. I have a major problem."

He rolled his eyes. George was a waiter at the club. He'd also worked at Midnight Eclipse, and I considered him one of my very best fanged friends. Totally gorgeous, too. He had shoulder-length sandy blond hair, a square jaw, high cheekbones, full lips, and bedroom eyes. A body like a Chippendales dancer, or one of those hottie male models on the covers of romance novels. Yeah, George was damn hot.

Too bad he played for the other team.

"Marco dumped me," he announced.

"Who's Marco?"

"My boyfriend." He frowned. "You knew that already."

I shrugged, feeling too distracted to fully concentrate on what he was saying.

"He was one of the construction workers who worked on the club," he said.

"Oh. Well, I'm sorry. I'm sure you'll . . . I don't know . . . meet somebody else." I glanced around the dimly lit club. "So where's Thierry?"

He sighed and leaned against the table. "Your lack of compassion for my acute depression is duly noted. What's your *trauma du jour*, anyhow?"

I quickly explained what had happened, starting with the jog and ending with my new nickname. George whistled.

"Well, that explains all these crazy rumors I've been hearing," he said. "About some badass vampire in town. I never realized it was you. No offense."

My anxiety increased another notch. "There are rumors? Already? What am I going to do?"

He appeared to think about it. "You should probably talk to Thierry."

"Well, *duh*."

I felt a rough tap on my shoulder and I turned around. A husky man wearing a dark blue ski jacket presented me with a fang-filled grin. "You Veronique?"

I stared at him blankly. "Not even remotely. Who are you?"

"I'm her ride to the airport."

There was a sudden change in the air and I knew without a doubt the woman in question had just entered the room. The scent of expensive perfume wafted under my nostrils. I'd been turned into a vampire exactly seven weeks ago and my sense of smell had been growing daily. This was sometimes a blessing and sometimes—depending on where in the city I was walking—not so much.

I turned to watch her glide through the club.

Veronique eyed the driver and her red lips curved up to the right. "If you could give me one moment to say good-bye to my friend I would greatly appreciate it."

He nodded, immediately intoxicated by the gorgeous woman with long raven hair, flawless skin, and remarkably white and sparkly fangs.

She glanced at the leaning tower of George and her eyes narrowed. "Shouldn't you be working?"

"I was . . . I was just going to . . . " he stammered, then gave me a stricken look. "Um . . . I'll go find Thierry." He scurried away.

Well, her charms didn't work on everyone.

But I liked Veronique. Actually I liked her a lot, but there was one big thing about her I wasn't terribly fond of.

She was Thierry's wife.

I had been assured that their marriage was in name only after more than six hundred years. Frankly, I couldn't imagine knowing somebody for thirty years, let alone six hundred. But I still wasn't thrilled with the situation. Dating a married man, even though the wife was fine and dandy with it, just seemed . . . *extremely* wrong.

I'd recently summoned enough courage to ask if she'd ever considered getting a divorce. Veronique had waved off my question with a laugh and said, "After so many years, why would I want something like that?"

Yeah. I'd managed to refrain from digging my fingernails into her perfect eyeballs. Barely.

So, as I said, I liked Veronique. But her recent decision to go back to her fabulous life in France wasn't the most heartbreaking news I'd heard all year.

She gave me a tight hug, followed by a brief kiss on each of my cheeks. "*Au revoir.*" She leaned back. "Are you all right, my dear?"

I forced a smile. "I'm fine. Have a nice flight. Bye now."

"Are you quite certain? You look a little . . . *malheureux.*"

"I failed French in high school. But I feel fine." I shrugged. *Well, other than narrowly escaping death only hours ago*, I thought. *Again.*

I looked over my shoulder. Where the hell was Thierry?

"I think I know what it is." A smile played at her perfectly outlined lips. "You are afraid to admit how much you will miss me. I understand. But the time that I was needed here has passed and yours has just begun."

My eyebrow perked up at that. Was she talking about Thierry? Maybe she'd given the divorce thing more thought. I shifted my feet, which now, instead of the Reeboks from my near-death jog, sported low-heeled, rubber-soled Tender Tootsies that looked okay with my black jeans. My trendier footwear was currently piled up at the back of my closet to make way for that which was consistently comfortable and easy to run in.

Proactive = Me.

Veronique reached into her tiny Fendi bag, pulled out a business card, and handed it to me.

"That is the number to my home in Paris. If you ever need to talk to someone, please don't hesitate to call me. I know things will soon be difficult for you."

I glanced at the card and then tucked it into the pocket of my jeans. "So you've heard about the hunters' special new interest in me, too? Wow, rumors sure spread quickly, don't they?"

Her forehead creased prettily. "No . . . though that is certainly cause for concern. I was referring to how distraught you will be when my Thierry leaves you."

"Huh?" My forehead creased less prettily, and I scanned the nearly empty club again. "What? He's leaving me? When did this happen?"

She shook her head. "No, not yet, my dear. I'm simply saying that when it does happen, please feel free to call me. I can dispense invaluable advice to help mend your broken heart."

My eyes widened with every word.

The driver approached her. "We should be leaving now to catch your flight, ma'am."

I just stared at Veronique. "Did Thierry say something to you? Is that why I can't find him tonight? Is he avoiding me?"

She smiled patiently at me. "It is so sweet how taken you are with him. I am not saying this to upset you, but it is quite obvious that this will only be a short-term relationship."

"Short-term?"

"You have known him for what . . . less than two months, yes? I know he feels a great sense of responsibility for your safety. From the attention he has paid you, it is understandable that you would become greatly smitten with him."

"Smitten?" I sputtered. "You think I'm *smitten*?"

She frowned slightly at my words. "Thierry is almost seven hundred years old. You are . . . what? In your mid-thirties?"

"I AM TWENTY-EIGHT!"

"There is no reason to shout, my dear. I am trying to be a friend to you and tell you how things truly are, so you will not be shocked by how things inevitably turn out. I have known Thierry for so, so many years. I know him better than anyone else. I am simply warning you to prepare for his interest to wane." She touched my arm. "I am sorry."

The driver cleared his throat loudly. "If we don't leave soon, ma'am, I'm afraid you'll miss your flight and then I'll—"

I spun around. "And then you'll *what*?" I snapped.

He took a step backward. "Never mind. Take all the time you need."

Veronique shook her head. "*Mon dieu.* I should not have said anything. It is simply my desire to see those I care about happy. Being in love with a man such as Thierry will not bring you happiness. He is too old for you. There are too many secrets. Simply too much against you. I apologize for being blunt, but I have only done so as a friend."

It was difficult to be friends with somebody who had been effortlessly perfect for seven centuries. She'd seen everything and done everything at least once. Plus, she had really great hair.

She also had a nasty habit of being right.

I ran a quick hand under my nose, sniffed, and tried to compose myself. "You'd better go. Don't want to miss your plane."

Veronique nodded. "Of course. Take care, my dear."

She looked at me with concern for a moment longer. Then, with a single glance at the driver, she left the club without another word.

I took in a deep breath and let it out slowly and shakily as I tried to compose myself.

"*When my Thierry leaves you.*" Her words kept repeating in my mind like a bad burrito. "*It is quite obvious that this will only be a short-term relationship.*"

I shook my head. No. Thierry wasn't going to break

my heart. Our relationship was on solid ground. Rock steady.

Even though he was absolutely perfect and I was far from it, I wanted us to work out. I'd do whatever it took to prove to him that I was the right woman for him. Long-term.

Sure, he'd been a little distracted lately with trying to open the new club in record time. I'd barely seen him at all for the last couple of weeks, but that didn't mean a thing.

Not a damn thing.

It was only a little over two weeks ago that we'd gotten back from a fantastic trip to Mexico. Romance. Margaritas. Sunscreen.

It could have been better, I suppose. Even while staying mostly out of the blaringly bright sun, I'd still managed to get a serious burn on my back that made it difficult to move without screaming. Thierry warned me about staying out of the sun, but I hadn't listened to him. Vampires are not killed by sunlight as is the popular myth. However, it still makes us a bit weaker physically and annoyed by the brightness of the "big ball of fire death" in the sky, which is what I call it now, ever since the sunburn from hell. Especially after going through vats of Noxzema during the healing process. Talk about putting a major crimp in your love life.

After getting back, Thierry focused all his attention on the club. But now that it was open . . .

I glanced around. Where in the hell was he, anyhow?

No. I couldn't think about this right now. I had rumors to worry about. Hunters to hide from. Etcetera.

Veronique was crazy. Thierry and I were just fine. Sure he was a little distant, but that was just the way he was. We had a deep, romantic *connection*.

Well . . .

Except for the fact that we hadn't had sex since Mexico. Oh, didn't I mention that? Yeah. Might be a problem.

I swallowed hard.

Maybe Veronique wasn't so crazy.

"Sarah—" a deep, familiar voice said from behind me. "George says you're looking for me?"

Chapter 2

I turned around to face Thierry. Sometimes when I'm out of his company for a while I forget how easily he takes my breath away.

He was, without a doubt, the most handsome man I'd ever seen in real life. Dark, almost black hair framed his face. His skin was pale—he tended to avoid the sun as much as possible even though it didn't hurt him—but glowed with an inner power. His intense eyes were gray, with thick dark lashes—gray eyes that sometimes seemed silver. And it wasn't just his looks: tall, dark, and handsome; a man who moved with grace and presence. It was his very essence. Without even trying, he became the focus of any room he was in. All eyes, female and male, were immediately drawn to him.

"Thierry," I said, my voice sounding awkward all of a sudden. "I . . . I've been trying to find you."

"I know." His forehead furrowed and he stepped closer to me, close enough that I could breathe in his cologne—

spicy and masculine. "I'm glad you're here. Are you all right?"

I let out a long, shuddery sigh. I didn't like to appear too shaken by anything that happened. I guess I thought it made me seem weak and needy. Therefore I ended up coming off a little flippant to some people. Covering my fears with a sarcastic comment. It usually worked. But the events of the day were tough to shake off. "I've been better."

He closed the remaining distance between us and brought a hand under my chin, prompting me to meet his silver-eyed gaze. "Tell me."

So I did. I told him all about Chad the hunter. About my new "Slayer of Slayers" nickname. About the taxi driver who'd dropped me off tonight and how he'd freaked out when he looked in the rearview mirror and noticed it didn't reflect anyone in the back seat. Really had to remember to only use the vampire-owned cab companies. It was such a hassle waiting for them to show up, but definitely worth it for the lack of screaming.

I told Thierry everything except for the doubts Veronique had managed to wedge into my brain about him and me. The stuff that made me want to both fight like crazy to keep him and run away and hide. He listened to my tirade right through to the end without saying a word.

Then he nodded. "I feared this."

"You did?"

"Yes. Sarah, I would like to tell you not to be concerned, but this is very serious. I have been on the telephone for the last two hours dealing with this very situation." A shadow crossed his expression. "I was worried that what happened at Midnight Eclipse would not go unnoticed—that the hunters would see you as more of a threat to their safety than you truly are."

I didn't like how serious he looked.

"So I've got a reputation." I tried to make my voice sound way lighter than I felt. "Just like back in high school. By the way, that one was a big lie, too."

He frowned at me and held my gaze, then ran his fingers through my shoulder-length brown hair. I caught his hand in mine.

"Look," I said. "It'll be okay. I got away from Chad. It was no big deal. I'll just avoid going anywhere hunters may be hanging out. It'll blow over, right?"

"I sometimes forget how young you are."

"Veronique seems to think I'm in my midthirties. Is it wrong for me to say I'm glad she's gone?"

A small smiled played at the edge of his lips. "You have only been a vampire for a short time. There are still many things you need to learn."

"That's why I have you."

"Then I have failed you. For hunters are not the only things in this world to be wary of. So many things would do you harm now. Even those of your own kind."

"My own kind?" I blinked with confusion. "Other vampires?"

He nodded. "Yes."

"But vampires are just like regular people. I just told Chad we're like pointy-toothed bunnies. Cute and harmless."

He raised an eyebrow. "You actually said that to him?"

I shrugged. "I was grasping at straws. I admit it."

"I have spoken with several of my informants who tell

me that the rumors quickly spreading about your skills as a vampire have caught the attention of hunter and vampire alike. There are those of both factions who would see that as a threat. Also, those who would like to use your skills and reputation for other purposes."

I nodded slowly. "In other words, I'm screwed."

His gaze flicked to mine. "In a word, yes."

I felt a line of perspiration slide down my spine. "So we just spread the word that it's all a big fat lie. No harm done."

He shook his head. "It's too late for that, I'm afraid. Too many hunters know. And . . . " he paused, "there are other vampires . . . *elder* vampires who will be interested in learning more about you as well. One of whom, I am told, is en route to Toronto as we speak. If they find out the rumors are a lie and that you are no more dangerous than you truly are, they'll . . . " He trailed off.

"They'll what?"

He took a deep breath and let it out slowly. "It is likely that they will kill you before it gets out . . . so your reputation will remain intact and you will become a martyr to vampires worldwide."

"You are shitting me." I blinked hard. "Why didn't you tell me about this?"

"Because I only learned of the depth of this problem today."

"So what am I supposed to do?"

He glanced around the club. We were completely alone for the moment. "You have told me you were an actress once, correct?"

"*Aspiring*. Then I realized I needed to eat daily, so I had to get a real job."

"You must not tell anyone that the rumors are not true. You must act as if you are a dangerous vampire whom no one should trifle with. If we hold up this façade for a few days, I feel that all will pass without harm. The elders will be satisfied, and most hunters will fear you enough to leave you alone."

I let this sink in. "This is your plan?"

He nodded gravely.

"Your plan sucks. No offense."

He raised a dark eyebrow. "I am well aware of that. But it is the best I have at the moment."

"So I'm just supposed to walk around like nothing's wrong. And when a hunter moseys by and stakes me, I'm just supposed to ignore the big piece of wood sticking out of my chest?" My voice shook with every word. The line of perspiration along my spine had turned into a small waterfall.

He hesitated, then his worried gaze met my own. "I have just now arranged for bodyguards to follow you for the next couple of days. They are not the ones I originally requested, but they come highly recommended. They arrive tomorrow and will ensure your safety."

"Bodyguards." I repeated. "Great. Just great. I think I'm going to be sick."

"Do you trust me?" he asked.

"Of course I do. But what should I do tonight?"

He glanced at the bar. "I do need a bartender to fill in. The new bartender I hired seems to feel that it would be too dangerous to work here, so he resigned early this afternoon."

"You want me to make drinks all night?"

"It will keep you close to me. And safe. And yes, I want you to make drinks."

I glanced over at the long, shiny bar—an exact replica of the one that had been in Midnight Eclipse. "Okay, fine. If you say it will be okay, then I believe you. I'll go along with this plan. I'll let your bodyguards guard my body." I paused and let it all sink in. "But I want something in return for being all agreeable."

"What's that?"

"Tomorrow night we spend some time together. Just you and me."

A trace of amusement slid behind his silver eyes. "You are asking me out on a date?"

"I need something normal in all of this craziness. And you've been so busy that I haven't spent any quality time with you in weeks. So what do you say? A little wine, a little music, a little . . . *privacy*?" I gave him a shaky, yet hopefully flirtatious smile.

I wanted to spend some much-needed alone time with the man I was crazy about. Show him that there was more to me than just a sunburned, ex-actress, substitute bartender. Prove that I was the woman he wanted to be with now and in the future.

It would also be the perfect way for me to find out if Veronique was right in her prediction. And, truth be told, I really didn't know a great deal about the beautiful man in front of me. He was a true master at avoiding questions. When I asked him something about himself, about his past, he'd turn it back around on me and I'd end up telling him about my life instead. Everything I knew about him, other than what was plain to the eye, I'd been told by other people. And I wanted a chance to change that. I wanted to know everything I could about him.

I actually expected him to say no. That things were too serious to have some fun. That would be so him.

He studied me for a moment, and then nodded with the smallest motion of his head. "Tomorrow, then."

"Really? I mean, great. That's great. Tomorrow." I tried to refrain from smiling too widely at the thought of having Thierry all to myself without any other distractions. "Okay, so I'll make drinks. You win. And if anyone wants to know more about the Slayer of Slayers, I'll lie my ass off."

"Just make the drinks and try not to draw too much attention to yourself."

"But, you said—"

"The bodyguards do not arrive till tomorrow."

I nodded. "Good point. Fine. I'll be as quiet as a little booze-serving mouse. With pointy teeth."

He smiled. "Very good. I'll be in my office."

I smiled back and closed my eyes waiting for a kiss. But no kiss came. I opened my eyes.

Thierry was gone, as if he'd never been there in the first place, leaving me standing there in the middle of the floor all alone.

"He's completely wrong for you, you know."

I blinked and tried to focus my wandering thoughts. "What did you just say?"

George gave me a look of annoyance over the bar. "These drinks. They're completely wrong."

I frowned and glanced down at the drink tray. "They are?"

"Yeah. Sarah, honey, pull it together, would you?"

I gave him a dirty look. I'd been on my feet making drinks for nearly three hours by then. A quick check of the little clock that sat between the Margarita blender and the keg of O-negative told me it was almost midnight. I was starting to feel a strange sense of gratitude toward my comfy shoes.

"Okay, give me a break. I'm new at this. What was the order again?"

He looked at the pad of paper in his hand. "Well, let's see. Three vodka shots, five A-positives on the rocks, and a bowl of tortilla chips."

I looked down at the tray, which held two Margaritas and a Coors Light. "I was close."

Another waitress came up to the bar and I filled her order while George waited. He didn't seem to be in that much of a rush to get back on the floor. Thankfully, it was a slow night. Only a few tables were filled with blood-thirsty vampires. The sound system played a mix of easy-listening music. I could hear Michael Bublé crooning "Kissing a Fool."

When we were alone again, I fixed his drinks, then as he was about to turn away, I grabbed his arm. "George, about that Slayer of Slayers thing I was telling you about?"

"Personally I like it. It sounds super sexy."

"Um. Thanks, I guess. Listen, don't tell anyone it's not true."

He looked at me quizzically. "Why not?"

"Just trust me, okay?"

He shrugged. "Honey, I got a ton of my own problems to worry about without adding yours to the mix. No offense."

I sighed. "Just don't tell anyone it's not true. Got it?"

"Gotten. I see since Barry isn't here tonight, you've taken on the title of Little Miss Bossy?"

"And I wear that title proudly."

He left with his drinks and I absently ran a wet cloth along the surface of the bar top. I was overthinking everything. That's all this was. Ever since I'd been fired from my last job for sucking a drop of blood off my boss's injured finger—I still shudder at the embarrassing and rather disgusting memory—I'd been "in between jobs," aka *Very Unemployed*. I'd helped out where I could in getting the club up and running, but other than that I had a lot of time on my hands for worrying, thinking, and letting things fester away in my mind until they grew completely out of proportion.

My meager savings account was slowly dwindling away. I didn't particularly want to bartend at Haven for the rest of my immortal life. I mean, George had recently told me he'd been a waiter for over twenty-five years. Yikes. I needed to start making some decisions about what I was going to do to make ends meet. I couldn't live on credit forever.

Well, maybe for a couple more months.

Out of the corner of my eye, I saw a blond-haired male sidle up to the bar.

I didn't look up. "George, can you watch the bar for a sec? I need to go on a bathroom break."

"Who's George?"

My eyes widened and I looked up at the unfamiliar, lightly accented voice. Was that Russian?

A very attractive, well-over-six-feet, muscular, blond

vampire gazed at me from the other side of the bar. He smiled.

"May I have a Jack Daniels on the rocks before you head to the ladies' room?"

Feeling embarrassed, I nodded, and reached under the bar to grab the bottle and pour out the drink. I slid the glass across the bar to him.

His eyes were green. Very green. Like little green laser beams that fixed directly on me, making me acutely self-conscious. "This is a nice place. You just opened?"

"Last week."

"I had some trouble finding it."

"That's sort of the point. We don't want just anyone walking in here unannounced."

"No, wouldn't want that."

George appeared next to the man. "Well, hello there, handsome. Welcome to Haven."

"Thank you."

"You should come and sit in my section." He eyed me. "You don't mind, do you Miss *Slayer of Slayers*?"

"Um." I blinked. "Of course not."

The man glanced at George, and then back at me. "Slayer of Slayers?"

"That's right," George confirmed, with a knowing wink at me. "Our little Sarah here's been kicking some hunter butt. She's totally my hero."

Now the man's attention was focused completely on me. "You're Sarah Dearly?"

I tensed. "Maybe. Who are you?"

He stared at me long enough that I felt like I wanted to crawl away and hide. I felt goosebumps form on my arms.

After another moment he flashed his fangs at me and finally spoke. "You are not at all what I expected."

"You were expecting something?"

"Yes, of course. What I have heard led me to believe that you'd be larger, older . . . and *much* less attractive."

Hmm. Maybe this guy wasn't so bad after all.

"Well, you know what they say about rumors," I said.

"Slayer of Slayers. Yes, this is good. Very good." He stood up from the stool and leaned over the bar, his face coming within inches of my own. I froze in place, not knowing if I should back away from him or not.

A hand clamped down on his shoulder, bringing him firmly back down to a seated position on the barstool.

Thierry stood next to him. "Nicolai." His voice was void of expression.

Nicolai tore his gaze from me and turned to the other vampire, surprise registering on his face for a split second. "Thierry."

I watched them as they stared at each other and felt tension rising in the air.

Thierry finally broke the silence. "What are you doing here?"

Nicolai regarded him for a moment, his expression far from pleasant. "Is that any way to greet an old friend? I'm disappointed in you."

"You haven't answered my question."

Nicolai glanced at me. "Thierry, after so many years, you still manage to surprise me. I had no idea this club was yours. And hiding an angel away in a dark place such as this? What an absolute waste."

Thierry's gaze flicked to me. "Sarah is my bartender." And that's all he said.

I felt the blood drain from my face. His bartender.

"Yes," Nicolai said. "I can see that much. It all begins to make sense to me now. It was at one of your other clubs that the confrontation with the hunters took place in early December?"

Thierry crossed his arms. "An event I wish to leave behind us, for the sake of everyone's safety. That is why we moved to another location."

"I have heard all about it." Nicolai turned to me again. "Such power in such a petite form. I am very impressed."

"Thanks," I said. "By the way, that drink was five bucks."

He grinned and took a wallet from the inner pocket of his jacket. He placed a hundred-dollar bill on the bar. "Keep the change."

"I think I like you," I said.

"The feeling is entirely mutual."

"Who are you, anyhow?"

"Nicolai is a vampire elder," Thierry said. "Whom I hope is only passing through town."

That surprised me. I'd expected a vampire elder to have a long white beard and walk with a cane. Not look like that Russian boxer who kicked Stallone's butt in *Rocky IV*. Live and learn.

"Yes, I will not be here long. I have been in town on other business, but I wanted to investigate the rumors I've recently heard before I leave. Of the Slayer of Slayers." His gaze moved leisurely down my face and neck to my chest. "Is it true that you killed eight hunters that night without sustaining a single injury?"

"It was nine," I lied. "And I *did* break a nail. See? Rumors can't be trusted."

One hunter named Peter who wanted me dead. One gun. Me or him. Nightmares ever since that woke me almost every night in tears.

Yeah, it was good being the Slayer of Slayers. Big fun.

I glanced over at Thierry. Thierry, my boyfriend, who had referred to me just a minute ago as his bartender. I didn't think I liked that very much. But maybe he figured that our personal lives were none of Nicolai's business. Plus he said some vampires were dangerous, and I knew this dude was one of them. I could feel it. His age, his power, crawling up my arms like dancing ants.

Nicolai nodded. "Your talents are being wasted here. I would like you to consider joining the Ring."

"Forget it," Thierry said quickly.

"What's the Ring?" I asked. "Does it have anything to do with that scary movie with the creepy little girl in the well? Because that really freaked me out."

He laughed. "The Ring is a group of vampire elders who act as counsel to the vampire community."

"A useless organization of self-involved, power-hungry opportunists who love to hear themselves talk," Thierry growled.

Nicolai's smile grew cold. "We do what we must to survive. And we do what we must to help others of our kind survive. However, we prefer to do so in the open, not hiding in the safety of the nearest dark corner." He looked around the club. "Interesting that this place is so hard to find, isn't it? Still hiding from the past, my friend?"

George approached with another drink order, but the look Thierry shot him was enough to make him quickly scamper away.

"As you said, we all do what we must for survival," he

replied simply, his face and voice regaining a lack of any discernible emotion. However, I could have sworn the temperature in the club had just dropped about ten degrees.

My eyes had widened at their exchange. "Time for another drink?"

Nicolai glanced at me with a tight smile. "That would be nice."

I poured another shot of Jack Daniels. Nicolai produced another hundred-dollar bill that he held out to me. I reached forward to take it but he pulled it out of my reach.

"As I was saying, the Ring is interested in meeting with you to discuss your future with our organization. Your involvement would, with your admirable reputation, inject the Ring with new energy in our fight against the hunters. The fact that you also appear to be young, beautiful, and charismatic will only help."

Beautiful, huh?

"She will not consider it," Thierry said.

"I believe that is a choice for Sarah, not for you." He turned back to me. "I will be in town for three more days. Think about it. I will be in contact again."

"No," Thierry said.

Nicolai frowned at him, then a smile curled up his lips and he glanced at me. "I think I see what is going on here. The two of you are romantically involved, I take it? I believe I have also heard rumors that Sarah is involved with a master vampire."

I opened my mouth to answer, but before I could, Thierry did it for me.

"No, we are not involved in that way. I am simply concerned for Sarah's future safety."

I blinked as my breath caught in my chest. Right. Not involved. There it is, then. Veronique was right.

I tried to meet his eyes, but he wouldn't look directly at me.

Nicolai laughed at that. "I believe Sarah has proven that she needs no one to look after her."

"I disagree."

"Of course you do." Nicolai stared at him for a long moment before he spoke. "You owe me, Thierry. Do not get in the way of this. Unless there is some other reason you wish to protect her?"

He owed him? What was that supposed to mean?

I watched Thierry to see his reaction. His face was so tense I thought it might shatter. His throat worked as he swallowed. He broke the staring contest between the two of them first.

"Of course Sarah can do as she likes," he finally said.

I let all of it wash over me and ended up feeling dizzy. This was all happening too fast for me to properly register what was going on.

Nicolai wanted me to consider joining the vampire elders because he believed the rumors about me to be true. I wasn't supposed to reveal that it was all a big misunderstanding, otherwise I would be killed so the reputation would stay intact. Got that. Crappy corner to paint myself into, to say the least, but I was on board with that.

Thierry didn't refer to me in mixed company as his girlfriend or even hint that I was any more to him than an employee.

Not on board with that. But there were more important things to focus on at the moment.

I cleared my throat. "So you want my answer before you leave town."

"That's correct," Nicolai said. "It is quite an honor to be asked. To be honest, I expected you to agree right away."

He thought I'd jump right on the vampire bandwagon of rallying the troops by joining some organization I'd never heard of? Who did I look like, Bob Hope?

What a mess.

Ever since being turned into a vampire, all I had wanted was my normal life back. For a short time, I even thought there was a cure for vampirism, which I pursued with great gusto. That ended in disappointment and betrayal. I was sick of being disappointed and betrayed.

It seriously caused wrinkles.

I didn't want this reputation. I didn't want to be constantly hunted like a monster in a video game. I didn't ask to be a vampire. So far, not too impressed with the whole deal.

I just wanted a normal immortal life with my six-centuries-old boyfriend. Was that too much to ask for? And what did I have to do to get it?

Even if the rumors *were* true, there was nothing Nicolai could say to persuade me to consider joining this Ring thing. Nothing at all.

"If you agree," Nicolai said, "we are willing to pay a salary of one hundred thousand dollars a year plus living expenses for your time."

"One-fifty," I said.

"Done." He nodded, smiled, and downed the last of his

drink, leaving the hundred dollar bill behind. "I'll be in touch for your final decision."

And then Nicolai, vampire elder and my potential new benefactor, strolled out of Haven as if all he'd come in there for was to have a couple of drinks.

Chapter 3

"Well," I said after a moment. "That was interesting."

Thierry glared at me.

I cleared my throat. "So you two are old friends?"

"Our history has nothing to do with what just happened here."

"What did he mean when he said you owed him?"

He ignored the question. "Why did you just agree to his offer?"

"I didn't. I'm thinking about it. What? I thought you wanted me to pretend to be tough."

"I had no idea that he, of all the elders, would come here. And so soon." He shook his head. "This isn't right. I fear for your safety."

"You said I'll have bodyguards to keep me safe from the hunters. And Nicolai seems nice enough. He'd probably understand if I told him the truth."

Thierry grabbed my arm and stared into my eyes with concern etched into his handsome features. "Nicolai cannot know the truth. Ever. He is a very dangerous man, don't let his charm fool you." His frown deepened. "You should leave the city. Tonight."

I pulled away from him. "Let's not get carried away. I'm not going anywhere. Not yet anyhow." I smiled. "However, it is so nice of you to be so concerned for the well-being of your employees. We really appreciate it, *boss*."

He gaped at me for a moment. Then, despite all that had just happened, a smile twigged at his lips. "I see."

"Well that makes one of us. Anyhow, I'll do as you say. I'll keep lying, and when Nicolai contacts me I will tell him I don't want anything to do with his Ring thing. Now, if you'll excuse me, I have a bunch of drinks to make. George looks like he's about to go postal. And I've had to go to the bathroom for the past ten minutes. I believe my bladder is only seconds away from exploding, so if you wouldn't mind, *boss*."

The small smile remained. "This is an incredibly serious and dangerous situation. And you choose to fixate on one small thing I said."

"It doesn't matter." I shrugged and began to work on a stubborn stain on the top of the bar with a rag.

He sighed. "Sarah, if Nicolai knew the two of us are involved, it could have dangerous repercussions."

"If he's heard the rumors he already knows we're together. Chad did. But whatever. Me. Bathroom. Got to go."

He sighed. "Fine. I have a few more phone calls to make, myself."

"You do that."

He opened his mouth to say something else, but then

closed it, nodded, and turned away to disappear in the direction of his office.

I swallowed. I actually felt like crying right there in the middle of the club, but instead I took several long, deep breaths.

Pull it together, Sarah, I thought. *He was just trying to protect you. It didn't mean anything*.

I grabbed an ice cube and ran it along my forehead. *There, that was much better*.

Well, not really, but I could pretend, couldn't I?

Both George and the other waitress hurried over, both looking extremely pissed off for being kept waiting, and placed their latest drink orders. I got them ready before I hit the ladies room, did what I had to do, washed my hands, and returned to the bar feeling incredibly tense.

Maybe I should have stayed home.

Maybe I should have stayed in university and gotten my degree.

Maybe I shouldn't have given up on acting after a few lousy auditions and that embarrassing feminine hygiene commercial I'll never live down.

Maybe I never should have gone on that goddamned blind date that got me into this situation in the first place.

Hey, hindsight is always twenty-twenty.

It's also always there to laugh at your mistakes while you duck under the bar to suck back a shot of tequila with a B-positive chaser.

I'd made a lot of stupid decisions. I never claimed to be a rocket scientist. I knew that. But there was no going back now and wishing things could be different, was there?

I stood up from behind the bar.

"So, what's a nice girl like you doing in a place like this?" a voice said from behind me.

I turned slowly around.

Michael Quinn leaned against the bar. He gave me a big smile.

A matching smile landed directly on my face. "What makes you think I'm nice?"

"You're not?" he replied.

"To the right people I am."

He cocked his slightly scruffy, dark blond head to one side. "Why does this conversation sound strangely familiar?"

I moved out from behind the bar to give Quinn a big hug. I was surprised at how glad I was to see him. "You are a sight for sore eyes."

"I am?"

"Hell yeah. When did you get in?"

"A couple hours ago."

"Where have you been?"

"Down south. Had some stuff to take care of." He grinned. "But I'm back now."

"I see that." I smiled back at him. "You know, you just missed Veronique. She left for her flight back to France a few hours ago."

He didn't look overly disappointed by the news. Quinn and Veronique had had a short-term relationship last month. Short-term in the fact that it had been about six days, after which, Quinn had left town.

"I hope she sends a postcard," he said. "But I didn't come back for her, you know."

I froze. "Quinn . . ."

His grin widened. "Relax, Sarah. I'm back in Toronto for other reasons. I'm not going to go all stalker on you. Well, not again, anyhow. I know you and what's-his-name are still together. You made your choice and I respect your decision."

I raised my eyebrows. "Really?"

"Not even remotely. If I had any say in the matter you would be making out with me right now." He glanced at an unoccupied booth in the corner. "Over there. But I'm not going to press the issue."

"No pressing of the issue," I told him. "Any issue pressing would be wrong. But I'm glad you're back."

"That makes two of us."

I'd met Quinn just after I'd been turned into a vampire. Since he was a hunter at the time, he'd tried to kill me. Twice. Then he was turned into a vampire. It was a rather traumatic experience for everyone involved. I helped him out, and he'd . . . become a bit fixated on me. Go figure. And, believe me, it would have been a mutual fixation—Quinn was hot and sweet and wonderful—but I only had eyes for Thierry.

Yeah, *Thierry*.

The one who didn't acknowledge me as his girlfriend or show any public displays of affection. The man I barely knew anything about because he was so damn secretive about everything. *That* Thierry.

I gave Quinn another hug. It felt good to be in his arms. Somebody who actually wanted to touch me. In public, even.

Very public.

It felt as if somebody was staring at us and I pulled away from Quinn. Yes, somebody *was* staring. The whole club was. Including Thierry, who'd just emerged from his office again. He approached slowly, eyeing Quinn.

"You're back." His voice was flat and he slid an arm around my waist to pull me a little distance away from the other man. I looked up at him with surprise.

"I am," Quinn replied simply.

They stared at each other in silence. I could feel the gazes of everyone in the club still on us, but then I heard the buzz of conversation start up again as the CD version of Diana Krall sang about "The Look of Love."

I cleared my throat.

"So," I began. "I guess I'd better get back to the bar."

Thierry and Quinn continued to size each other up.

"I was under the impression that you had departed the city for good," Thierry said.

Quinn nodded. "I considered it."

"You did?"

"Briefly." He took a deep breath in and glanced at me. "But I kind of like it here. Just can't get enough of these Canadian winters."

"What are your plans?"

"What do you mean?"

"Now that you've returned. You are no longer a hunter," Thierry said the word with such distaste it was nearly palpable. "You have no current employment, do you?"

"Are you offering me a job, Thierry?" Quinn gave him a smile that didn't reach his eyes.

Thierry matched the expression. "I am always looking for janitorial staff."

"I'll think I'll pass. Don't worry about me, buddy. I know how to take care of myself."

"I'm sure that you do. Well, it is a great pleasure to see you again. And you found the new club so easily. I am surprised."

Quinn nodded. "Sarah told me where you were going to be set up."

There was an interesting new painting on the wall I was currently and conveniently studying, but it didn't stop me from feeling a burning sensation on the side of my face that signified Thierry was staring intently at me. I raised my eyebrows. "Hmm? What was that? I wasn't listening."

"It is good of you to let Quinn know where to find us."

I nodded. "Sure. I do what I can. He . . . uh . . . called about a week ago. Didn't I mention that? And I . . . let him know where Haven is."

Thierry nodded. "You are a good friend to him."

"I try to be a good friend to everyone." I glanced over at the bar. "Anyhoo, George is flagging me down over there. Got to go."

Thierry's fingers dug into my side. Not enough to hurt, but enough to keep me in place. I was still floored that he was touching me in public. Should I feel special, or annoyed? Not quite sure but I was leaning toward "annoyed."

I didn't remember him and Quinn being quite so un-friendly before, though they were definitely not best buddies. In fact, while Quinn was briefly seeing Veronique they'd considered joining Thierry and myself down in Mexico for a couple of days.

That never happened.

It was probably for the best.

Thierry regarded Quinn again. "It was nice of you to stop by tonight."

He crossed his arms and glanced around the club. "Well, you'll be seeing a lot more of me. I'm moving to the area permanently. Do what I can to help the other vampires out. Saving the ones who've gotten themselves into scrapes with the hunters. It's going to be my thing now. Redeem myself a bit for being on the wrong side for such a long time."

"Is that so?"

Quinn shrugged. "In fact, I've been following a lead on a vampire serial killer that led me back here. He's taking out hunters and humans alike. Even ripping the throats out of other vampires. Some young ones have been found still intact. Doesn't seem to have any preference for species. This is the kind of killer that has given vamps the stigma that they're all monsters. He has to be stopped. I wanted to ask you about it, Thierry, since you're the go-to man with answers around here. Know anything about this?"

Wow. Talk about an exaggeration. There must have been a memo or something that went out to everyone today about my new rep. Now I was supposedly killing humans and other vampires, too? Wonderful.

I opened my mouth to clear the matter up, but Thierry spoke first.

"I've heard of this, though I haven't seen any proof. What does it have to do with you?"

Quinn shrugged. "I just want to help. I want to keep innocents safe, be they human or vampire. When I find out who this vamp is, I'll put a stop to it."

"A noble endeavor."

"I try."

"Though it does nothing to erase the crimes of your past. All of the innocents that you, yourself, slaughtered with your hunter friends for fun and games."

Quinn's eyes narrowed. "It was never fun and games to me."

Thierry waved his hand dismissively. "No matter, it is ancient history."

"That's right."

"You know, that killer vampire might be just a rumor," I said. "Nothing to worry about."

Quinn smiled at me. "Maybe. But I'm going to check it out anyhow. Listen, I'm going to take off. I found a motel room nearby that they're willing to rent to me on a weekly basis until I find something a little more permanent. I want to grab some shut-eye. It's been a long day."

"Good seeing you again," I told him, trying to ignore the tightening of Thierry's hand at my waist.

He nodded, shot a last extremely unfriendly look at Thierry, and headed back to the door past Angel the bouncer.

Thierry finally released me. And said nothing.

I looked at him. "I take it you don't want him to know I'm the Slayer of Slayers."

His lips thinned. "You could have mentioned you spoke with him on the telephone."

"So . . . " I cleared my throat, feeling my face flush. "We're still on for our date tomorrow night?"

He raised an eyebrow at me. "I am looking forward to it."

"Super."

*   *   *

Three long and tiring hours later, I was home at my apartment, doors double-locked, trying my damnedest to get to sleep. Even considering that I was exhausted, it seemed to be an impossibility to clear my mind.

George gave me a ride home from the club as opposed to my taking another expensive cab. He said he'd stay on my couch, but I told him I was okay. I regretted it as soon as he left.

I wasn't even sure if Thierry knew I'd left the club, he was so busy talking on the phone with his office door closed up tight.

My mind raced. From my new reputation, to Nicolai's offer . . . to . . . well, I didn't really want to think about Quinn. Although maybe I should. The reaction the ex-hunter had elicited from Thierry had been very interesting. Did Quinn make him jealous? Or did he just not like the guy?

I heard the padding sound of footsteps outside my bedroom. The door, which was already open a crack, creaked open even farther. The footsteps grew nearer. I couldn't see anybody in the inky darkness, but I wasn't scared it was a hunter. I knew what it was.

I felt a wet tongue lick up my bare arm, which was hanging off the side of my bed.

"Gross." I turned to look at the floor. "How many times have I told you not to do that? Bad dog."

Barkley wagged his tail innocently.

"Don't give me that. I know you can understand me."

Barkley scratched the side of the bed and whined.

I sighed. "It's the middle of the night. You have to go out *now*?"

I was currently dog-sitting Barkley, since his regular keeper was spending some much-needed time relaxing in a special hospital near Niagara Falls. Some might call it an insane asylum, but I preferred to look at it as a "special hospital." He'd been charged with the murder of Roger Quinn, who just happened to be Quinn's zealous, vampire-hunting father. When the police arrived, apparently Dr. Kalisan (former fake-o cure-for-vampirism doctor, but actually a pretty nice guy) went on and on about vampires, which made the court decide a little time in the hospital would be a good thing.

Anyhow, Dr. Kalisan needed somebody to look after his werewolf while he was away. This is a phrase he used in front of the other doctors, which did nothing to make him look non-insane.

The fact that Barkley actually *was* a werewolf really didn't make any difference in the situation. I'd never seen him in human form. Apparently he was stuck this way: as a big, shaggy, scary-looking, but friendly, black dog.

Who had to go out to do his business many times a day.

"Don't you think you can hold it?" I asked him. "All I need is a few hours' sleep. I've had one hell of a day. Why don't you know how to use the toilet?"

Barkley whined and scratched at my bed again.

I stared at the dark ceiling for a moment. And sighed. Well, it wasn't like I was getting any sleep anyhow.

"All right, I'll take you out." I swung my legs over the side of the bed, and then hunted around for my fuzzy slippers and ratty blue terrycloth bathrobe. "But you better make it a quick one."

I grabbed my keys off the kitchen counter. My cell phone was right next to them so I grabbed that too and slipped it into the deep pocket of my robe. More of a habit than anything.

He was scratching at the door by the time I got there.

I tied my robe and glanced at the nearest clock: 5:35 A.M.

Then I unlocked the door, slipped out into the hall-way, and pushed the down button on the elevator. Barkley was still whining, now scratching on the eleva-tor doors.

"Okay, almost there," I told him. "Relax, would you?"

Outside, it was freezing. Nobody should be out in January before 6 A.M. Even creatures of the night like me. Even though the cold didn't really bother me much anymore, it just felt wrong. Especially while wearing pink fuzzy slippers and after recently learning I was a potential walking target.

I found the spot I usually took Barkley, a ten-foot-by-ten-foot patch of snow with a tree he seemed to enjoy. I absently glanced up at my balcony on the tenth floor.

And frowned.

"What the hell?" I said aloud.

A dark figure was scaling the side of the building. It stopped briefly at my floor, bracing itself on the balcony railing, and threw something. I heard the sound of glass shattering.

"Hey!" I shouted. "What the hell do you think you're doing up there?"

The figure swung over to another balcony and then another, and then it was out of my line of sight.

Barkley hadn't done his business yet. He looked up at me and whined.

And then my apartment blew up.

Chapter 4

My apartment.

Blew. Up.

In a great big ball of fire.

I couldn't believe my eyes.

Barkley started to howl. Doors slammed. I heard voices around me in the cold early morning and after a while a blanket was wrapped around my shoulders. I smelled the smoke, sharp and pungent, and it made my eyes water. Sirens, loud and migraine-inspiring, assaulted my ears. My mouth felt dry. People started asking questions, touching my shoulder, staring at me with concern.

"You're so lucky you got out," one voice said. I don't know who it was. I don't even know if I answered.

The apartment complex was evacuated and people milled around me, looking confused and afraid.

I just stared up at what used to be my apartment, now a smoking black spot on the side of the building, ten floors up, and I burst into tears.

"Nobody was hurt, thank God!" another voice said.

Then in lower tones. "She must have had a gas leak. Poor girl."

Poor girl. They were talking about me.

The pale girl standing outside in the cold in her bathrobe, crying like a baby, with a red blanket dangling from her shoulders. In shock, not moving, not thinking. Just staring at everything she had in the world that had just gone up in smoke.

Barkley nudged my hand. I looked down at him.

"Woof," he offered in a concerned tone.

"The hunters," I said to myself, or to Barkley, or just out loud. My voice sounded odd. Kind of creaky. Broken. "The hunters did this, didn't they?"

Vampire hunters had just blown up my apartment.

And they'd been two minutes too late to take me with it.

"Shit," I whispered. "I really am in serious trouble, aren't I, Barkley?"

Behind me, I heard a car door slam. I didn't know how long I'd been standing there, but the sun was now beginning to come up, casting a pinky orange glow along the ruined side of the apartment building.

Pretty, I thought absently as a shiver went through me.

"Sarah." A hand touched my upper arm to slowly ease me around. Thierry's brow was creased, his face and shoulders tight. His frown deepened when he saw my face.

I turned to glance at the building again. Despite the warm blanket, I was shaking.

"Are you okay?" he asked.

"*Okay*," I felt the word on my tongue, but said nothing else.

His gaze slid down the front of me, then back up to my face. "Answer me, Sarah." His voice sounded harsh with concern. "Are you injured?"

I looked down at Barkley and sniffed. The damn dog had saved my life. I suddenly felt guilty for deciding not to buy him the steak-flavored dog biscuits because they weren't on sale this week.

He deserved special, overpriced biscuits. It was the least I could do.

Thierry shook me then, hard enough for me to take notice.

"Are you injured?" he asked again, sharper.

I shook my head. "No. Not injured."

He pulled me to his chest, and I wrapped my arms around him, his warmth taking my chill away for the moment. He didn't say anything else.

"Barkley had to do his business," I murmured against him. "I'm just lucky, I guess." I laughed suddenly, and it came out sounding pinched and slightly hysterical. Then I took a deep breath of the cold morning air and looked up at him.

Thierry's expression relaxed a little, though his jaw remained tight. "I shouldn't have let you leave the club without me."

I totally lost it. I started sobbing against him for a good five minutes while he held me. He kept talking, but I couldn't hear him. So much for staying all strong and sarcastic.

Everything was gone. Everything. All of my worldly possessions, all of my shoes and clothes and makeup and shampoo and my bed and my TV. My entire life had just been destroyed right before my eyes.

Except for my ratty bathrobe and fuzzy pink slippers. And my new red blanket that they'd have to pry out of my cold, dead hands to get back. *My* blanket. My new favorite possession in the world.

After I'd pulled it together enough to stop wailing, Thierry stroked the hair back off my face and looked down at me. "I need to get you out of here. There could still be hunters around, watching."

I leaned back to look up at him. "So you think this was definitely them?"

"Of course." He nodded grimly. "They will be disappointed to learn you were not in your apartment."

"Guess I showed them."

"Indeed." He gently moved his thumb across my cheek to wipe away the tears.

"If I knew you were coming by I might have rescued a nicer bathrobe. But seeing that this is now the full extent of my wardrobe . . . " I sighed, glad I no longer had a reflection to show me exactly how hellish I looked at the moment.

I suddenly had a thought.

Out of everything I'd just lost—so much that I didn't even know where to start—there was one thing that was up there I wouldn't be able to replace. I felt the thick lump in my throat move down to become an ache in my chest.

"My shard," I said quietly. "It's gone."

It was a gift Thierry had given to me when I'd first lost my reflection. Usually it takes years for a new vampire to lose his or her reflection, but since Thierry had used his superstrength master vampire blood to help me not die after my sire bit the biscuit, the process had been sped up for lucky ol' me.

A shard was a special mirror vampires could see themselves in. It was also, allegedly, ridiculously expensive, and mine was my most prized possession, both for its practical use and because of the sentimental value. I took it everywhere with me, but not to take Barkley out for a quick walk, of course.

And now it was gone forever.

"Sarah," Thierry spoke as I began to cry again. He held me tightly against him and stroked my messy hair off my face. "Everything will be fine. I promise you."

I continued to cry. The well was not yet dry. It would make my face all red and puffy and majorly unattractive to match my new eternal nightwear from hell, but at least I wouldn't have to look at myself. Ever again.

"How is everything going to be fine?" I managed after a moment.

He held my face in his hands and gazed down at me with his captivating silver eyes. "I know somewhere you can stay. Somewhere you'll be protected by someone who cares very deeply for you."

My breath caught a little in my chest at his words. I swallowed and looked up at him while I ran the back of my hand over my face to dry it up a bit. "Is that right?"

Was this the catalyst? Was this the event that was going to make Thierry realize he wanted to be with me? That he was madly in love with me? Because if so, then this was totally worth it.

You know, in a majorly messed-up way.

"Yes," Thierry leaned forward to kiss me lightly on my

lips. "George has an extra bedroom he is willing to share for as long as necessary. I have already spoken to him on the way over."

Going into shock again.

The tears started to pick up where they left off.

"It's going to be fine," Thierry assured me as he hunted in his jacket pocket for a handkerchief, which he handed to me. He patted me on my back as I blew my nose. "A few days and all will be taken care of."

Fine, I thought.

That's a nice little four-letter word that begins with an F.

Let's think of another one, shall we?

"Sarah!" George exclaimed as he opened the door to his small rented house. "My little charred vampiress! Come in, come in!"

George lived three blocks away from Haven. I figure that's why Thierry thought that it was the perfect place for me to shack up. You know, other than with him.

But beggars couldn't be choosers. And this beggar chose to stagger into George's place without saying a word.

Barkley padded in after me.

"I don't remember saying anything about a dog." George looked down at the mutt with disdain. "I don't like dogs. Or cats. I'm a 'none of the above' person."

I slumped down on the first available seat, in this case, a rather stiff, red vinyl sofa. I'd never been there before. It was small for a house. Kind of like my dearly departed apartment only with a couple of extra rooms. George had recently moved there after getting evicted from his last place. No idea why he'd been evicted. He didn't tell me. I didn't ask. The house was littered with moving boxes and bubble wrap as it slowly made its way into being a livable space.

"He's not a dog. He's a werewolf."

"And that makes it better?"

Barkley turned around three times and flopped in a gangly pile in the corner, next to a pile of Styrofoam packing popcorn.

"It is only for a short time." Thierry closed George's front door behind him. "We'd appreciate if you made an exception."

George sighed. "I have allergies. It's not going to work."

I burst into tears. Pretty much anything was setting the waterworks off now.

George looked stricken at my soggy reaction. "Okay, okay. The dog can stay. But I just had these rugs cleaned."

I nodded wetly. "He's very good. You know, he's never once made a mess."

Barkley whined.

"Anything for you, Sarah," George nodded. "Damn hunters. You really lost everything? Even those fabulous Jimmy Choos?"

I had one pair of Jimmies. Secondhand. Comfortable, even. They looked great with absolutely everything.

I cried harder.

He plopped down beside me and patted my arm. "But you're okay and that's all that matters. *Mi casa es su casa*. For as long as you need." He glanced up at Thierry. "Though why you're not staying at *his* place, I have no idea."

I glanced up with surprise at Thierry. Good old George. Always had a way of putting my thoughts into words. We were like soulmates. Only . . . *not*.

Thierry's lips thinned and he avoided looking at me. "It is best this way."

And that's all he said.

It is best this way.

And how exactly was I supposed to interpret that? Or was I supposed to interpret it at all?

I had no bloody idea.

And frankly, at that very moment, I was too exhausted to care.

George showed me into his guest room. Very small, with a bare mattress on the floor and not much else. All things considered, it looked comfortable enough for me to crash for the next thousand years or so. Wake me up when life gets easy again.

In other words, *never*.

I gave him a quick hug. "Thanks, George. Thanks for letting me stay with you."

"For you, gorgeous? Anything." And then he was gone, leaving me and Thierry alone.

Thierry stood by the doorway. He seemed so calm and silent it was as if he was made of stone. I wrapped my arms around myself, hugging my new red blanket closer to me (they'd wanted it back, but I won in the end). I wanted to demand that he elaborate on what he'd just said. Why didn't he want me to stay at his place? His townhome was more than large enough, from what I could tell from the very few times I'd been there. I wouldn't be any trouble at all. Quiet as a little mouse. With tiny fangs.

Isn't that what normal couples were supposed to do? When one of their apartments blows up, the other one takes her in?

Then again, normal couples' apartments don't tend to blow up.

And normal couples usually aren't a pair of vampires with an age difference of 650-plus years.

Yeah, I guess that was a couple of strikes against us from the get-go.

I sighed, so tired I was practically swaying on my feet.

"I'll make arrangements at a few local stores for you to visit tomorrow," Thierry began, cutting through the silence of the room. "You will need new clothes. And to get back out in public the very next day after this incident . . . " his throat worked as he swallowed. "It would show the hunters that they are no threat to you. As I said earlier, you will have bodyguards to ensure your safety."

"Much as I'd love to rub those bastards' noses in their failure to launch me off the face of the planet—" I pulled the blanket tighter around my shoulders "—until I get some insurance money I'm going to have to depend entirely on the kindness of strangers. I'm broke. Do you know any strangers who are my size?"

He shook his head. "I will take care of any new things you may need."

I raised my eyebrows. "You're going to buy me a new wardrobe?"

"Would that be all right?"

"I appreciate the thought, but you really don't have to. Me and Amy are almost the same size. I could probably borrow from—"

"I want to," he cut me off. "Let me do this without argument, Sarah."

I didn't know what to say. Thierry was generous. I never would have asked him to do this, but since he was offering . . . what could I say except, "Hell yeah"? "Thank you."

"Is there anything else I can do for you, Sarah?"

Anything else? I shook my head, then looked up at him. "Actually, yes. Our date tomorrow. I still want it to happen, if that's okay. I don't want this to get in the way."

"Are you certain?"

I nodded.

"As you wish." Thierry leaned over to kiss my forehead. "Now, we must only wait until Nicolai leaves town. After he is gone, I know of a safe place you can stay until the rest of this nonsense blows over."

"A safe place?"

"It is a nunnery in France."

I almost laughed at that. It would have sounded hysterical, but still. Laughter. "You've got to be kidding me."

He didn't look as if he was trying to be funny. "For now, you are of special interest to the hunters. Their curiosity will eventually wane and move to something new. Until then, we must be extra careful."

"A nunnery?"

"If you would rather leave immediately, I can arrange that. I will deal with Nicolai. Your safety is the most important thing to me."

There was silence for a moment. When I'd first met him I thought he had the most expressionless face of any man I'd ever met. But now I knew you just had to look a little closer. It wasn't just my imagination that I saw concern slide behind his silver eyes. That worry etched a few fine lines into his forehead.

Or maybe I was just really, really tired.

And I *had* inhaled quite a bit of smoke.

Finally, I spoke. "I don't want to go to any nunnery."

He sighed. "Why not?"

"Because I'll miss you." I paused, then looked up at his painfully handsome face. "But if I go, will you visit me?"

His eyebrow arched. "Visit you?"

I shrugged and found myself, despite the horrific night I'd had, smiling at him for his completely bizarre but strangely sweet suggestion to keep me safe. "I'll get kind of lonely, you know. With all those boring nuns. I'll need some company."

"Is that so?"

I nodded slowly.

"I should leave." Thierry glanced at the door. "There are things I must do and you've had a very traumatic night."

I grabbed the lapel of his jacket and pulled him toward me. Not thinking, just acting. A little spontaneous. That used to be me. I used to be spontaneous. I didn't always think over everything I said, everything I did— being careful to do the right thing at all times. That's just the recent me, but not necessarily the real me.

Thierry didn't resist. He drew nearer, leaning over to gaze directly into my eyes. My hands tangled in his black coat, and I felt the heat of his delicious body underneath.

"I was very worried about you," he breathed against my mouth, his lips only a whisper away.

"I know."

And then I kissed him. Full and deep and hot and open-mouthed. His fingers twined into my hair, my hands went down to his waist as I pulled him against me.

After a moment we crashed down to the mattress on the floor, and, *oh yeah*. Being with him like this, touching him freely, desperately, like it hadn't been like since Mexico—hell, this was *better* than Mexico—was like a glass of water after wandering through the desert for weeks.

Very refreshing.

And extremely tasty.

Enough to make a girl forget all of her problems.

I felt his hands on my bare skin, moving lower, kissing down my neck and along my collarbone, parting my bathrobe.

My own hands slid down his back, under his jacket, to slip under his shirt, trying to pull him closer against me. Aching with the need that I usually tried to ignore so as not to scare him away by how much I wanted him. But he wasn't scared. He wanted me as much as I wanted him. I arched against him, as my hands drifted lower, receiving a ragged gasp from his lips as he moved slowly down my chest, my stomach, to my—

Then he suddenly stopped. He pulled away to look up at me and I groaned out loud with frustration. "What is it?"

He frowned, his gaze trailing off to the side of the room. "Your werewolf is staring at us."

"My—?" I glanced to the right. Barkley sat, not four

feet away, panting and wagging his tail. "Barkley! Shoo!"

Barkley didn't shoo. His tail began to make a "thwack, thwack" sound against the hardwood floor.

Thierry shifted slightly. "Shall I remove him from the room and—" he looked down at me and our eyes locked "—then return?"

I couldn't help smiling at that. Here I thought this would be his excuse, yet again, to leave me all alone.

"He might need to go outside first, if you know what I mean."

He brushed his mouth against my cheek in a knee-weakening line to the curve of my ear and whispered, "Then I'll be right back."

And he stood, slowly, and with a glance down at me lying on the mattress, took Barkley out of the room.

Oh, this was very, very good.

Maybe whoever blew my apartment up was acting under strict direction from Cupid himself. It could happen. All of my earlier doubts about Thierry were starting to get all blurry and difficult to remember. He was wonderful, giving, fabulous, perfect. And unbelievably sexy. I was a lucky, lucky girl.

And about to get even luckier.

Veronique could stick her words of wisdom. Stick them! Ha!

I smiled and then stretched out long and languidly on the mattress, raising my arms high above my head.

As soon as Thierry came back I was *so* going to rock his world.

However, after waiting for a few minutes, I yawned. It had been such a long, draining, exhausting day.

Very, very, very long.

Very exhausting.

So tired.

So very tired.

No . . . I thought, but it sounded a million miles away. *Don't you dare close your eyes* . . .

. . .

Zzzzz.

"And then I fell asleep," I explained to my best friend Amy the next day. "Like Rip Van-freaking-Winkle. And ruined what could quite possibly have been the most incredible night of my life. The end."

Amy shook her blond head in silence. "What's a Rip Van Winkle?"

I blinked, then looked both ways as we crossed a busy intersection after visiting the fourth clothing store of the day. "He's an old man with a long white beard who fell asleep for twenty years and missed out on some hot vampire loving."

"What does this have to do with what happened to your apartment?"

"Nothing."

"Isn't that more important than this Rip Van Winkle guy?"

I cleared my throat. "Maybe you're right."

I was homeless. Still twitching from watching the sum total of my twenty-eight years go up in flames. The twitching could also have a lot to do with the morning phone call to my parents to tell them that I was okay. Just a little gas leak, is all. They took it like good parents should, and freaked out—long-distance style. Offered to come and get me and bring me back to my hometown for an extended stay. After I declined, my mother gave me a fifteen-minute lecture about how I needed to be more careful.

I could just imagine the lecture I'd get if I ever got around to telling them I was a vampire.

Now I was on the streets of Toronto on a brisk January day with Thierry's Platinum American Express card in my preapproved clutches. The last thing I felt like doing today was shopping—and that's saying something—but I'd decided to go along with the "plan" as best I could.

Some plan.

Stupid hunters.

Amy'd also freaked out when I called her earlier and told her what happened. She'd brought over some clothes for me to borrow so I wouldn't have to go shopping in slippers and nightwear. I told her about the bodyguards. She decided that it would be worth putting our lives at risk in order to acquire some new threads. It's all about priorities.

I wondered if the hunters in general even knew what I looked like? Did they just know me by name? Chad hadn't recognized me until he found out my name.

It was an odd feeling knowing people wanted to kill me. "Edgy" didn't begin to cover it. Sure, Peter had wanted to kill me. Before I turned the tables on him. He wanted to kill me *badly*. And if it wasn't for the golden horseshoe of luck I obviously had jammed up my butt that night, then I really shouldn't have gotten out of that in one piece, nickname or no nickname.

But I did.

And here I am.

With bodyguards in tow.

I'd spotted one large hulking beast about ten paces be-hind us. I would have thought it was a coincidence, but he had followed us into the lingerie department of Sears just a half hour ago.

He was either my brand-new bodyguard, following us on a crowded downtown sidewalk near the Eaton Centre, or a huge man who enjoyed the feel of silk against his skin.

Or maybe both. I'm not here to judge.

Plus, I'd seen him tackle a guy who'd asked me for the time as I passed a bus stop a block back.

"Why didn't he wake you up?" Amy inquired.

"Thierry?" I glanced over my shoulder nervously, then back at Amy. "I'm thinking he knew I was ex-hausted. He was trying to be a gentleman. I did wake up with his credit card on the pillow next to me. It was very *Pretty Woman*." I froze as a large man who was eating a mustard-drenched hot dog bumped into me. "Maybe we should get off the streets for a while. It's kind of crowded around here."

"Speaking of Richard Gere, I have to admit that Thierry is definitely gorgeous."

I looked at her out of the corner of my eye. "And your point?"

She shrugged. Just one shoulder clad in fake white fur. "No point. Just . . . "

"Oh, *God*. What is it? You're doing that half-shrug thing. And that's never good."

She shrugged the other shoulder this time. "It's just . . . other than the fact he's nice to look at, what ex-actly do you see in him?"

I stopped walking. With a quick glance, I noticed the hulk also stopped walking. I faced my shrugging best friend. "Excuse me?"

"Don't get defensive. And don't get me wrong. Thierry's great. He's generous and . . . um . . . *tall* . . . and, uh . . . wait, I'm sure there's something else . . . "

"Not you, too." I shook my head, feeling a wave of anxiety fill me.

"Not me, too, what?"

"You, *of all people*, are not going to tell me that me and Thierry aren't going to work out."

"I'm not saying that."

"Yes, you obviously are. Besides, I believe you're the one who's about to turn thirty. The day after tomorrow. You should be more concerned with yourself. And you know, *getting old*. That's almost worse than losing all your worldly belongings."

When in doubt, change the subject. Always a good rule of thumb.

"Sure, rub it in." She pouted. "But I'm a vampire. I'll never look any older than I do right now."

"But you're still turning thirty. Ha."

She looked thoughtful for a moment. "Do you know who you were great with?"

Oh, God. Please make it stop. Doesn't she know I'm mentally fragile today?

"Quinn," she continued, despite my giving her the evil eye. "He was so hot and he really liked you, didn't he? Where'd he go, anyhow?"

My head. *Throbbing.* "He's actually back. Just returned last night."

She actually clapped her hands together and smiled brightly at me. "Oh, good!"

I shook my head. Vigorously. "What part of 'I'm with Thierry' don't you understand?"

She looked thoughtful. "You know, I bet he could have protected you last night. He wouldn't have just left you all alone with that dumb dog."

"Amy, you don't know what you're talking about. And Barkley's a werewolf."

She sighed. "I just want you to be as happy as I am. With Barry." She gazed down at her tiny diamond ring.

"So everything's cool between you two? I know you said last week you were a little . . . how did you put it?"

She took a deep breath and let it out slowly. "Insanely jealous and paranoid. Yeah, I was a little concerned for a while. I thought he was going to be another man who treated me like crap, but so far so good. I just need to be more confident." She grinned. "Being married to a wonderful man like Barry is everything I ever thought it would be."

"So you thought being married would be the first sign of the short man apocalypse?" I paused. "Wait, I can think of a better one. Just give me a minute. My brain is seriously fried."

"Sarah! Barry likes you now, you know. I thought you two were friends now?"

I glanced around the busy street. The bodyguard was keeping his distance. Trying to look all incognito even though it must have been obvious I'd already spotted him. "He doesn't like me. Your husband rubs me the wrong way. There's just something about him. He's just so—"

"Wonderful, charismatic, and wonderful?" She beamed.

"You said wonderful twice. And no, I was thinking more along the lines of troll-like and annoying."

She frowned.

I raised my hands. "But you're the one who has to share a bed with him, not me."

Her frown turned upside down. "And let me tell you. Barry is seriously a sex god."

"I am going to throw up."

"I know you don't like talking about this sort of thing, but seriously." She appeared to quiver. "Sometimes he bites my neck when we're in the middle of, *you know* . . . and it is *so* amazing. That man can curl my toes like nobody's business. I don't know why I would ever doubt that he loves me."

"Where is my barf bag?" I made a face. "Hold on one moment, I think I need to deal with something."

I turned around and walked quickly over to the hulk, who had raised a copy of the *Toronto Star*'s entertainment section up to cover his face. He lowered it just in time to see me approach, and his eyes widened slightly with surprise. He had a brown crew cut and wore a black leather jacket and blue jeans he probably had to buy at the Big & Brawny store.

"Hi there," I said. "What's your name?"

"What?"

"Your name. You have a name, don't you?"

"I . . . " He looked confused. "My name . . . uh . . . "

"Listen, buddy. I'm having a difficult week, to say the least. I get that you've been hired to keep an eye on me so I don't get murdered or blown up again. And I appreciate that. Really. But I want you to know that I know that you're here and I want to know your name."

His shifted his weight to his other very large shoe. "Uh . . . it's Lenny, ma'am."

"Lenny." I repeated. My bodyguard's name was *Lenny*. "All right, Lenny. Thank you. You're doing a good job so far. Still alive. Hooray. Keep it up. Me and my friend are heading into Starbucks for a coffee. Can I get you something?"

He tucked the newspaper under his arm. "Um. No thank you, ma'am. I'll wait out here."

I turned back to Amy, who'd raised her penciled-in eyebrows at me. "Wow. You're getting all demanding. Very impressive."

"Thank you. Now I demand that you stop talking about Thierry, your sex life, and anything else that makes me want to throw myself into oncoming traffic. I need caffeine in the worst way."

"Mmm. I'm having a major craving for a brownie." She practically skipped across the street toward the coffee house.

Some vampires could still eat solid food. Like Amy. She was blessed with the ability to chow down on whatever she wanted. Me? Lately eating a kernel of corn made me hurl. Coffee seemed to be where the line had been drawn.

I guess it's because Amy hadn't been lucky enough to partake in a master vampire's blood like I had. Much like wine, a vamp's blood was more precious, rare, and potent the older he was. And Thierry was damn old.

If I let my mind wander a little, I could still feel him

against my mouth. Drawing a wet line against his warm skin with my tongue. My teeth grazing the surface.

Drinking deep, so deep.

Filling my mouth with the dark, delicious taste of him.

I blinked and shook my head to try to clear it.

"Coffee!" I shouted, my voice suddenly a little pitchy. "Right now! Make it an espresso!"

Chapter 5

W ould you look at that line?" Amy said as we entered the crowded coffee house.

"What did you expect? It's a Saturday afternoon." I glanced around, feeling immediately claustrophobic and more than my share of paranoid. We were surrounded by a lot of people I didn't know. Buzzing on caffeine and biscotti. Why did I come out today again?

Death wish, table for two.

"Oo, I see a table." She beelined to one near the window that had been abandoned all of two seconds ago. I sat down. The chair was still warm. And oddly sticky.

"Look," I moved to the seat next to me and shifted to get comfortable, "I don't want to spend a lot of time here. I have things to do. Assassination attempts to avoid. Besides, I have a date with Thierry tonight so I need to have time to prepare."

"How do you prepare for a date with Thierry?"

Since I'd never really had an "official" date with him,

I wasn't entirely sure. "Um. A little red lipstick and a calming meditation CD?"

She eyed the lineup. "It won't be long."

"Famous last words." I cleared my throat and thought of the smoking remnants of my life. "Wait, let me take that back. That's a phrase I never want to say again just in case it happens to be true."

The wide hips of a passing woman bumped into my shoulder and I glanced up to make sure she wasn't carrying any concealed weapons along with her caramel macchiato.

Suddenly a sound rang out above snippets of conversations I could catch with my surprisingly sharp vampire hearing (to match my increased sense of smell) —though some conversations, like the one about body piercings between an older woman at the table in the far corner and her much, much younger boyfriend, were not ones I really wanted the chance to overhear.

The sound was coming from Amy. From her purse, specifically. She reached into it and pulled out a thin pink cell phone, which was the cause of the odd sound, a sound I now pinpointed as a tinny rendition of "I'm Too Sexy" by Right Said Fred.

"This is Amy," she chimed into the tiny contraption. "Uh huh?"

There was a long silence and I watched her face lose its happy Amy glow.

"I see. Well, alrighty then. Thanks for letting me know. No, I appreciate you telling me. I really do." She shut the phone up and stared at it. "That heinous *bitch*."

"Who's a heinous bitch?" I inquired. Amy rarely, if ever, got mad enough to call somebody else a bad

name—a trait I didn't happen to share with her. I didn't
even think she knew the word "heinous." But obviously I
was wrong.

"My neighbor." She looked down at the small, expensive piece of technology as if it was the cause of every
problem she'd had since birth. "My *nosy* old bag of a
neighbor."

"And? What did she say?" I glanced outside at Lenny,
who'd just started to chase two kids with deadly looking
skateboards down the street.

Skateboards in January? There should be a law.

She slumped down into the seat across from me. "She
just saw Barry."

"Oh, I feel badly for her."

Amy glanced at me sharply. "I wasn't finished. She
says she saw him with another woman."

"*Your* Barry."

She nodded stiffly.

I frowned, trying to focus my wandering thoughts
enough to understand. "I'm sorry. She saw Barry doing
what with another woman?"

"Talking. Closely. And touching each other."

I shuddered at the thought. "I'm sure it's nothing."

"Yeah, of course. It's nothing." She nodded. Then a
frown creased her pretty face. "Why would you assume
that it's nothing?"

"Well, this is Barry we're talking about."

"I know you don't like him, but that doesn't mean he
isn't an incredibly desirable man, you know. He's had
many girlfriends over the years." She sighed. "Women
are irresistibly drawn to him. It's not his fault. He's
blamelessly charismatic."

I blinked at her. "If you say so. But really, you guys are newlyweds. So if you're thinking that something fishy is going on—"

She nodded, looking suddenly sad. "I was right to be worried. He's cheating on me."

"Amy! How can you say that?" I shook my head. "Weren't you just doing the 'Barry's so hot' cheer outside?"

She slumped down in her chair. "I'm trying to fool everyone into thinking I'm fine. That my marriage is wonderful. But I can't take it anymore. It's all a sham, Sarah." She let out a long breath. "I was afraid of this. But I'm not surprised."

I reached across the table to grab her hand and squeeze it. I'd never seen Amy so down, so ready to accept defeat without even putting up a fight for the man she married. "Maybe you're just overreacting. Maybe this is nothing at all."

A tear slid down her cheek. "I'm not enough woman for him. I told you before that he is a very sensual man. He has needs that I'm just not able to fill."

I tried to cover up my shudder by squeezing her hand harder. "Don't say that."

"I thought he was *the one*," she continued. "That after all these years I'd found my knight in shining armor. But . . . " She sniffed and her voice grew shaky. "I've just set myself up for a-a-another h-h-heartbreak."

Now I leaned over the table to give her a hug, before I got up in search of a napkin that I returned with and handed to her. "Listen to me, Amy. Barry may be a lot of things. Gross things. At least to me. But I seriously don't believe he's cheating on you. I want you to be happy.

Listen, if you're that upset about this, I'll check things out. I'll be really subtle, too."

She blinked and a tear splashed down to her cheek. "You'd do that for me?"

"Of course. I'd be happy to spy on your husband for you. What's a friend for?"

"I really appreciate it."

"Anything to help distract me from the fiery pit of despair of my own life is a good thing. And then I'll be able to tell you that there's no way he'd want to be with another woman. Even though I still feel like staking him for turning you into a vamp on your first date."

She pouted. "I just don't know."

I shook my head. "You guys might have your problems, but I think Barry's in this for the long run."

She dried her face with the napkin, and nodded. "I hope you're right."

Frankly, so did I.

Amy left me to look after the table and scare off anybody looking to steal it. She joined the end of the long lineup. I sat there by myself and glanced out of the window at Lenny, who was back from his skateboarder takedown and pacing in front of Starbucks, trying to look inconspicuous and failing miserably.

It was good to know he was there. He seemed like a bit of a musclehead, but he was a musclehead who was going to look out for me.

After five minutes I glanced up at the line. Amy was still waiting and was on her cell phone again, talking to who knows who. Maybe Mr. Charismatic Barry himself.

It was going to be a bit of a wait. I put my head down on my folded arms with the intention of resting my tired eyes and trying to put my problems briefly out of my mind, but found myself quickly spiraling off into dreamland.

I was all alone at Midnight Eclipse. The chairs were placed upside down on top of the tables so the floor could be easily cleaned during the off hours. The long, black lacquered bar hugged the wall. The stage was to the right—small but adequate enough to put on a good show.

I felt a hand on my shoulder that trailed warmly down my back, stopping at my waist to turn me around.

"Sarah," Quinn said, staring down the length of me before meeting my eyes. He smiled and I could see his fangs glint in the soft light of the club. His dark blond hair was brushed off his face. His blue eyes flashed. He wore a dark suit with a pale blue shirt.

"You should know that this isn't real," I told him. "I'm dreaming right now."

"Yeah, I know." He grinned wider and raised an eyebrow. "Interesting, though, that you're dreaming about me, isn't it?"

Then he crushed his lips against mine, his strong hands sliding down my body to pull me against him. I didn't fight it. My fingers worked their way up to tangle in his hair and I opened my mouth to the deepening kiss.

After a moment, I pulled away from him, feeling confused, turning as if in slow motion to look at the stage. The lights were on, flooding the performing area with bright light, almost too bright for me to register what was up there.

But then I saw.

It was Peter, eye patch and all. The vampire hunter

who'd wanted me dead. The one that I'd shot in self-defense. But instead of me onstage with him, as it had been that terrible night, it was Thierry.

His face was rigid and emotionless. But his eyes weren't. Those bottomless silver eyes watching me and Quinn were filled with pain.

Peter approached the microphone. "Hey, bitch. Remember me? I haven't forgotten about you. Not by a long shot."

Icy fingers played along my spine and I shivered. "You're dead."

He grinned. "Yeah, I am. Some things do change. But some things never do. You think you could get away with what you did to me with no consequences? You've got a world of pain headed directly your way, darlin'. A *universe* of pain. And it's only just begun."

"You deserved it," I told him, feeling both guilt and anger fighting inside me. "You tried to kill me. That's all you did—kill vampires. For fun. Don't even try to tell me that you believed we were all monsters."

"Nobody's perfect." He shrugged. "We're all monsters down deep, darlin'. Every one of us. You gotta embrace that monster. I did. If you believe any differently, then you're fooling yourself."

"Let Thierry go."

Peter started to laugh. "You think you're in control of anything? You're all fools. And you," he regarded Thierry. "You should have killed yourself when you had the chance."

"Peter," I took a few steps closer to the stage. "You want me. Why don't you leave him alone and come and get me?"

He stared down at me. "Oh, I'll have my revenge, darlin'. Don't think I won't. And you'll never see it coming. But I don't want you to forget about me in the meantime." He glanced out at Quinn, then back at Thierry. "Two men, huh? Aren't you the lucky one?"

My hands curled into fists at my sides. "Go to hell."

Peter laughed louder. "Why don't I make things a little easier for you?"

He turned and plunged a wooden stake into Thierry's chest. Thierry gasped, his silver eyes widened, and he fell to his knees. I ran up to the stage.

"Thierry!" I reached up to touch his face.

"I'm sorry, Sarah—" His pain-filled words sliced through me like knives. "—I'm so sorry I couldn't protect you."

And then he dissolved before my very eyes. His handsome face melting into nothingness, his body collapsing on itself until there was nothing left of him but a dark stain on the stage. I could hear Peter laughing. Quinn tried to pull me into his embrace but I pushed him away.

I shook my head and felt the hot tears cutting lines down my face. And then I screamed—

"—NOOO!!!"

I woke up and stood up from the table at the same time, flailing about from the intensity of the dream. I hit something and heard an "oof" sound. And then a crash. Followed closely by a splash.

My heart beat wildly and my breathing came in rapid bursts. I glanced around as I got my bearings, my hands still clenched into fists. Ready to fight.

Still in Starbucks. It was just a dream.

Just a dream.

I let out a long sigh of relief.

"That was a double espresso moccaccino, I'll have you know," a female voice said. "Five bucks and now it's gone. Oh God. Look at my shoes."

I glanced in the direction of the voice. A blond woman glared at me. I looked down. Next to her stained Manolos was a mocha-colored puddle.

"I am so sorry." My voice was shaky and a little raspy. My heart was pounding so hard that I felt it in my eye-balls. "I'll buy you a replacement. For the coffee, that is. A little . . . club soda might be able to clean your shoes up. Are those suede?"

She jabbed a finger at me. "You have something stuck to your face."

"I do?" I reached up to feel around and touched paper. I peeled it off my forehead to find that it was a yellow sticky note with Amy's handwriting on it.

Had to go. Didn't want to wake you, looked like you were having a good dream. Talk later . . . Amy

She stuck a sticky note to my forehead while I was sleeping.

I wish I could say it was the first time she'd ever done that.

I glanced at the girl. She was pretty. Somewhere in her midtwenties, with long hair—alternating streaks of darker blond and platinum—done in two haphazard braids hanging well past her shoulders. She wore a three-quarter-length red leather coat. One of her high-heeled, stained shoes tapped angrily against the tiled floor.

Those were some nice shoes.

Too bad they were now ruined.

I glanced at the table. Amy had left me my coffee. Alas, not a moccaccino. It was a tall regular coffee that smelled like it might have brushed past some hazelnuts somewhere between here and Colombia.

I grabbed it and glanced at the angry blonde, feeling rather sheepish and still shaky from my visit from the nightmare fairy.

"Okay, then." I nodded. "Lovely to meet you."

"We didn't meet."

I smiled and nodded again. Usually the best way to deal with an unfortunate situation just before you escaped.

And then I grabbed my bags and left. Pushing open the front door of Starbucks and feeling the cold air hit my face.

Lenny tried to be all subtle again in following me. He kept far enough back that after a minute, I didn't notice him at all as I hurried along the street.

"Hey!" a voice called out behind me. "Stop!"

I glanced over my shoulder. It was the blonde. *Oh, great.* Probably wanted me to pay for her shoes. Well, it wasn't as though I'd banged into her on purpose. I picked up my pace. All I wanted to do was get back to George's. That dream had seriously freaked me out. I needed recovery time away from hunters and pissed-off, caffeinated fashionistas.

Her heels clicked against the cold pavement as she began to chase after me.

I turned the next corner and waded through a small swarm of warmly dressed sidewalk stragglers and looked over my shoulder just as I tossed my untouched coffee into a passing garbage can. It was too hard to juggle with my other bags. Even though the stupidly bright sun made me a bit weary, my slightly increased vampire speed (plus comfy footwear) helped me to move at a definite clip.

But moccaccino-girl was still coming.

After a minute when I couldn't lose her, I stopped and turned around. "Listen, I don't know why you're following me, but—"

She skidded to a halt, panting a little, and held up a shopping bag in front of her. "You left this in Starbucks. Damn, you sure can walk fast."

Talk about sheepish. "Oh," I took the bag from her. "Thank you. Sorry, I didn't realize what you wanted."

She shook her head. "It's okay. Nice store, by the way." She raised a matching bag of her own.

I smiled—closed mouth so as not to show off my *pearly frights* to an unsuspecting stranger. "Great minds think alike. And sorry about the shoes. Really."

"To tell the truth, these are fairly old." She glanced down at them with a sigh. "I guess I can use this as an excuse to buy another pair. What was the problem in there anyhow? Do you lose control of your bodily functions like that all the time or was I your first victim of the day?"

I shifted my bags to my other arm. "I fell asleep waiting for my friend to come back from the lineup. Had a bad dream and woke up flailing like an octopus. If octopuses flail."

"You're lucky you're able to fall asleep so easily," she said.

"I didn't get much sleep last night."

I felt uneasy standing there in the middle of the sidewalk in the broad daylight. It wasn't safe. A hunter could be watching me right now while trying to figure out how to kill the Slayer of Slayers in a way spectacular enough to impress his buddies. I suddenly got a visual of a thousand tiny wooden Sarah-seeking missiles flying through the air. Or just one big one. Either way, not a good place to be for long.

"I'm going to grab a taxi," I told her.

"Do you mind if I share one with you?" She glanced up at the surrounding skyscrapers with a confused expression. "It's so hard to get used to things around here."

"You're not from around here?"

"No. Actually, I'm from Florida."

"And if you're from Florida, why would you come to Toronto in January?" I asked. "If I had a choice I'd rather be sitting on a beach right now."

"You can get sick of beaches."

"That's crazy talk."

"Then call me crazy. I'm Janelle, by the way. Janelle Parker." She shifted her bags to offer me her gloved hand. "You can call me Janie."

"Sarah," I told her, as I shook her hand. I left off the last name. Nobody needed to know my last name. It might get me in trouble, and it didn't matter who I was talking to. Nope. From now on I would just be *Sarah*. Much like Madonna. Or Cher. Or Mary-Kate and Ashley. "Welcome to Toronto. Which is actually Cherokee for 'we will ruin your designer footwear upon arrival.' Where are you staying?"

"The Royal York."

I whistled. "Fancy. How long are you in town for?"

She shrugged. "It's business related so it could be a day or two. Maybe more. I've got some personal stuff to attend to as well."

"Do you have family here?"

When she didn't say anything right away, I glanced at her sideways to see her moisten her lips and blink hard.

"Family's one thing I don't have to worry about anymore," Janie said grimly, but then seemed to shake her melancholy moment away. She turned to offer me a bright smile. "You just never know what's behind the next corner, do you?"

I nodded. "Ain't that the tru—"

As we passed the next corner—ironically enough—a hand reached out to grab my coat and yank me into an alleyway. I went sprawling onto the ground in a heap, surprised, with the wind knocked out of me, the contents of my shopping bags spilling out onto the pavement.

Something blocked out the sun. Was it an eclipse? I squinted up, feeling dazed. No, no eclipse. It was a behemoth of a man blocking the sun and my potential escape.

"You're Sarah Dearly, right?" he asked.

My thousand tiny missiles dissolved and were replaced by the image of one huge man who'd just pulled me into an alleyway, away from the maddening crowd who were apparently the only thing keeping me alive until now.

Yup.

Spectacular death. Right here. Right now.

Oh, shit.

Chapter 6

The behemoth had a knife in one hand. "Slayer of Slayers. I've been following you all day, waiting for this moment. I'm a very patient man."

My eyes widened, and my gaze darted around the darkened alleyway. Where did Janie go? Where the hell was Lenny? "Uh, I think you have me confused with somebody else. It's okay. I get that all the time. No harm done."

"I don't think so."

"You want my purse?" I said again, my chest tightening. "Here. Take it."

He fixed me with a narrow-eyed stare. "I don't want your purse, vampire." Then he eyed my brand-new handbag. "Hold on. Maybe I will take it. Then I can have some proof that I was the one who took you down."

"Hey, what's your name?" I asked through chattering teeth. Maybe he wanted to talk a bit like Chad did. Buy some time.

"Shut up, bitch."

Maybe not.

I glanced around the narrow alleyway. No doors. No other way out. Where was Lenny? Shouldn't he be swinging in on a vine like a big hairy Tarzan to save me?

The hunter grew nearer and so did his knife. A silver knife. Every bit as deadly as a wooden stake to your average vampire.

"Hey, Sarah! You okay?" I heard Janie shout from behind him.

He bared his yellowed teeth and turned to face the blonde, then grabbed her leather jacket and shoved her in my direction. I heard a rip.

Janie looked down at herself. He'd ripped her jacket along the right underarm seam.

She looked up, her eyes flashing angrily. "Oh, no, you did not just do that. First my shoes today and now my jacket?" She took a step forward.

"Janie, he's dangerous—" I tried to catch her arm to stop her from doing anything too stupid, but by then she was out of my reach.

Janie's eyes widened. "He has a knife."

He looked at it and moved it around in the light. "Yeah, bitch. And I know how to use it."

"Good to know." She swiveled and kicked him directly in the chest. He staggered back a couple of steps, coughing, with an expression of shock on his face.

She closed the distance between them and he sliced the knife upward, catching the bottom corner of her jacket before she moved away. She spun around and punched him in his stomach. He let out an "ughh!" Then she grabbed the arm that had the knife, twisted it behind him, and brought her knee up against his elbow.

I heard a sickening crack and a surprisingly high-pitched scream of pain for such a large, scary man. The knife clattered to the ground.

He stared at her in silence for a few long seconds, clutching his broken arm against his chest. And then turned and ran away.

I think he was crying.

During the entire duration of this unexpected action sequence I stood against the cold brick wall with my mouth open long enough and wide enough that my fangs had dried out.

Janie leaned over and picked up the knife. She breathed on the blade and wiped it against her ripped jacket. Then she looked at me and there was a fierce, fiery expression in her eyes, which quickly extinguished back to a cool blue.

She shrugged. "I hate vampire hunters."

"Holy crap," I managed. "That was the most impressive thing I think I've ever seen. Who are you, *La Femme Nikita*?"

She shrugged again and slipped the knife into her purse. "It was nothing."

I shook my head slowly. "No, that was definitely not *nothing*. Did I say 'holy crap' already? Hold on . . . did you say you hate vampire hunters?"

"They're just so . . . indiscriminate. You know? Well, most of them, anyhow. Are you okay?"

I frowned at her. "You're my other bodyguard, aren't you?"

She smiled. "Guilty as charged."

"So you know I'm a . . . a . . . "

"Bloodsucking monster. That's right."

My eyes narrowed. "Why didn't you say anything?"

"And miss the fun?"

"You call that fun?

She shrugged. "Kinda. Still not thrilled about the ruined shoes, but I'll just include it in my fee. By the way, that's actually the third hunter we've taken down today. This one got a little too close for comfort, but all is well."

"The third?" I let it all sink in. "So you're not a distance kind of bodyguard like Lenny. You like to get up close and personal."

"Total mistake. I just wanted some caffeine. You were the one who initiated contact."

She was right about that, I guess. "Who taught you how to fight like that?"

She picked her shopping bag off the ground. "My brother. He was into all that *Kung Fu* shit. Needed a sparring partner so he taught me some moves. He always called me Grasshopper, like in the TV show. He was a total geek." She got a faraway look on her face, but then seemed to shake it off and smile at me. "Listen, we should probably get you off the streets. As much as I love a little afternoon workout, we've had enough face time for today. I've got something else to take care of, but Lenny will see you safely home." She turned and left the alley, merging onto the sidewalk as if nothing out of the ordinary had just happened.

"Wait a minute." I had to hurry to catch up to her. She was walking faster now. I guess when you kick a guy's ass without even breaking a sweat you might get some adrenaline flowing.

If I knew how to protect myself like that I probably wouldn't even need to rely on any bodyguards at all. The fitness classes I've been taking with Amy didn't come anywhere near what I'd just witnessed. Amazing. The mugger had been easily twice Janie's size. And he hadn't been wearing heels. That was a definite disadvantage. In this case, for him.

"You know," I began, a plan formulating in my mind as I tried to walk and juggle my shopping bags without dropping anything. "Since you're already being paid to hang around me, maybe I could get you to teach me some self-defense."

She studied me for a moment, shifting the bag to her other hand. "You must know how to protect yourself, don't you?"

"Yeah, that's why I was standing there wearing my 'I'm the Victim' T-shirt while you took care of business."

She frowned. "I don't know, I'm not much of a teacher. But, like you said, I am going to be around—I guess I could, if you like."

"I would like." I smiled, feeling as though this was the best idea I'd had all day. All decade, really.

"Sarah!" I heard somebody shout, and I turned to look, surprised to see that it was Quinn on the other side of the street waving at me.

He wore dark sunglasses, a black leather jacket, and faded blue jeans and was smiling so widely I could see his fangs from a distance. I waved back, and he started to cross the street.

"What the hell is he doing here?" I said, mostly to myself. "Janie, I'm going to have to introduce you to Quinn."

I turned to look at her and realized that she was gone. Gone. Disappeared.

I frowned. Where did she go?

"What's wrong?" Quinn asked, when he reached me. "You look a little disturbed."

For a second I thought about my dream. It had been so vivid. Both the kissing of Quinn and the staking of Thierry. But it was only a dream.

Only a dream.

I shook my head and tried to smile. "That's a look I will probably have a lot in the future. 'Disturbed' is my new middle name. What are you doing here?"

"Looking for you."

I nodded. "Do the words 'needle in a haystack' mean anything to you? How did you find me? This is a big city."

"When I put my mind to something I can accomplish a lot." He grinned. "Plus I saw Amy a minute ago. It's her birthday the day after tomorrow, you know."

"Well aware."

"Actually, the motel I told you I was staying at isn't that far from here. It's not bad, really. Soda machine just down the hall. Total luxury."

I hated to admit it, but I'd really missed Quinn when he'd been gone. It was only for a couple of weeks, but he'd definitely wedged his way into my life in the short time that I'd known him. And he'd had a rough time of it, too. Even worse than me, if I had to admit it. All his life he'd spent under his father's thumb, traveling from town to town with the rest of the hunters, taking down vampires.

Then he'd been made into one very much against his will.

And just before he died, his father had confessed that he was responsible for Quinn's mother's murder—instead of her being killed by a vampire as Quinn had been led to believe since he was just a kid.

Yeah, Quinn's life had been one lie on top of another, on top of another. And now it was all tied up with a pretty bow of soul-wrenching guilt from his past deeds.

Despite all this history and pain, all I could think about, standing here in the middle of the sidewalk facing him, was how it had felt to kiss him in my dream.

I shouldn't be dreaming about kissing Quinn. Not with everything else going on.

No way. No how.

I shook my head as if to shake out the mental image and turned around one more time looking for Janie. "It's so weird. I was just talking to somebody and she disappeared."

"Like magic, disappear?"

"No." I frowned. "Like she waited for my back to be turned so she could escape from me. But, since she's one of my bodyguards, that wouldn't exactly fit the job description. I'm not that annoying, am I?"

"Truthfully?" His grin widened, then slowly disappeared as a frown swapped places with it. "Bodyguards? What do you need bodyguards for?"

I cleared my throat. "Mostly to keep me from getting killed."

"No, seriously."

"Actually, I'm being totally serious." I let my shopping bags rest on the sidewalk for a moment and scanned the general area for any sign of Janie or Lenny. Neither was anywhere to be seen.

I told Quinn everything. Absolutely everything, from the rumors, to Nicolai's offer, to my damn apartment blowing up, to my currently MIA bodyguards. I let it out in a long tirade that left me exhausted just by saying it, let alone living it.

Actually, once it was all out, I felt a bit better. It was like verbal therapy.

I looked at Quinn to get his reaction. His face was red, his expression tense. "Why are you walking around on the streets? You should be inside somewhere safe, instead of . . . " He eyed my bags "You're *shopping*? Why the hell are you shopping at a time like this?"

I bit my lip. "Thierry gave me his credit card to buy some new clothes, since all of mine have gone up in smoke."

His expression darkened and he swore loudly. "That son of a bitch. What the hell is he thinking, letting you expose yourself like this?"

I stiffened. "Well, for one thing, nobody *lets me* do anything. I make my own decisions."

"Do you?" He glowered at me and let a long breath hiss out between his teeth. "Sarah, don't take this the wrong way, but you're being a total idiot."

My eyebrows shot up. "Gee, why ever would you think I'd take *that* the wrong way?"

"Dammit, Sarah. I'm seriously worried about you. Thierry obviously isn't worried enough." He looked around. "He's the real idiot. Maybe more than that, if you ask me."

"What's that supposed to mean?"

"The reason I was looking for you . . . " he hesitated and glanced around our general surroundings at a few people passing us by like we were nothing out of the ordinary. He adjusted his sunglasses. "There have been five highly suspicious murders in Toronto alone in the past week. Bodies drained of blood. Puncture marks on the necks. Same MO as a few cities I've visited the last couple weeks. Two were hunters. I recognized them when I snuck into the morgue last night. Two were human. One, I'm positive, was a vamp. But an old one. Nothing much left once the bastard finished his meal."

I frowned. "Why haven't I heard anything about this? Hold on, you snuck into the morgue?"

"The police will try to keep it out of the papers until they have some leads. They obviously don't. And they won't. This guy is good. He's wandering around taking whatever he wants, whenever he wants it. Probably has been doing the same thing for hundreds of years."

I shifted my weight to my other foot, feeling uncomfortable just thinking about something so terrible. "And you said you've been looking for me, because?"

He licked his lips before he continued. I couldn't see his eyes. "Where was Thierry the night before last?"

I actually laughed. "You can't honestly believe he had anything to do with this."

Quinn shrugged. "I originally wanted to talk to him to see if he could hook me up with some of his informants. But then I got thinking. I've read some interesting things about your boyfriend's long life. He hasn't always been a cranberry-juice-drinking nightclub owner, you know. I'm not ruling out any suspects."

"Yeah, well Columbo, you might want to check out

this Nicolai guy who just came to town. Thierry says he's a dangerous elder vamp. He does look a bit shifty."

"Oh, Thierry says that, huh? Well it must be true then."

I gave him a look. "I'm not even going to have this discussion with you."

"So he was with you the night before last?"

"That's none of your business. Look, Quinn, I know you're trying to be helpful. But Thierry's a good man. Almost too good, if you ask me. He hired bodyguards to keep me safe till all of this blows over. One of them even said she'd teach me some self-defense."

He waved off my words. "Forget them. Consider *me* your new freelance bodyguard."

"You'd do that?"

"Of course I would." He glanced around the street and then met my eyes. Well, our dark sunglasses met each other, anyhow. "If you really trust Thierry, then I'll give him the benefit of the doubt. I'll look elsewhere. See what I can dig up. And if you want to learn some self-defense, I can teach you. That's sort of what I do, you know."

"Well—"

"In fact, I think that's an excellent idea. If you insist on putting yourself into these dumbass situations . . . "

I frowned. "Dumbass?"

"Let me rephrase that." A smile twigged at his lips. "*Stupid* situations . . . "

My frown deepened. "Hey!"

"Then you should at least know how to protect yourself." His smile got bigger. "And I'm an excellent teacher."

"You're willing to teach me self-defense."

He closed the distance between us with a step and

reached out to stroke the side of my face. "Of course I would. And we can start whenever you—"

Lenny appeared out of nowhere and tackled Quinn to the sidewalk. He had a knife out, pressed to Quinn's throat.

"Lenny, no!" I grabbed his huge python of an arm. "He's a friend of mine."

Lenny eased the pressure of the blade off Quinn's neck, leaving behind a thin line of red. Quinn bared his fangs and growled angrily at his attacker, pushing him off so he could stand up.

We'd attracted a bit of attention. People were passing us—at a safe distance—with their mouths open in shock. Cars slowed on the street as they drove by.

"He grabbed you," Lenny explained.

I frowned at him. "He didn't grab me. And besides, where were you a while ago when I got dragged into the alleyway by the hunter?"

"I . . . uh . . . had to . . . um. Nature called." He touched his right ear and I noticed that he wore one of those tiny communication earpieces. "Janie said it would be all right."

I felt frustration welling up inside me. "Quinn, are you okay?"

He gingerly touched his wounded neck. "Never better."

I shook my head. "You probably regret coming back to Toronto, don't you?"

He tore his narrow-eyed gaze away from the body-guard to look at me. His expression softened. "Not at all. Shit like this just makes life a little more interesting." He turned back to Lenny. "Touch me again, ass-hole, and it'll be the last thing you do. And if you're being paid to watch Sarah's back, I suggest you pull your head out of your ass. If she comes to any harm, you'll have me to answer to."

Lenny smirked. "Oh, yeah, and who in the hell do you think you are?"

"I'm a lot of things, depending on my frame of mind. And right now, I'm thinking I could be your worst nightmare."

Lenny's eyes narrowed. "Funny, you just look like a nobody to me." He glanced at me. "Ma'am, I think it would be best if I saw you home. I've called a taxi."

He didn't wait for an answer, instead moving away to give us a little privacy.

I glanced at Quinn. "I guess I'll go back to George's for now. That's where I'm staying. I'll be okay."

He didn't say anything, instead nodding stiffly, his arms crossed in front of him.

"Listen," I said after a moment. "Don't pay any attention to Lenny. He was just being a jerk."

Quinn snorted. "Lenny? Is that his name?" He shook his head and sighed slowly, a long exhalation that froze the cold air in front of him. "He's right, you know."

"About what?"

"About me being a nobody."

"What are you talking about?"

He was quiet for a moment. "I deserve it. I . . . " He absently rubbed a hand over his mouth. "I thought coming back to Toronto, looking into the murders, would give me purpose again, but I'm just . . . I don't know what I'm doing anymore."

I touched his shoulder. "Is everything okay?"

"With what? Adjusting to my new status of being a little long in the tooth?" He took a shaky breath. "I'm managing."

"No cure for what ails us, you know."

Quinn had been my partner in trying to find the cure for vampirism. Unfortunately, the trail led us to a dead end. Emphasis on the dead. And that was the end of that pipe dream.

"No, there isn't. So I guess we don't have much of a choice in the matter, do we?"

"No, I guess we don't."

He adjusted his sunglasses and managed to smile a little at me. "That's why people like us have to stick together. We've got a lot in common, you and me."

"Yeah, I guess we kind of do."

He looked at me fiercely. "That's why I don't want you to do anything stupid and get yourself killed. You hear me?"

The cab pulled up alongside us. Lenny approached and stood, arms folded, beside me.

Quinn helped me get all my bags into the backseat. I was about to get in, but he grabbed my hand to stop me.

"Sarah . . . " His voice trailed off and he looked at me so intensely that for a second I thought he might bite me.

"Uh huh?"

"When I'm with you I don't feel like a nobody. I want you to be safe, Sarah, no matter what. I promise to teach you a few things that will bring any man to his knees." A grin curled up the side of his lips. "That came out a little differently than it sounded in my head. I meant 'teach you self-defense moves,' of course."

I nodded a little too quickly and despite the chill in the

air, felt my cheeks warm. "Of course. Self-defense. Kung fu and all that. I totally understood what you meant."

"Good."

I nodded again. "Okay, I guess I'll see you soon, Quinn."

He brought my hand to his lips and kissed it, sending a hot tingle coursing all the way through my body.

"You can count on it," he said. Then he turned, and walked away.

I sat down heavily in the backseat of the cab thinking that I just might be in deep, deep trouble.

Chapter 7

Thierry called," George announced as I got back to the house. "You left your cell phone here."

"What?" I said, too distracted and flustered by seeing Quinn and by the rest of my afternoon to focus.

George was sprawled on the sofa. Barkley was sprawled out next to him. They were both watching *What Not to Wear*. "He says to meet him at the club at six-thirty. Oh, and your insurance agent called, too. I wrote her number down somewhere."

"The *club*?" I frowned. That's where Thierry wanted to meet for our date? I was hoping for something a little less familiar.

He eyed my shopping bags. "So, did you buy anything for me?"

I dropped my bags by the front door. "No. Sorry. But I did buy a great black dress for my date with Thierry."

"That's why you're meeting him at the club? For a date?" George eyed me with bland curiosity.

"So?"

He glanced back at the TV screen for a second. The makeover candidate was crying over her shortened hair as if the world was ending. "I'm sorry, but don't you have way more important things to worry about right now than that?"

I blinked at him. "Can you be more specific? I have so many things to worry about I think I'm forgetting to worry."

He blinked back at me. "I mean attending to me. Hanging out with me. I am morbidly depressed about my lacking love life, remember?"

I almost laughed at that. Not quite, but almost. "Of course. I'm so sorry. I guess I got so distracted with my apartment getting blown to smithereens, thus throwing my life into a state of confusion and uncertainty, that I forgot about how lonely your Saturday night was going to be."

"I forgive you. But I'm free tomorrow night if you want to do something." He shifted position on the sofa so he could see me better. "So is Quinn available?"

"Pardon me?"

"I would go out with him sometime if he was interested."

"Quinn's not gay."

He gave me a knowing smile. "Just give me time."

I nodded. "And this conversation is now at an end."

"Not that I could wedge myself between the two of you. Seriously, honey, it's just not fair for the rest of us when you monopolize two hot men."

"Excuse me?"

"The way you draped yourself over the poor boy last

night just to make Thierry jealous. Shameless." He shook his head. "I totally and completely approve."

I felt my cheeks flush. "I wasn't trying to make him jealous."

"Uh huh. Right. Well, when you end up breaking poor Quinn's heart—*again*— I will certainly be there to help him pick up whatever pieces he wants me to handle with care."

I frowned deeply. I wasn't trying to make Thierry jealous last night. I wasn't. That was ridiculous.

Or was it?

Time to change the subject.

"Amy told me today that she thinks that Barry's cheating on her."

George's back straightened and he twisted to look at me. "You don't say."

"I do say. But I'm sure it's not true. Maybe if I clear the guy's name he won't hate me so much. I'm going to investigate the situation tomorrow. Can you believe it?"

He nodded slowly. "Of course I can. Barry is undeniably charismatic."

I scrunched my nose. "Seriously?"

"Not as charismatic as Thierry, but I suppose you already know that. Even though I was surprised he wasn't here when I got up this morning."

I shuffled my feet. "He had to leave."

"Obviously."

"I've known him for two months and I feel like I don't know anything about him. That's part of the reason for the date tonight. I want to know everything I can about him."

George grabbed the TV guide and flipped through it. "He's very private about his past, you know."

"I know. But —"

"Sometimes you just have to accept people for what they are up front. Dig too deeply and you might not like what you find. Sounds superficial, but that's just the kind of guy I am. I mean, look at me and Barkley. I've decided to tolerate him because I know that *you* like him."

I smiled at the two of them. "You guys look like you're getting cozy."

George leaned forward to scratch Barkley's head. "I don't like dogs."

"Yeah, keep telling yourself that. Dog lover."

He shot me a look. "Oh, by the way, somebody tried to deliver something for you earlier but nobody was home. He left a slip that said he'll be back tomorrow. On a Sunday? Who delivers on a Sunday?"

I froze. "Who was it? What were they trying to deliver? Was it ticking? Did the delivery guy look like a hunter?"

He shrugged. "I didn't really pay that much attention. You know, you're getting a little paranoid, Sarah."

"*Paranoid*," I repeated. "Paranoid is just another word for *proactive*, my friend."

"Whatever you say."

I took a deep breath and let it out slowly. "All right, this is me getting ready for my date now. If that's okay with you?'

He waved a hand. "You do what you have to do. Just remember what I said. Don't try to pry too deeply in Thierry's business. Even though he doesn't look it, he's really old and set in his ways. Old guys get crotchety about their privacy."

"I'll keep that in mind."

I dragged the bags into my temporary bedroom and then went through my loot from the day's shopping spree. All things considered, I'd done okay. It came nowhere close to replacing my old wardrobe. God, I was going to mourn that for a long, long time, along with everything else I'd lost—especially my shard. Somebody had to pay, and I'm not just talking credit.

I'd bought something special to wear tonight, even though the thought that we weren't going anywhere better than Haven an hour and a half before it opened to the general vampire public was a little disappointing.

I wasn't sure I wanted to set foot in any club for the next few days after that horrible dream I'd had. Even though I know it wasn't real, seeing Thierry staked right before my eyes had really shaken me to my core. And my core was already shaken to begin with. I wish I could just forget about Peter once and for all. I shouldn't feel guilt for what happened. He'd deserved it. It had been self-defense—it was him or me.

I shivered at the memory.

Thierry had taken care of the body. All the bodies, really. He had some serious contacts pretty much everywhere, so when he needed something done, all he had to do was flip open his silver cell phone and call those who would assist with whatever problem there might be.

Just like he'd been on the phone last night with his contacts dealing with his latest problem. Otherwise known as me.

I sighed. He probably thought I was just one big bother.

I pulled out the black dress I'd bought during my shopping extravaganza—the kind of black dress that was chic and sophisticated while still being low-cut and sexy enough for me to not want to wear in front of my mother.

Maybe it was wrong to go through with my date with Thierry after everything that had happened. I mean, it was less than twenty-four hours since my apartment and all my belongings had gone up in flames. I think if that had happened when I'd still been a normal office gal things might have been different for me. Instead of going on a shopping spree the next day I would be curled up in a corner of a dark room rocking myself back and forth. Drool may have been involved.

But I wasn't drooling. It was a miracle.

Or maybe I was still in shock. That was a definite possibility.

But I did want to see Thierry. Actually, I couldn't wait. I wanted to spend some time alone with him to remind him how much I wanted him in my life.

And not just that. I needed some answers. I had so many questions—about him, about us, about Nicolai, about the hunters, about everything, really. And getting him alone with no other distractions might just be the prescription for getting exactly what I needed to know to keep me happy and alive.

Yes, relationship issues and murder plots. Let the romantic evening commence!

At the end of the day, I guess there was only one person who needed to be focused on keeping me not dead. And that was me.

Well. And maybe Lenny, too. He had that big knife.

Lenny dropped me off at Haven a few minutes after six-thirty. He said he'd be back to guard the door after he grabbed a burger for dinner. I hadn't seen Janie since that afternoon. I had a spare key to the place, and I used it to let myself in through the nondescript front door.

I wore my new black dress (frankly, a little itchy) under a new black leather trench coat, and a borrowed-from-Amy pair of black four-inch heels. Black. That was my theme for the evening. But it didn't look like I was in mourning. Not too many people would wear a dress this low-cut to a funeral unless they were the twenty-something widow of the ninety-year-old billion-aire who just went toes up.

I peeled off the coat and draped it over my arm as soon as I stepped inside the darkened club. There was a short hallway before you got into the main area. That's where Angel the bouncer normally hung out. Walk down the hallway and go through another set of doors, and boom . . . welcome to Haven.

A dark and empty Haven.

I frowned. Maybe George got it wrong. Was I sup-posed to be there? I knew that nobody usually showed up until about eight o'clock to get things ready for the nine-o'clock opening. The club was silent, still, and vacant.

Then I saw something over in the corner. Candles. Actually, a whole lot of candles. It was the table Thierry usually sat at when not in his office. The table was sur-rounded by lit candles that gave off a warm, flickering glow as I approached.

On the table were two red roses. A bottle of champagne chilled in a silver bucket. Two fluted glasses waited on the white linen tablecloth.

"Sarah. I'm glad you got my message." Thierry's deep voice moved through me from head to toes.

I turned around to face him, sucking a breath in at how tall, dark, and delicious he looked. The memory of his kiss early that morning came back to me in vivid, Technicolor, R-rated detail.

I smiled. "Hi there."

He looked very serious. "I've been worried about you today. I tried to call your cell phone but I kept getting George."

"I know. Sorry about that. I'm fine."

His gaze trailed down the front of me, then back to my face. "New dress?"

I shrugged. "Since it's not made of ashes, I'm going to go with a yes. Do you like it?"

"I believe I got my money's worth."

"Despite the fact that you really have no idea how much this cost you, I choose to take that as a compliment."

"A wise choice. Please have a seat."

I glanced at the table as I slid into the booth. "This is beautiful."

He shook his head. "I wanted to take you somewhere a little more extravagant, but feel that this is the safest place right now." He sat down across from me. The candlelight reflected softly in his silver-colored eyes.

"So we have an hour and a half before anyone shows up?"

He poured me a glass of champagne. I noticed that his glass was already filled with what seemed to be his favorite drink—cranberry juice. "Will that be enough time?"

"That all depends." I smiled. "You know, you could have woken me up last night."

He gave a small shrug. "You were sleeping so peacefully. And after the shock of what happened, you needed your rest."

"I really would have made an exception." I pushed aside my uncertainty and reached across the table and entwined my fingers with his. "Trust me on that."

He raised an eyebrow. "I must admit, I did consider it. But after listening to your snoring for a short time, I decided not to disturb you."

I gave him a stricken look. "My *what*?"

"Your snoring." He gave me a half smile. "Just a soft sound. A snuffle, really."

"A *snuffle*?" I felt my cheeks start to burn.

He nodded. "It's nothing to be ashamed of. It's quite adorable."

I felt the sexy dress vibe skidding off of me like eggs on a nonstick frying pan. "I *don't* snore."

"You do. Trust me." His eyes flashed with amusement and I gave him a dirty look, which only served to amuse him further. Oh, good. I guess I was the entertainment for the evening. Well, a guy who seemed amused by my unconscious bodily noises was probably actually a good thing if I could shake my embarrassment. I don't snore. I'm almost completely positive I don't.

The amusement faded from his eyes. "Perhaps this should have waited for a better time. If you want to leave, I'll understand completely."

"Things are a little crazy right now," I agreed. I picked

up my glass of champagne. I'd never really acquired a taste for the stuff. Kind of like caviar. But I could fake it with the best of them. "But it was my idea we do this, and I stand by it. Should we toast to anything?"

He raised his glass of cranberry juice. "Anything you like."

"Okay." I thought about it for a moment. "To the future. May it be filled with six-hundred-year-old vampires making an exception and waking me up, for which I will make it well worth their while."

"You know many six-hundred-year-old vampires?"

"A lady has her secrets."

He smiled and touched his glass to mine. "That is a toast that is sure to come to pass."

I smiled inwardly. Maybe this date was a good idea after all. I took a long sip of my champagne. It didn't taste bad, actually. Maybe the stuff I'd had in the past was just the wrong kind. I glanced at the bottle. Roederer Cristal. Hundreds of dollars for one bottle. More depending on the year. Yeah, I'd *definitely* never had that kind before. That was the kind of alcohol worth fighting somebody for.

Which brought up a subject I should probably get to right away, now that I thought of it.

I put the glass down on the table. "Thierry, do you happen to know any self- defense? Like karate or kung fu or anything like that?"

He studied me for a moment. "Why do you ask?"

"I'm thinking about learning how to protect myself. I've considered it for a while, but lately . . . I think it's the only way I can feel safe being out and about with everything that's going on."

He shook his head. "The best way to stay safe is to *stay* somewhere safe. Right now you have the bodyguards. That should be enough. The only reason you would need to learn self-defense is if you continue to thrust yourself into dangerous situations."

I shrugged. "It happens. Sometimes it can't be controlled. Quinn said he'd teach me, but—" I stopped talking and cleared my throat. "How about a little more of that champagne?"

"He did, did he?" He poured me more champagne, but his gaze didn't leave my face. "You could have told me you've been in contact with Quinn since he left town. That you told him where the club was located."

I found that I couldn't meet his eyes. Why did I feel guilty? "Why does that matter?"

"He has ties to the hunter community. Even if he is no longer fully affiliated with them, that doesn't mean that they aren't tracking his every move."

I sighed. "You are such a worrywart."

He raised his eyebrows. "A *worrywart*?"

"That's right. You take simple situations and blow them *way* out of proportion. Quinn's had a hard life, you know."

He nodded, but his expression was cold. "Yes, poor boy. Such a hard life he's had with his rich genocidal father, spending every waking moment killing vampires while they screamed for mercy. And now to have you as his number-one advocate. Poor Quinn."

"He regrets his past."

Thierry took a sip of his cranberry juice. His knuckles were white on the glass. "I suppose I find that one month is not enough to redeem a decade of his previous actions."

"And how long would be the right amount of time for you? A decade? A century?"

"Sometimes an eternity is not enough."

I studied his tense expression. "You sound like you're speaking from personal experience."

He stared at me for a moment, but didn't reply. What George had said to me earlier came back: *Dig too deep and you may not like what you find.*

This date was taking a serious nosedive. I had to turn it back around while I still could and get it back to how it was at the beginning. Focus, Sarah, I told myself. And no more talking about Quinn. Definitely a hazardous topic.

"How about a new subject?" I announced, forcing a smile to my lips after a moment of uncomfortable silence.

"An excellent suggestion."

"What's your favorite color?"

He looked at me for a moment, and then started to laugh. "Favorite color?"

I shrugged. "It's a new subject, isn't it?"

"I don't know that I have a favorite color."

"My guess would be black. You wear a lot of it."

He looked down at his staple outfit— black shirt, black jacket, black pants. All designer and custom made to perfectly fit his tall, lean frame. "It all matches."

I nodded. "So you pick black to help you have a no-brainer wardrobe?"

"Why else?"

"It does suit you."

"You think so?"

"Yes, it gives off that slightly sinister, but very sexy look."

His gaze moved slowly down the front of my dress. "I

see that you are also wearing black tonight. Are you trying to look sinister?"

I looked down to be faced with my cleavage. "Not so much."

He raised an eyebrow. "So just sexy."

I slid out of my side of the booth and slid in beside Thierry. "We sort of match, don't we?"

He paused and met my gaze. "Yes, I suppose we do."

I slipped my hand under his jacket and against the warmth of his chest. "How much time do we have left?"

He glanced at his watch. "A little over an hour."

"That should be enough."

"For what?" he asked with mock innocence, as he slowly ran his fingers through my hair and tucked it behind my ear.

"Maybe that's enough small talk for one night." I grinned and moved my hands up to draw his face closer to mine to kiss him. After a moment, I traced my tongue over his fangs—small and sharp, just like mine. Something else that matched.

Thierry could kiss. And this was such a wonderful kiss that whispered promises of things to come, but still . . . there was something missing. It wasn't like last night. He was restraining himself again. I could feel it. He was only giving a percentage of himself. It might have been 90 percent, but I could tell that it wasn't a hundred.

But 90 percent of Thierry was 1,000 percent of any other guy I'd ever kissed. If I'd been standing up, my knees would have gone weak.

I inhaled his cologne. Woodsy, musky, undoubtedly male. Not like some of these fruity, floral colognes men wear that smell like clones of women's perfume.

Thierry's was different, and I associated the scent with him completely. I slid my hand down to his waist as I buried my nose into his neck.

He tensed. "What are you doing?"

"Smelling you." My hand moved down to his thigh.

"Why?"

"Because you smell so damn good. And it isn't just because of my new vampire nose."

"Your senses are heightening?" he asked.

I nodded. "I've noticed smell and hearing," I kissed him again. "Taste, too. I'm still disappointed that I won't be able to turn into a bat, but I'm moving on."

"All earlier than expected," Thierry said, his expression darkening a little. "My fault, I'm afraid. I never should have given you my blood."

"If you hadn't, I'd be dead right now. So I appreciate it."

"There were other options. I simply wasn't thinking."

I moved even closer to him. "You think too much."

Our lips met again and I allowed my hands to wander freely along his delicious body. I wanted him so badly it hurt. It had been two long weeks since we were in Mexico. And this was so perfect. Why had I doubted things between us?

He grabbed my hand just before it started to make any unladylike maneuvers and brought it to his lips to kiss. "Do you have anything else you wanted to know about me, or were you simply wondering what my favorite color was?"

I smiled at him. "Okay, I do have another question. Where did you get that wonderful cologne?"

He placed my hand on the tabletop and poured me

more champagne. "Veronique gave it to me. She has it specially made every year."

Cold shower. Right here. And I didn't even have to get wet.

I scooted a little away from him so we were no longer touching. "Veronique."

"Yes."

Yes, despite the fact they weren't together anymore, that woman would always be the dark little rain cloud over our relationship.

"Why don't you divorce her?" I asked.

My eyes widened. Yikes. Did I really just say that out loud?

Yeah, I did. So what? It's about time somebody did.

Oh, God. Can I take it back?

Thierry looked surprised at my question. "Divorce?"

I swallowed hard. "Um. Well, it's not like you two are living together anymore. Your marriage is in name only. Isn't that what you told me?"

"Of course. But a divorce—"

I shook my head. "No, just forget I said anything. You two have so much history that I guess it doesn't make sense to get a divorce. I mean, it's not like you'd ever want to get married again."

Why was I still talking? Things had been so great a second ago and I had to go ruin it bringing up something that didn't even matter.

Yes it did.

No it didn't.

He was going to think I was a completely possessive idiot.

"May I finish?" he asked. I nodded meekly. "As I was

saying, divorce would be extremely complicated, due to our unusual circumstances. We were married over six hundred years ago. Any official record of our vows has probably been destroyed. It is not as simple as hiring a lawyer and filing papers."

"Of course." I nodded, not looking directly at him. "That makes total sense."

I seriously had to focus. Forget Veronique. Forget Quinn. There were more important things to discuss. Including that champagne that I could seriously use another glass of it right about now.

I tried to smile. "Let's just forget I said anything, okay?"

Thierry shook his head. "It's true that I have not revealed much about myself personally to you. I will admit that. I am a private man and always have been. But . . . " His expression tensed and he looked down at the table, then up to stare intently into my eyes. "Sarah, there . . . there are things I wish for you to know about me. Things you must know."

I put my hand up and shook my head. This was the dangerous territory George warned me about. "Maybe we should talk about Nicolai."

That stopped him. He frowned. "Nicolai . . . "

"Yeah. The reason I'm not immediately hightailing it out of town? You said that he's dangerous. Why is that? Where do you know him from, anyhow?"

"I will tell you about Nicolai in a moment." He paused and took a sip of his drink. "But first I want you to know some things about me I should have told you long ago. It simply didn't seem the time."

His expression was very grave. I braced myself to hear

some horrible news as he looked down at the tablecloth and his glass of dark red cranberry juice.

Then he looked up at me and grabbed my hand so suddenly that it scared me. Instinctively I pulled away, managing to knock my champagne glass off the table. It shattered on the ceramic tiled floor.

"Shit. Sorry." I slipped out of the booth and crouched over to start grabbing at the pieces, but I wasn't concentrating completely on what I was doing. I flinched as I felt a slicing pain and realized I'd just succeeded in cutting the tip of my index finger with a broken piece of glass. "Oh, great. Just my luck. I'm sorry, I'm so clumsy."

Thierry stood up from the booth and grabbed a napkin. He took my hand in his, his brow furrowed. "I broke a glass last night, too. Nobody noticed, but I did. So we're even."

I smiled up at him. "You're just trying to make me feel better."

He studied the wound. It was deep and the blood dripped steadily to the floor. I had a bit of a love/hate relationship with the red stuff. It still made me squeamish. I'd never been able to watch any of those operation shows on TV, but at the same time, now whenever I saw it, my stomach rumbled, seemingly recognizing it as my main food source. Talk about gross. Welcome to my life.

Yeah, I'd done a great job of hurting myself. I didn't need hunters. I could probably kill myself by accident before too long. I could just hear the hunters discussing it over a beer. "Yeah, she fell on a sharp pencil while doing a crossword puzzle. It was spectacular!"

He tossed the napkin, unused, to the table. "It will heal shortly."

"Right." I squinted down at the blood and grimaced. "Super-speedy healing. Good to know I can add that to my arsenal of vampire powers."

Thierry frowned. "Sarah . . . it is very important that you stop me right now." His voice was strained and his grip on my hand increased. "I don't know if I can stop myself."

"What are you talking about?"

He kissed the back of my hand. Then he kissed the injured finger, and slowly drew the length of it into his mouth.

I gaped at him, frozen in place. Heat flooded my body at the feel of his tongue swirling around my finger. My knees weakened and my brain stopped working.

This was finger sucking the way it should be! Hell yeah! Forget about that horrible incident with my boss and her letter opener. This was definitely the way to go.

He gazed at me as he concentrated on my injured finger. There was an expression on his face I don't think I'd ever seen before. I didn't even know how to explain it. Something wild and unpredictable. Dangerous. His eyes narrowed slightly and appeared to darken, the darkness bleeding out to the whites of his eyes until they were fully black.

I frowned. "Thierry . . . "

Against my finger I felt his fangs—normally small and innocuous and barely noticeable like mine—thicken and elongate as he attended to my injury. After a moment he finally let my finger slip out of his mouth.

"Sarah . . . " His voice was raspy and deep and filled with the edge of an unfamiliar emotion. He slid his hands down the sides of my dress and pulled me closer.

"Thierry, your eyes—"

"Are they my favorite color now?" He pulled me against him, hard, and crushed his lips against mine, taking my breath away.

One hundred percent. No restraint. I melted against him.

After a moment he broke off the kiss with a growl. He looked down at the table we were leaning against, then with a sweeping movement pushed everything off it to the floor. The bottle of champagne shattered like the crystal glasses. The candles hit the floor and extinguished, making the room even darker. Then he pressed me backward, down onto the surface of the table.

I wrapped my arms around his shoulders, sliding my fingers into his dark hair, hoping that we had enough time to explore black-eyed Thierry before somebody walked in on us. That would be extremely embarrassing.

But, hey, I think it might be worth it. I was beginning to like this black-eyed Thierry a whole lot. And he wanted me to stop him? Like hell, I say.

He buried his face in the crook of my neck. "You smell wonderful, too."

"Thank you. It's *Amarige* by Givenchy. Bought it today."

"Mmm. Yes . . . wonderful. Good enough to eat."

"What did you—?"

And then he sank his fangs into my neck. I clutched at his back, surprised and shocked by the sharp intense sensation. But it wasn't pain. I was surprised. I couldn't exactly remember what it felt like getting bit by my blind date, I guess I'd blocked it out because he'd been just nasty, but it hadn't been like this, I was sure of it.

This was . . . *damn*. This was just as hot as all those sexy books made it sound. Having your neck bitten by a vampire was like a total metaphor for—

I frowned.

No . . . wait.

No . . . this wasn't good. Not good. He was taking too much. Drinking too fast.

"Thierry . . . stop." I pushed at him. He responded by sliding his hands up my body to grab my wrists and hold them down against the table. He said nothing, continuing to focus completely on my neck.

After another moment, what started as a sensual experience began to hurt. It felt as if somebody had just bitten into my neck with long, sharp teeth, a searing pain turning to agony as his fangs dug deep into my flesh so he could pierce my vein. To drink my blood.

Not sexy.

"It is important that you stop me right now," he'd said just a moment ago.

Maybe I should have listened to him.

I squirmed under the weight of him. "Thierry . . . let go of me . . . "

But he didn't. He held me there and drank from me until I began to feel weak, until I started to feel cold. I stopped struggling.

"Thierry . . . " my voice was weaker now.

Cranberry juice, I thought absently. He normally drinks cranberry juice. I'd never seen him drink blood before. Never.

Suddenly he jerked away from me, bringing a hand up to his mouth, but not before I could see my blood on his lips.

He shook his head and stared at me with wide black eyes. "No. Oh . . . Sarah. I'm so sorry. I . . . damn it. *Damn it*. I didn't want this to happen. Not with you. Never with you."

And then he turned and ran from the club.

I could barely move. I sat up weakly and pushed myself off the table, absently adjusting my dress. I had to go after him. He looked so distraught about what just happened. I had to go . . .

I took two steps before I fell to the ground unconscious.

Chapter 8

When I woke up I noticed that somebody's wrist was in my mouth. Which, to say the least, is an odd thing to notice. I grabbed the wrist and extracted it, only then realizing that, one, the wrist was bleeding, and two, it belonged to Nicolai.

"Gross!" I scrambled away from him. "What exactly do you think you're doing?"

"Saving your life." He rolled his sleeve down and picked up his jacket from a nearby table.

"How do I know where your wrist has been? That's disgusting."

He stared at me. "I gave you some of my blood."

"Yeah, got that. Thus my 'disgusting' comment?"

He frowned at me. "You are a very strange vampire."

"Where's Thierry?" For the first time since I woke up I looked around the club. It was still dark. There didn't seem to be anyone around except for me and the Russian vamp.

"I don't know."

"How did you get in here?"

He didn't say anything for a moment. "I have ways of getting where I need to be. And it's a good job that I did. You had lost a great deal of blood. Too much. You didn't have much time left."

I touched my neck and flinched. What in the hell had happened? That was most definitely not the way I'd expected things to turn out tonight.

"Thierry did this," Nicolai said. It wasn't a question so I didn't answer it. He shook his head. "So many years and so little has changed."

"What's that supposed to mean?"

"Sarah, please sit. You should get off your feet. You're still weakened. I can give you more blood if you like."

I waved him off. "No thanks. If I need any more I can go tap a keg." A wave of dizziness came over me and I swayed on my high heels.

"Sit. Please."

"I think I'm going to hurl." The backs of my legs found the nearest chair and I sat down heavily. I took a moment to compose myself before I looked at Nicolai. "What do you mean that not much has changed over the years?"

He took a seat across from me. "What happened tonight?"

I shook my head. "Who are you, anyhow? And don't just give me that elder vampire Ring crap."

He spread his hands. "I am simply someone who wishes to right the wrongs of the world. To make sure that those who are innocent do not pay the price for those who are guilty."

"Right."

"You don't believe me?"

I rubbed my temples. "I don't know what to believe right now. What time is it?"

"It's twenty after seven."

I looked at him sharply, feeling tense and more than a little bruised. "Were you spying on us?"

"I was concerned."

I made a face. "You were spying. You're a total weirdo. Well, I hope you enjoyed the show."

"I saved your life."

I nodded and tried to relax a bit. "Yes, I guess you did. Thank you."

He raised a blond eyebrow. "I am surprised that one known as the Slayer of Slayers would find herself in such a predicament."

I felt a chill go down my spine. "Well, sometimes I slip up a bit. That's never happened before. I'll kick his ass next time."

"Thierry was lying to me when he said you weren't romantically involved, wasn't he?"

"Not that it's any of your business . . . but our relationship is an *undefined* one."

"Undefined."

"That's right. Now, if you came here for an answer to your little job offering with the Ring, I haven't made up my mind yet. You don't have to stay in town. Just leave a number where I can reach you and I'll be in touch."

He studied me for a long moment. Until I began to feel very uncomfortable. If I'd had the energy I would have stood up and left the club, but I didn't think my legs would carry me very far before having another ceramic tile nap.

Where had Thierry gone? Was he okay?

Hell. Was I okay?

"What really happened at Midnight Eclipse that night?" he asked.

I crossed my arms. "I killed eight vampire hunters. And I'd do it again."

"I thought you told me there were nine."

Oops. "Eight, nine. What's the difference?"

"How did you kill them?" His eyes narrowed. "With your bare hands? With a weapon?"

When I didn't answer right away, he stood up abruptly. "I think that your relationship is not the only thing Thierry has lied about, has he?" He turned to look at me. "I am going to surmise that he said that I would kill you if I learned that the rumors were false, correct?"

"No comment." My mouth was dry. "Let's just say there are video cameras everywhere in here. Don't try anything or you'll be a stain on the floor in less than thirty seconds."

I was such a terrible liar.

He didn't look too worried. "So typical of him. Well, you don't have to worry, Sarah. My plans do not include killing you. My disappointment, however, is vast. I had hoped that it was true. That I had finally found another who could help vampirekind find the strength we seem to have collectively lost."

"I'm sorry. Really." I touched my now-injured neck and flinched. "Plus that Ring salary would have been great right about now. Did you happen to hear about my apartment?"

He nodded. "The hunters still perceive you as a threat. In fact, I have heard that their leader, Gideon Chase, has taken a special interest in you, though how long that will last before he, too, finds out the truth . . . " He looked away with a grim expression. "I had hoped to use your reputation to our advantage. Thierry may find that ironic if he ever learns of it."

"What do you mean?"

He fixed me with a steady look. "You don't know who Gideon Chase is?"

"No. Should I?"

"He is the leader of the vampire hunters—a billionaire who is from a long line of those who kill us without conscience."

"What's he got to do with Thierry specifically?"

His lips made a move to smile, but seemed to change their mind. "Gideon is one of the many reasons Thierry hides himself away. Gideon is the man who put the price on Thierry's head. Thierry has managed to surround himself only with those he trusts, and has avoided being captured or killed. Quite an accomplishment. But he is still highly sought after. I believe the current price tag is three million dollars?"

"Something like that."

"That price is for Thierry captured alive. Gideon wishes to claim the kill for himself. His riches have made it possible for him to make a hobby of hunting down the oldest vampires. He has many kills to his name. All vicious, sadistic, and excessive, for his own entertainment. He is a fearsome man."

"I hate him already." Sounded like this guy was responsible for a good chunk of the way Thierry acts. His safety measures. His secrecy. Sounded like the kind of guy the world would be better off without.

"You should, as he is on his way to Toronto as we speak to hunt and kill the Slayer of Slayers."

I blinked. "Say what?"

"It is true." Nicolai paced toward the bar, stood there for a moment, then turned around. Oddly enough, he was smiling. "I had a great plan. It is almost humorous now. I was going to use your reputation to lure Gideon to be captured. Seize this opportunity. The Slayer of Slayers could have been instrumental in changing the dynamic between hunter and vampire. Thierry, too, would have been safer with the price off his head. Not completely safe, but without such a reward, it is unlikely that the average hunter would seek out a confrontation with a master vampire so old and powerful."

"This guy is coming *here*."

Nicolai nodded, the smile fading from his face. "Not that it matters. Stay inside, away from danger, and you can avoid him easily. He will move on to his next challenge. As will I."

My mind was working overtime. Half of me, well, more than half, wanted to do just what Nicolai suggested. Now that I didn't have to put on an act for him, I didn't have to put myself in danger anymore. I could leave the country. Go live with those nuns, like Thierry suggested. Stay away till things cooled down and my insurance money for the apartment came through.

Or . . . I could do something else.

"Nicolai . . . do you think the plan would still work, even though the rumors about me are all a big lie? If I still showed my face out there and Gideon showed up . . . how likely is it that I would get killed?"

He shook his head. "You would be safe. I have a team in place as of this evening, ready when he appears to capture him. I doubt that he will be expecting anything like that."

"You have a team? Seriously?"

"Of course. Your life was never in danger, from me or from anyone else. But I wouldn't expect you to agree to such a thing now, despite my assurances. You don't know me. My reception from Thierry was not overly friendly, as I'm sure you noticed."

"I did notice that. But he's not overly friendly with too many people, so to tell you the truth, the 'grain of salt' was invoked."

He glanced over at the table in the corner. Two candles were still lit. The rest had joined the champagne, cranberry juice, and broken glasses on the floor. "And you shared blood with him tonight."

I grimaced. "It was an accident."

"It's never happened before?"

"No. Not like that, anyhow. And I'm thinking rather strongly that it won't be happening again."

He paused and studied me for a moment, his face hard and expressionless. "So you didn't know about his . . . little problem."

"Oh, the fact that he turns into a blood-crazed Nosferatu when he gets a taste of the red stuff? Yeah, doesn't everybody?"

Nicolai's lips thinned. "Sarcasm is well known to be the lowest form of humor."

I shrugged, which was actually a bit of an effort. "But I'm so good at it."

He studied me for a moment. "Did he tell you that we were once good friends?"

I could use another glass of that champagne. Too bad it was currently coating the mosaic-tiled floor. "The subject didn't come up."

"One hundred years ago, give or take a decade, Thierry was one of the elders of the Ring. In fact, he founded it."

I tried not to show I cared, but any information about Thierry perked my ears up like Barkley's. "Really? The Ring? No, he definitely didn't mention that."

He nodded. "He and Veronique had gone their separate ways by then. He was interested in finding a way of stopping the hunters, who had made life for a vampire so unbearable in large parts of Europe that he'd come to North America. He searched for those who were interested in making a change. I was one that he recruited."

"Where was this?"

"In the States. California. After a while he had six vampires who had formed the Ring. So called because there was a vampire elder on each continent who would in turn solicit interested parties in their areas. These are the same elders that Gideon Chase's family has been systematically slaughtering for decades." His expression hardened for a moment. "I was a newlywed at the time. I married the most beautiful woman I had ever seen. An actress." His fingers twisted the long gold chain around his neck. "To this day I wear her locket."

"Where is she now?"

He took the locket in his hand and squeezed. "She is

dead. She's been gone for nearly a century, and I miss her as much today as when I first lost her."

His face held great pain and my heart twisted. "I'm sorry."

He opened the locket and showed me a small black and white photo of an elegant-looking blond woman. "Her name was Elizabeth."

"She was very beautiful."

He gazed at the picture. "Yes, she was. I should never have left her alone that week. I felt that something was amiss. That something was going to go wrong. And it did. And I'll regret what happened for the rest of my life."

"What . . . what happened?"

He tucked the necklace under his shirt and met my gaze. "Thierry killed her."

I gasped. "What?"

His face contorted and it looked as if he was about to cry, but he held it together. "I know it was an accident that he regrets. I know it. But in my heart I've never been able to forgive him. I haven't seen him since it happened. I've avoided him. He has avoided me. Until last night."

I shook my head. "No. I don't believe it. He wouldn't do something like that. It's not possible."

He rubbed the back of his hand across his mouth. "It is possible. My wife was very beautiful. Thierry was alone. She was kind to him and he became obsessed with her. Then . . . " He broke off for a moment and I saw his gaze lower to my wounded neck. "One night when I was away he bit her as he just did you. Old vampires like Thierry should not drink blood anymore. Any vampire over five hundred years old has no need for it; their bodies have evolved to such a level that they are capable of living without it. When they do taste it, it's like a drug that turns them feral and wild. Like animals who have no choice but to feed until their prey is dead."

I touched my neck again, but said nothing.

Nicolai continued. "I don't believe Thierry meant to drain my Elizabeth. If I thought him capable of such an act, I never would have left. But it was an accident. When I returned, she had been dead for a week. It is the greatest regret of my life."

I never would have believed what Nicolai said. Not if I hadn't just witnessed a blood-crazed Thierry for myself. If Nicolai hadn't been around to revive me, would I have died? Thierry would have been responsible for killing me. The thought sent a chill through my body.

"What did he say to you when you got back?" I asked.

"Nothing at all. He resigned from the Ring and simply left. My hate has subsided over all the years, but seeing him again affected me more than I ever would have believed. And to think that after all this time, he has finally found someone who cares about him as my Elizabeth cared for me." His expression tensed. "I must admit it bothered me that he should be allowed that luxury."

Was this one of the reasons why Thierry was the way he was? So guarded? So restrained? Unable to share himself fully with another person? Because of this ton of guilt he carried around for killing a friend's wife a hundred years ago?

For what happened to him if he had a taste of blood?

No. I couldn't think about this now.

"We were talking about Gideon and your plan," I said before I paused for a moment. "I still want to help if I can."

He shook his head gravely. "I don't think that's a very good idea."

"You said that there are people ready to grab him when he comes for me, right? That this would make a big difference to vampires—help them stop being hunted a bit. If I have a chance to do something to make that happen, then I can't exactly turn my back on that."

"I don't know, Sarah."

"This reputation of mine won't last much longer. The truth will eventually get out. Gideon and the other hunters will see that I'm nothing special. So it's now or never. Plus, if doing this will take the price off Thierry's head, then I have to do it."

"You're in love with him." It wasn't a question. "Even after what he just did to you. Even after what I just told you."

I swallowed hard and didn't answer directly. "He can't know I'm doing this. He can't know about Gideon. Just grab him when you get the chance and then we can all try to live happily ever after."

"You are very brave."

"I've lost a great deal of blood, you know."

A small smile tugged at his lips, and he glanced again at my neck. "Vampires worldwide will thank you."

I sighed. "Just have them send flowers to the funeral. And listen," I stood up from my chair and touched his arm. "I'm so sorry about what happened with your wife. Really."

He was still looking at my neck. His eyes appeared to darken a shade and he took a step closer to close the space between the two of us.

The door to Haven opened up to my left and we both looked over. It was George.

"Hey Sarah, how did your date go?"

I exchanged a glance with Nicolai, who stepped away from me and looked over toward the empty bar. "It was so much fun that I might have to be hospitalized."

He nodded with approval. "Glad you had a good time. Where is the boss now?"

"He had to leave."

"As I must, as well." Nicolai stood up from his chair. "We will speak again very soon."

"Definitely."

With a last look at me, Nicolai turned and left the club.

George looked over at the broken bottle of champagne on the floor. "Do I even want to know what happened here?"

The phone began to ring.

"Probably not." I slipped behind the bar and picked up the phone. "Haven. Hello?"

"Yes, I wish to speak to my husband," a sexy, lilting, lightly French-accented voice said. "He's not answering his cell phone."

"Veronique? This is Sarah. Thierry's . . . out." I adjusted my dress, noticing that there was a rip in my thigh-high nylons.

"Oh, Sarah, my dear. You're still there."

"Yes. It's only been a day since you left."

"Are you well? You sound distraught."

"I do?" I reached over to pour myself a shot of B-positive and knocked it back. "That's strange, since everything's so incredibly wonderful around here. The fun never ends."

"You are sure?"

"Quite sure."

"Very well, my dear. You have my number should you need to talk."

"Yes, I have it."

"Please let Thierry know that I called."

"Sure. Listen, Vee, can I ask you a question?"

"Anything. I am an open book to aid those who need my advice."

"Thierry's got a price on his head, right?"

She hesitated. "Unfortunately this is very true. One of the reasons he is so conscious about keeping those close to him safe."

"I've heard some guy named Gideon Chase is responsible for it. Is that true? And would taking this guy out of the picture mean that Thierry's life is a little easier?"

"Gideon is a handsome, powerful man who indulges his sadistic pleasures. His family for generations has loved to bring any elder vampire down, and Thierry is unfortunately at the top of their list. So am I, for that matter."

A simple yes would have sufficed, but whatever.

"Veronique—"

She cut me off. "Dear, speaking of Gideon upsets me greatly. Could you please tell my husband I called? I must get back to the party."

There was a click as she hung up.

That was rather rude. She could afford the long distance.

"Okay, miss, if you would clear out of the way, I need to set up now."

I glanced up at a very tall vampire who looked pissed off that I was in his space.

"Are you the new bartender?" I asked, feeling shaky from blood loss and information overload.

"Move it."

"Geez. Okay." I moved away from the bar. The rest of the employees began to arrive.

"Where's Barry tonight?" I asked George.

"He asked for it off, Sarah. Again. Can you believe it? Which means more work for the rest of us. Note my lack of enthusiasm."

Barry wasn't here again? What was he up to?

He couldn't be cheating. I didn't believe it for a minute. But I had to find out what he was up to. If I could prove his innocence and get rid of Amy's doubts about her diminutive husband, the guy would owe me. Plus, he might start liking me a bit. Since he was Thierry's number-one advisor, it would be nice to have him on my side. Barry, more than anyone, could tell me all I ever needed to know about Thierry. If he was properly motivated, that is.

I'd check him out tomorrow. I was going to find out the truth.

"Sarah?" the sullen new bartender asked. "You're Sarah Dearly?"

"Guilty."

A big smile spread across his face. He came out from behind the bar and before I knew it he was shaking my hand vigorously. "Oh, my word! You're the Slayer of Slayers I've been hearing so much about."

I glanced at George. "Really, it's no big deal."

"No big deal, she says. No big deal? It's a big deal. Sorry I was a little rude earlier. I didn't know who you were! Gosh. The Slayer of Slayers. It's a pleasure to be in your presence." He didn't let go of my hand. "Ooo. I can feel it. Your powerful vibe. It's coming off you in waves. It gives me shivers. But in a good way."

"Um . . . "

He frowned. "What happened to your neck?"

George looked at me curiously.

I wrenched my hand away from the enthusiastic new bartender and covered up my neck. "Oh, it's nothing. Just a bruise. You know, with two deep puncture marks. Into my jugular. No biggie."

George pulled my hand away and inspected the wound. He frowned. "Sarah, honey, what happened?"

I cleared my throat. "I fell on some barbecue prongs."

He looked so concerned that I started to feel uncomfortable. "Sarah, this is serious. What happened?"

"It's nothing. Just a little accident."

He glanced around the club. "Where is Mr. Barbecue Prongs, anyhow?"

I waved my hand absently. "Gone. I don't know. He'll be back. I'm going to take off, too. I'm kind of tired and I think I may be a tad anemic. Big day tomorrow. Plus, I'd better take Barkley for a walk."

His expression didn't change. "We'll talk about this. Later."

I nodded with fake enthusiasm and then felt a little dizzy. "Sure. Sounds like a plan. Okay, I'm out of here."

I left Haven to find Lenny waiting outside scribbling in a notebook under a nearby streetlamp. He waved when he saw me. I walked toward him as briskly as my high heels would take me away from the relative safety of the club.

Yeah. Where I'd just been nearly bled to death by my date who was also a confirmed murderer, where I'd volunteered to be bait to trap the leader of all hunters, and where I'd met my biggest fan.

All in all, a productive evening, I'd say.

Chapter 9

I slept for more than twelve hours. When I woke up it was almost noon. I didn't want to get up. I wanted to pull the covers up over my head like I did when I was a little girl and make the world go away.

But it didn't look like the world was going anywhere.

George wasn't home, but he'd left some nearly un-drinkable coffee and half an apple danish. I ignored the pastry and filled a mug with the dark, lukewarm liquid, sipping it slowly while I mentally assessed my current problems.

Thierry couldn't find out what I'd agreed to do. If he knew what Nicolai's plan was, then I was off to live in a nunnery as Sister Sarah.

I had no idea where he'd gone last night. I grabbed the phone and dialed his cell phone number, but I hung up after the first ring. Later. I'd talk to him later.

I touched my neck. The bite marks were still there.

Strange that they hadn't healed yet, since most of my cuts and scrapes were gone within hours lately.

My wardrobe and everything I owned could now fit comfortably in two suitcases. From the small selection I picked out some black jeans, a white T-shirt, and the leather jacket from last night to wear.

Ready for the day. Ready to face all challenges head-on. Fearless and self-assured. That was me. Bring it on. Come and get me, Gideon Chase.

I stood in place staring at the front door for a good twenty minutes before I finally opened it and went outside.

Lenny and Janie were waiting. Janie eyed my neck but didn't say anything other than "Good morning."

"I don't know about good, but it is a morning," I replied. "Listen, if you're willing to give me some of those self-defense lessons today that we talked about, I would be eternally grateful. And as a vampire, that isn't just an empty promise."

She glanced at Lenny, then back at me. "Sure. No problem."

I'd decided that learning self-defense was now essential. I needed to feel more secure. Leaving my life in the hands of other people was not a good thing. And I needed to learn how to protect myself as soon as possible. At least a little. And though Quinn had offered his enthusiastic services to me, I would have to decline. Being around Quinn was extremely distracting. It wasn't good for him or for me. Plus after what George had said about it looking like I was using him to make Thierry jealous, I thought I'd try to avoid the ex-hunter as much as possible. Because I *wasn't* using him.

Unless I was doing it subconsciously. My subconscious was a very devious thing.

And this had nothing to do with my dreaming about kissing him. Because that was just a dream. I wasn't interested in Quinn. No way.

I never bothered to consider the fact that being with Quinn would cause me way less stress and emotional pain than being with Thierry. Or that we might be better matched, from the fact that we're both fledgling vampires, to our ages, to our interests. Or that it was strongly possible that I had made a mistake in choosing to be with my bloodthirsty boyfriend who had scared the crap out of me last night and seemed to have enough issues to open his own magazine stand.

Nope. Hadn't considered any of those things. Not at all.

"When do you want to start?" Janie asked.

"I have a little something I need to take care of first. But right after that would be perfect."

"After we take care of your chore do you mind if we grab some lunch?" she asked. "It's very unprofessional, I know. But I've been working a couple jobs while I'm in town and haven't had a chance to grab anything this morning. And if I'm going to teach you some self-defense, I'd prefer to have some protein first."

Lenny tucked his notebook into his jacket pocket. "I could have picked something up for you. Why didn't you say something?"

She shook her head. "You're guarding Sarah. It's okay. Really."

"Remember when you picked me up that BLT sandwich because you thought I looked hungry? That was really sweet. I could do that for you, too."

She smiled. "Lenny, why don't you go get the car?"

"Can do." He nodded and jogged off down the street.

I raised an eyebrow.

"He's got a bit of a crush on me," she explained. "What can I say? I'm irresistible. And extremely hungry."

I'd decided that I liked Janie. We could probably become friends given enough time. And now she was going to teach me how to kick some ass. It was totally fate that she was hired as my bodyguard. Fate that I'd spilled a moccaccino on her expensive suede shoes.

And speaking of fate, I had a promise to fulfill.

When Lenny pulled the black sedan up to the curb, I instructed him on how to get to Amy's *Melrose Place*–like building. She'd left a message that she was going to be out all day at the spa with her mother as an early birthday present. Her mother apparently had recently learned her daughter is a vampire and didn't particularly mind since she was so excited about her little girl finally getting married.

Sounded like the perfect time for a diminutive, tuxedo-wearing, ass-kissing vampire to get some hot afternoon lovin'.

I squinted out of the backseat window of Lenny's car, which was parked across the street from the flank of modest townhomes.

Target: Barry Jordan.

Height: Four feet and change.

Charisma: Zero.

The front door to the unit he and Amy shared opened, and a tall, beautiful redhead emerged into the sunshine and put on dark sunglasses. I could see Barry standing in the doorway, shielding his eyes from the intense sunlight.

She kept talking to him for a minute. She had a briefcase under her arm. They laughed. Then she leaned over to give him a hug and she turned to walk away.

The door closed.

I honestly couldn't believe my eyes. Amy's suspicions were true!

"I'll be right back," I said, then let myself out of the car to march right up to the front of the house and knock on the door. It opened after a moment.

"Doris, did you forget something—?" Barry's eyes widened when he saw it was me.

"Doris, huh?"

"Oh, no." He tried to slam the door but I put my weight against it and slipped inside the apartment.

I jabbed my finger at him. "You are in big trouble, little man."

He held up his hands. "This isn't what it looks like."

"Oh? And what do you think it looks like?"

He frowned at me. "What are you doing here, anyhow?"

"Investigating your sorry little ass, that's what I'm doing. And I was on your side! I wanted to prove you were innocent. What do you think you're doing, cheating on Amy? Do you have any idea how lucky you are she even realizes that you exist, let alone allowing you to put that diamond smear on her finger?"

His eyes narrowed. "This is none of your business. You should go."

"Oh, we're not at the club right now. So don't even think you can boss me around. I want to know what you're doing, and what that bimbo was doing here. Just gloss over the top. Leave out the gory details or I might throw up."

His face reddened. "You weren't supposed to find out about this."

"Obviously."

He stared at me for another moment, his small fists clenched at his sides. And then he sighed. "Fine. But you better not tell Amy a thing." He turned away and walked into the kitchen.

"You have got to be kidding. You think I'm going to keep your seedy little secret?" I followed him. "I told her she never should have married you, you little—"

There was a huge birthday cake on the kitchen counter and several flower arrangements. Three packages of balloons and a helium tank sat nearby.

"I'm planning a surprise birthday party for her." Barry glanced at all the stuff before glaring at me. "Doris is the event planner who's helping me out. I want it to be really special since it's Amy's thirtieth and I know she's a little upset about it."

I deflated. "Oh, Barry. You have my permission to think I'm a total idiot."

"Way ahead of you."

"I'm so sorry. I thought you were . . . " I gritted my teeth.

"Cheating?" He raised his eyebrows.

"Well, yeah."

He shrugged. "I'm not."

I frowned. "So this is for a surprise party."

"That's right."

"For my best friend." My frown deepened. "That I

haven't heard anything about until now. Am I even invited?"

He sighed. "Of course you're invited. It's 6:30 tomorrow night at Haven. The master is closing the club to anyone but invited guests."

Thierry knew. He didn't mention it.

Then again, he was very good at keeping secrets.

I put a hand on my hip and looked around. "Does that cake really say 'Happy Birthday Snookums'?"

"So what if it does?"

"Why didn't you tell me about the party?"

"Because it's a *surprise* party."

"Yeah. And?"

He rolled his eyes. "You would have told Amy. And you better not tell her now or it will ruin everything."

"I wouldn't have told her."

He gave me a look that clearly stated that he didn't believe me.

I managed to look aghast. "Do you think I'm a gossip, or something?"

He shrugged.

I nervously tucked a piece of hair behind my ear. "Well, I'm not. I can keep a secret."

Barry's eyes shifted to my neck and narrowed. "Is that what I think it is?"

I grimaced and touched the bite marks self-consciously. "Barbecue-prong incident."

He stared at me.

After a moment I started to feel uncomfortable. "What?"

"Did the master do that to you?"

I forced an awkward smile to my face. "You know . . .

in the heat of passion and all that. Amy told me you guys
are into a little bite-play."

Mental picture. Bile rising. Inner shudder.

Barry had the decency to blush a little. "That's different."

"Is it?"

"Yes . . . I . . . " He pressed his lips together. "I'm
much younger than the master."

"So?" I did remember Nicolai mentioning that only
vamps over five hundred would have this little issue. So
glad to have it confirmed by Barry.

He shook his head. "You shouldn't encourage this sort
of thing."

"It's really none of your business."

"You'd be surprised."

"Oh, would I?"

He nodded gravely. "Has this ever happened before?"

"No."

"It must never happen again."

I swallowed hard. "Look, I don't mean to sound
rude, but what Thierry and I do is really none of your
business."

Any friendliness in his face dropped away. "You selfish little bitch," he snarled at me. "How dare you be so
flippant about such an important matter?"

I felt a flame of anger ignite in my chest at his tone.
"You are really asking for this cake to be thrown all over
your floor, aren't you?"

He stared at me for a moment, seething with rage.
What the hell did I say to set him off?

"I think I'm going to go." I turned to leave.

"Don't you take another goddamned step until I've had my say."

I turned around, heat rising in my cheeks, and this time it definitely wasn't from embarrassment.

"I was worried about this," Barry said. "From the moment you showed up and the master didn't send you immediately on your way. I was so worried that this would happen."

"That *what* would happen?"

He nodded at me, at my neck. "That. Where is the master now?"

"I . . . I have no idea." My mouth felt dry.

"I must find him. Did he . . . lose control of himself when you forced yourself on him?"

My eyebrows shot up. "Forced myself on him? I am going to put my foot so far up your little ass you'll need a tiny crowbar to remove it."

He waved off my protests. "I need to know what happened. It's important."

I crossed my arms. "Fine. He started to take too much blood. I tried to make him stop but he wouldn't. Or couldn't. Finally, he stopped and looked really distraught. Then he apologized and ran away and I haven't seen him since." I touched the mark absently. "I don't know why it hasn't healed yet."

"When an old vampire drinks, the wound is slow to heal. It may take days. I'm glad that you admitted what happened instead of trying to deny it. I respect that, Sarah."

I nodded. "Well, good. I guess."

He rubbed his chin. Then nodded firmly and met my gaze. "You must never see him again. Ever."

My eyebrows shot up. "And why is that?"

He glowered. "The master has not lost control like this for a hundred years. That event ended in tragedy."

"Nicolai's wife. I know."

"You know *nothing*." He looked at me sharply, scanned me from head to foot, then shook his head with obvious disapproval. "I must go find him and make sure he's okay."

"Yeah, you do that," I said. "And just as a reminder, *I'm* the one who got bit and nearly drained yesterday. Why aren't you concerned at all about me? I could be dead right now."

He glowered at me. "Sarah, get over yourself. Some things are more important." He moved to the phone on the wall and picked it up, pecking at a couple of numbers. "You can leave now."

Then he turned his back on me.

I turned and walked out of the kitchen and out to the sidewalk where Lenny and Janie were in the car waiting patiently for me. I got in the backseat so stunned that I couldn't talk for a couple of minutes. Janie eyed me curiously but didn't pry.

I pulled my cell phone out of my purse and dialed Thierry's number by heart. It went through to voice mail.

"Thierry . . . " I began. "It's me . . . Sarah. Listen, I'm really worried about you. Please call me when you get this message. I . . . we should talk about . . . things. I'll be at the club tonight, okay? I'll . . . I'll see you then."

I flipped the phone closed. No matter how much he'd scared me, I knew he hadn't meant to hurt me. I needed

to talk to him. Tell him I loved him. That everything was
going to be okay.

Stupid Barry. He didn't know me at all. I wasn't that
selfish, was I?

"Tequila sunrise," I told the waiter at Café Mirage.
"Actually, make it a double."

I'd picked a table that would allow me to keep my
back against the wall of the small restaurant. In the corner. So I could keep an eye on anybody who looked at
me a little shifty. Which, when you've become totally
paranoid like me, was pretty much everybody.

I hoped this would be a quick lunch.

Janie glanced at her menu. "I'll have a cheeseburger
with fries, and a Diet Coke."

Yeah. Those were the good old days. Solid food. Now
a distant, fading memory.

"You don't mind if I eat like a pig in front of you, do
you?" she asked, handing the waiter her menu.

I waved my hand. "Nah. I'm strong. I can take it. You
don't mind if I drink like a fish in front of you, do you?"

"Have at it. Hey, are you okay?"

I glanced out of the window. Lenny was waiting outside with the car. He'd wanted to come inside, but Janie
insisted that he "monitor the exterior." It was easy to tell
who wore the pants in their bodyguard partnership. And
it wasn't the one with the bigger muscles.

I sighed. "Let's just say I'm really looking forward to
those self-defense lessons I'm forcing you to give me to
let out some of my pent-up frustrations."

"Yeah, it must be tough to be a wanted woman. But

just chill. We have it under control. I won't let anything happen to you."

"It's not just that." I shrugged. "Let's just say I'm having personal problems."

She leaned back in her seat. "Oh, I see. The cell phone call in the car, right? Trouble with your love life?"

"Is it that obvious?"

The drinks arrived and she took a sip of her Diet Coke. "The double tequila sunrise gave you away. So what's the problem? Maybe I can give you some sage advice. Or maybe I'm just being nosy. You decide."

I smiled at that. "Well, let's see. First off, my boyfriend—the guy who hired you—is much older than me."

"How much older?"

I pressed my lips together for a moment. "Let's just say *significantly* and leave it at that."

She nodded. "Okay. So, a little age difference doesn't mean anything."

"He's also married."

Her eyebrows went up at that. "Hmm. That could be a problem."

"The wife is fine with our relationship."

"Well, that's . . . *friendly*. Okay, what else?"

I chewed my bottom lip for a second. "I think he might have a little substance abuse problem. When he drinks too much he gets a little crazy."

She nodded. "That is an issue. I had a boyfriend back in high school who smoked up every day. He wasn't abusive or anything, just really lazy."

I stared at her for a second. "This is a little different than that."

"Okay, so you have a much older, married boyfriend who has a drinking problem." Her lips twitched. "Sounds like a catch."

I looked at her sharply. "It's not funny."

"I'm sorry, I can't help it. Just when I think my life sucks, I find somebody who has it worse. Though, frankly, I'm still not convinced."

I thought about it. "Thanks to the hunters blowing up my apartment the other night, I'm currently homeless and living with a friend, since my boyfriend Thierry didn't invite me to stay with him."

"You're aiming for the blue ribbon in sucky life, aren't you? Well, I'm still in the running."

I watched a man take his toddler son to the bathroom. They looked fairly harmless, but you never could tell. "Your life is so bad? Go ahead and compare notes with me."

She played with her drink, absently pushing the ice cubes down with the end of her straw. "First of all, I have a boss from hell."

"Who, Thierry?"

She shook her head. "I haven't even met him face to face yet, so no. I have lots of jobs, lots of bosses, I'm afraid. A girl has to make ends meet somehow."

I played with the rim of my glass. "I've had lousy bosses, too."

"Yeah. Lousy. That's one way to describe him. Anyhow, I'm sort of in debt to this boss so it's not like I can just quit, but he makes me do things I really hate. And my jobs are taking up so much of my time I can't have a personal life. Which sucks. Plus, I have personal issues up the yin-yang, too. Family issues I'm dealing with as we speak."

I nodded. "You mentioned your brother who taught you self-defense."

"Yeah." She took another sip of her Diet Coke.

I grinned, not afraid to show off my fangs anymore since she already knew I was a vampire. "You know, maybe if things don't work out with me and my boyfriend, you can hook me up with your brother. And I'm only half joking."

She smiled, but it looked forced. "Sorry, but . . . he's dead."

I closed my big mouth and felt a chill go down me. "Shit. I'm so sorry."

"Yeah, me, too." She took another shaky sip of her drink. "You have no idea. He was murdered."

I shook my head. "I don't know what to say."

"Nobody usually does. But I'm dealing the only way I know how."

"Was the guy who did it caught?"

She shook her head. "Not yet. But I've been following up on some leads. His killer will get what's coming to them, that's for damn sure."

Her lunch arrived and she started absently chewing on a french fry.

I waited for the little black rain cloud that seemed to have set up house above our table to move away before I spoke again.

"This is fun, huh?"

She glanced up at me from her plate. "So, tell me, other than your mixed-up boyfriend, any other love prospects to distract you from your dangerous life as the Slayer of Slayers?"

I immediately thought about Quinn. I knew I shouldn't, but I couldn't help it. "Well there's one guy. He's pretty much everything that my boyfriend isn't. He's closer to my age, single, and no drinking problem. Well, not *yet*, anyhow."

"So what's the problem? Dump bachelor number one's ass and go on to him."

"It's not that easy. Number two is great, really, but I'm still crazy about number one. Even though he's not really a bachelor."

"Sounds like you might just be crazy."

I smiled wistfully. "That's what he said once."

"Maybe you should start listening to what people tell you."

I looked at her sharply. "Thank you, Ann Landers."

A cell phone rang. I grabbed mine and glanced at the screen hoping it was Thierry. But no, it was blank.

Janie grabbed her phone and flipped it open. "Yeah?" I watched her face change from lunchtime pleasant, to hard and cold. "Okay, I'll take care of it." She hung up, jaw tense, and then looked at me. "You said you wanted to learn how to protect yourself, didn't you?"

"That's right."

"You can learn by example. You're coming with me and Lenny on our next assignment."

"What kind of assignment?"

She grabbed her purse, threw a couple of bills on the table to pay for lunch. I noticed something else in her purse. A handgun. My eyes bugged.

"Why don't I just wait here?" I suggested.

She glanced down at the gun. "This is for my assignment. Don't worry. Come on, a fun time will be had by all. Trust me."

She stood up and grabbed my arm, literally pulling me along after her as she hurried out of the restaurant.

I didn't even have a chance to finish my drink first.

Chapter 10

Outside the restaurant, Janie tapped her left ear. "Lenny, where are you? We're out front. Come get us."

There was a squealing of tires and the black sedan screeched to a halt in front of us. The back door swung open. Janie pulled me into the car next to her.

"Paragon Theater. And step on it," she barked.

Lenny turned around to look at us. "Um. Do you have an address? I don't really know Toronto too well. And the GPS is broken."

I waved my hand. "I've heard of that theater before, I think. It's about ten minutes from here. Take a left at the lights up there."

Lenny nodded. "Cool. Thanks."

The car pulled away from the curb and began to move much faster than the speed limit suggested.

A huge headache had just announced its presence in the front portion of my brain with a throbbing hello. "Listen, Janie, like I said, I haven't been having the best of weeks. I don't need any additional drama. Can you just drop me off somewhere? I'll wait till you're finished."

"You said you wanted to learn self-defense, right? You can watch me in action. This won't take long. Just one more check mark on my long to-do list." She sighed heavily. "I *so* need a vacation."

Lenny glanced over his shoulder. "Where are we going?"

"What?"

"On vacation."

"I kind of meant my vacation *alone*," she said. "No offense."

He pouted. "Didn't you get my note?"

"What note?"

"The one I left in your coat pocket."

She reached into her pocket and pulled out a folded, lined piece of paper.

O beautiful Janie with your straw-colored hair
I would follow you anywhere
One so beautiful I will never meet again
And you're also much stronger than most other men
Which is hot, by the way
And I'm not intimidated by that at all

She blinked. "That's . . . nice, Lenny. Uh . . . are we almost at the theater?"

"We could go on a cruise. Somewhere tropical. It would be nice."

"Let me think about it." She glanced at me with a grimace.

I couldn't help but smile. Talk about *smitten*.

My cell phone rang. I fished it out of my purse and looked at the display, hoping it was Thierry.

It wasn't.

I flipped it open and held it up to my ear. "Hi, Amy."

"What's going on?" she asked.

"Oh, you know," I glanced at Janie, who was checking the ammo in her gun. "Just a boring afternoon. Same old, same old."

"So?"

"So what?"

"Did you investigate Barry? You said you were going to check things out."

"Oh. Um. Yeah," I switched the phone to my other ear. "Right. About that. I really don't think you need to worry about it. Barry . . . he doesn't strike me as the cheating type, you know?"

"But—"

"But nothing. Listen, Amy. He might have some stuff on his mind, but cheating? Nah. I don't think so."

"We're here," Janie announced as Lenny pulled up in back of a boarded-up, abandoned theater.

"Who's that?" Amy asked.

"Oh," I glanced at Janie as she got out of the car, holstering her gun under her red jacket, which I noticed still had the rip under the arm from her tussle with the hunter yesterday. "That's just Janie."

I heard Amy start to sob. "Oh, my God! You're . . . cheating on . . . me . . . too! You're seeing another friend I don't know about behind my back!"

"Amy, you're talking crazy. Janice's one of my body-guards. Just . . . just have fun at the spa and I'll talk to you later. Okay?"

She sniffed. "Okay."

I ended the call and put the phone away. Then I got out of the car. Lenny did, too.

"This isn't going to take long, is it?" I asked.

Janie shook her head. "Should be just a quick retrieval. He's supposed to meet us inside."

"Then what's with the gun?" I glanced at it nervously.

"Just a standard precaution." She looked at the theater.

Lenny leaned against the car and shrugged. "What do you want me to do?"

She looked at him. "Just stay out here. Make sure he doesn't leave out the back until we get what we came here for."

"You don't want me inside?"

"Just stay here." She looked at the back door. "But can you take care of this?"

He walked over to it and kicked the door in. I heard the old wood splinter as it met his left Doc Martens boot.

Inside it was very dark. Janie fished in her jacket pocket and pulled out a small flashlight that helped to light our way down a hallway. Old paintings hung on the walls, heavy with dust and age.

"What are you retrieving?" I asked.

"A necklace my boss wants. The delivery guy's supposed to be around here somewhere."

"And this is supposed to help me learn self-defense how?"

She turned to face me with a small smile. "The guy we're meeting isn't all that reliable. Let's just leave it at that for now."

"Seems like a strange place to meet somebody."

"He's a strange guy."

I stared at her for a moment. "Maybe I should wait outside with Lenny. I don't feel good about this."

Her smile widened. "For a vampire, you're a big fat wimp, you know that?"

I frowned at her. I wasn't a wimp. Well, not much.

We turned a corner and I realized we'd been parallel to the actual theater area and had come out to the front where the box office had been once upon a time. There was a man wearing a long black coat standing next to the ticket window up ahead. We approached him, Janie walking with a confident stride. The lights were on, but still fairly dim. She switched off the flashlight and put it away.

"Janelle," he said as she approached. "I didn't know you'd be the one sent."

"Long time no see," she replied.

The man wore a fedora pulled down low. He seemed very cloak and dagger. More cloak than dagger, though, I hoped.

He nodded in my direction. "Who's that?"

"A friend."

"I don't want to meet any of your friends, Janie."

"You picked the place, I brought a friend. Let's just get this over with. Do you have it?"

"Maybe."

I felt uneasy about being there so I just stood off to the side and tried to blend into the old art deco surroundings like a theatrical chameleon.

Janie beckoned to him. "Why don't you hand it over and we can make this nice and easy?"

The man laughed at that. "Janie, you don't make anything easy. I have a message for your boss."

"And what's that?"

"This is it. My last job. I'm quitting."

She shrugged. "It's got nothing to do with me, but I'll be sure to tell him. Do you have a note you want me to give him or should I just paraphrase?"

His coat parted and he pointed a big gun at Janie's face. "I figure your dead body should get my point across."

"Janie . . . " I managed, panic immediately welling up in my chest.

"Shut up," Fedora-guy said. "You're a vampire, aren't you? I can smell it from here. Why don't you go turn into dust somewhere?"

I swallowed hard and took a step back. "It's goo."

"Whatever. Even a vampire's too good to hang out with Miss Parker here. She's a liar and a cheat. She'll steal your soul and then laugh all the way to her boss's with a song in her cold, black heart."

Janie glanced at me and shrugged a shoulder. "My charm doesn't win every man over."

The guy laughed. "Janie, you're getting rusty. Never thought I'd get the upper hand so easily."

"Did you plan this?"

"Last-minute decision."

"So you didn't bring the merchandise?"

He hesitated. "No, I didn't."

"Liar. I'm willing to bet you have it on you. Somewhere. So I'll give you one last chance. Hand it over right now or I'm going to have to kill you."

"Brave girl with a gun in your face. And you're trying to make me believe that you'd let me walk out of here? I'm not that stupid."

Janie turned her head. "Yeah, Lenny. We're over here."

Fedora-guy looked over and Janie kneed him sharply in the groin. She tried to swing around and grab him but he slipped out of her grasp and started running away, thrusting open the doors that led down to the theater and slamming them behind him.

"Come on!" she yelled at me and took off after him.

Was she kidding? I wasn't following. Forget it.

My cell phone rang. I yanked it out of my purse to see that it was Thierry's number. My heart clenched. I was about to answer it just as an arm went around my neck.

"Hey," Fedora-guy said.

I dropped the phone to grab at his arms. The phone hit the floor and broke. Shit. Where had he come from?

"You don't mind if I use you as a hostage to get the hell out of here, do you?" he asked.

My heart thudded painfully against my ribs. "Actually, I'd really rather you didn't."

He chuckled. "So what's your story, morning glory? Hanging out with a bitch like Janie Parker? You feel too soft and cuddly for that kind of trouble."

"Are you calling me fat?"

"No, just right, actually. For a vampire. I'd do you."

"Gee, I'm incredibly flattered. I guess you're not aware of the whole vampire super-strength deal. I could break your arms like twigs right now if I wanted to," I lied.

He shifted and put the gun to my head. "And I could blow your brains out."

"So you're saying you would do me. Would you like to set up a time and place? Because you're way hot. I have a thing for dark, tortured murderers."

"I'm not a murderer. I just want to get the hell out of

here in one piece. I never should have come here. She can't have it. Not today. Not ever."

He grabbed my arm and began pulling me after him, farther into the shadows of the theater. He found a dirty window and broke it with kick. Sunlight streamed in and hit my face.

He glanced at me. "I thought vampires couldn't go out during the day."

I squinted out at the brightness. Good opportunity to try to save my skin. His lack of knowledge was my gain. "That's because I'm a special vampire. Have you heard about the Slayer of Slayers?"

He froze. "That's you?"

I nodded, trying to remain as calm as possible. "I'm very dangerous. I'm also a woman on the edge. So I would suggest you let me go before you get in any deeper than you already are."

"Janie and you are friends?"

"More like acquaintances."

He licked his lips. "Don't trust her. She's no good."

"If you say so."

He frowned hard, as if he was thinking something through. "Do you believe in fate, Slayer of Slayers?"

"Sometimes."

"I do. This is fate. You being here." He let go of me and reached into his pocket with the hand that didn't already hold the gun. He pulled out a gold chain that glinted in the sunlight and thrust it at me. "Take this. It's yours. You just can't let Janie have it."

"Listen, I don't think I want anything to do with this—"

"Take it," he pushed it into my hand. "And hide it."

"What is it?"

He smiled. "Just a necklace."

"Yeah, right."

"I'm outa here. Make sure to tell Janie—"

"Tell Janie what?" Janie walked over to us, holding her gun steady to the level of Fedora-guy's forehead. "Sarah, you okay?"

After catching the stricken look on his face, I slid the necklace into my pocket before Janie could see it. "Fine."

"Drop the gun, buddy. Now. Or you're toast."

The guy cocked his head to the side. "Oh, Janie, I love it when you talk like a two-bit clichéd action movie bitch. I've missed you."

"With every shot so far." She grinned, but it wasn't friendly. "Give me the necklace."

He stiffened. "You're going to shoot me one way or the other."

"If I don't get the necklace, then I'm the one who's going to be picking up my own pieces from the sidewalk. And since I'll be dead, that will be very hard to do. Now hand it over—" she pulled the safety back on her gun with a click "—or I'm going to kill you."

Chapter 11

With wide eyes I watched Fedora-guy's gun hand start to shake.

I could tell Janie I had the necklace. Stop this before somebody got hurt.

But there was something in the guy's eyes when he gave it to me. Like he trusted me. And he didn't trust her.

"Don't shoot him, Janie," I said suddenly.

"Why the hell not?"

"Because . . . you'll regret it."

"I regret a lot of things."

"Me, too. I totally regret spilling that moccaccino on you."

She snorted at that. "I almost forgot about that."

"Those were really cool shoes."

"They were, weren't they?" She lowered the gun a little.

Suddenly Fedora-guy turned to leap through the broken window and started running away from the theater.

Janie ran to the window and aimed at his back.

After a long moment she lowered her gun. "Damn it. I can't do it. I can't shoot somebody in the back." She looked at me. "Who's the wimp now, right?"

I watched his form become smaller and smaller in the distance. "Maybe he was right. Maybe he didn't have the necklace at all."

"I guess we'll never know."

I swallowed and pressed my lips together. "I guess not."

"My boss is going to kill me." She slid the gun back into her purse and then smiled. "I definitely need a drink."

A drink sounded like an excellent idea.

We had a drink. Actually three drinks. Alcohol didn't affect me and Lenny was the designated driver so it didn't really matter. I watched Janie for some clue that she was something to be afraid of. Somebody not to trust like Fedora-guy had said. But I didn't see any reason not to trust her.

Still, the necklace remained in my pocket. I didn't say a word.

I asked them to drop me off at Haven where I'd wait for Thierry to show up. He sometimes went there in the afternoon to take care of some paperwork. It was worth a shot. He'd called my cell phone before it broke at the theater. He obviously knew I wanted to talk to him.

Janie and I got out of the car next to the plain-looking, unmarked entrance to Haven.

"Sarah!" I heard a voice call to my right. I turned to see Quinn quickly moving toward me. "I've been looking everywhere for you. There was another murder last night. A vampire victim this time. A young female, dark hair, body still intact. With everything going on, I thought for a moment it was you and it scared the hell out of me."

I felt a chill at his words. "I'm here. I'm okay. Well, still breathing anyhow."

His jaw tensed. "I need to catch this bastard. But I'm at a loss. So many vamps in this city and they all keep to themselves. I might need Thierry's contacts after all."

I glanced at Janie and was surprised that she looked a little stricken.

"Um," she said. "I guess Lenny and I will wait out here."

"Okay."

"I, uh . . . I'll see you later."

Quinn glanced at her. "Sarah, aren't you going to introduce us?"

I sighed. "Yeah, Quinn . . . this is Janie. She's actually one of the bodyguards I told you about yesterday."

"Hi." Quinn extended his hand.

Janie ignored it. "Yeah. Hi. Okay, so like I said, we'll be close if you need us." She turned away and got into the backseat of the car without another word.

I glanced at Quinn. "She's shy."

"Whatever. So you're okay. Really?"

"I'm surviving. Hanging out with my odd bodyguards as a walking target for the hunters. Now I guess I'll be dodging a vampire serial killer too. Good times."

"You're with me now. And I won't let anything happen to you." He frowned, then reached forward to push the hair off my neck. "What the hell is that?"

I was seriously buying a scarf as soon as possible. When did Barry say this damn thing would heal up?

"Barbecue-prong incident."

Somebody had to go for that, didn't they?

He held his hand to the bite marks without saying anything, his gaze growing soft and worried as he searched my face for answers. I wrapped my hand around his wrist after a moment and pulled it away, turning toward the door to Haven.

"I'm thinking I feel like another drink." I glanced at him. "Want to join me?"

"A drink?"

"Yeah." I fished into my purse and pulled out a set of keys. "Look who just happens to have keys to Haven."

"Is that a good idea?"

"Nobody will be in there for hours. Therefore, it's an open bar."

He still looked disturbed about the state of my neck. "Sounds pretty damn good to me. I could use a beer."

I let us into the club and locked the door behind us. Flicked on a few lights.

"Can you give me a second?" I said to him. "I have to make a call."

I went over to the phone and dialed Thierry's number.

It immediately went through to voicemail.

"Thierry, it's me. Looks like we're playing phone tag. Listen, I'm at Haven right now. I'll . . . I'll talk to you later, okay?"

I hung up and stood there with my hand on the receiver for a few moments. I really wanted to talk to him. Make sure he was okay. Let him know that I wasn't upset about last night but there were definitely things we needed to talk about. I still didn't believe that he'd killed Nicolai's wife despite all evidence to the contrary. My gut was telling me there was more to the story. But, like everything in my life, the answers would have to wait.

I grabbed a couple of beers from the fridge and walked over to Quinn, who took one from me.

"So was that the bodyguard who said she'd teach you self-defense?" he asked.

"It was." I took a long sip of the beer. "Unfortunately, the day has not gone as originally planned."

Not by a longshot.

I slipped a hand into my pocket to feel the gold chain. What was I supposed to do with it? What was it, anyhow? I'd put it somewhere safe for the time being. Tell Thierry about it. Whatever it was, people were willing to kill for it.

It's not like it had a big diamond in it, or anything. It was quite ugly. Just a thin gold chain that Mr. T probably wouldn't even bother with. Whatever its value, it wasn't because it was from Tiffany's.

"Maybe I should just stay inside and avoid anything that might inadvertently get me killed," I mused aloud as I thought back on the experience with Fedora-guy.

"I agree."

I frowned at Quinn. "Great. Everybody wants me to stay inside. Don't get in trouble. Stay safe. Avoid living."

"That's not exactly what I mean."

"Then what do you mean?"

"I'm an advocate for awareness. If you're aware of the risks, and you know how to anticipate potential danger, then you can take care of yourself. You don't have to hide from life, you just need to approach it a bit differently."

"And how am I supposed to do that?"

"I'm going to teach you a couple of moves so you can go pretty much anywhere and if anybody gives you any problems, you can kick their ass from here to kingdom come."

I sighed. After the day I'd had, Quinn's offer sounded pretty good to me. And it didn't mean anything. Forget the dream. Quinn and I were just good friends. I'd be stupid not to take him up on his offer. "All right, you win. Teach me. I am but a student to the master."

"When?"

I shrugged. "What about right now?"

"You're not exactly dressed for a street-fighting lesson."

I looked down at my outfit. "What's wrong with jeans and a T-shirt?"

His gaze slowly trailed down to my feet. "I suggest you remove the shoes. The last thing I need today is a stiletto through my heart."

"These are hardly stilettos. They are sensible and highly comfortable. But okay." I slipped them off so I stood in bare feet on the cold, hard ceramic floor of the club.

He kept looking at me as he drained his beer and set the bottle down on the bar top. Then he went and started moving tables out of the way to clear a portion of the floor. Finally he stood in the center of a sizable empty spot. He pushed up his sleeves.

"Okay," he said.

I was still leaning against the bar. "Okay what?"

He beckoned to me. "Attack me."

I walked over to him. "How do you want me to attack you?"

"Well, first of all, would you ask your victim how he

would prefer to be attacked? No, I don't think so. Just try to punch me or something." He blinked. "You might want to put your drink down first."

I placed the bottle down on a nearby table. "Okay, mister. So you're looking for some pain from the Slayer of Slayers, are you?"

He grinned. "Bring it."

He looked so smug, so sure I couldn't do anything to hurt him that it bugged me enough to give me the gumption to approach him again. I curled my right hand into a fist and punched him in his left shoulder.

I frowned. "You didn't even defend yourself."

He laughed. "Against that? I'm not teaching self-defense against puppies today. You're going to have to hit me harder than that."

"I don't want to hurt you."

He laughed harder. "Don't worry, you won't."

I threw another punch and he caught it in his hand, then twisted my arm around against my back.

"See? Easy as that," he said into my ear.

"But I have yet to unveil the wrath of Sarah. You ain't seen nothing yet."

He let go of me. "I don't think I've ever seen the wrath of Sarah. You're way too easygoing. Even with all the trouble you've currently gotten yourself into. At least that's how you appear."

"Appearances are highly deceiving," I told him. "I am very stressed out right now. I just have a talent for hiding it. You obviously don't know me very well."

"Oh, I think I know you better than you might think."

I put my hands on my hips. "Is that so?"

"Yeah, that's so."

"Like what? Name something you know about me."

He studied me for a moment. "You can forgive really stupid mistakes."

"For example?"

"Me being a vampire hunter when we first met. Trying to kill you." His expression grew serious. "I can't tell you how sorry I am about that. I . . . I was a different person back then."

I shook my head. "You weren't different. You were you, only a little less educated in the way things actually are."

"That's a nice way to put that I was a complete idiot." He pulled a chair out and sat down heavily. "What am I going to do to make up for all the things I was responsible for?"

"You just need to put it behind you."

He looked up at me, his eyes moist. "I don't even understand how I could do it. Looking back, I see that it was wrong. But I truly believed . . . I believed that I was doing the right thing."

I went to the fridge and grabbed a couple more beers and brought them out. I put a hand on Quinn's shoulder. "Look, the way I figure it you have two choices. You can either dwell on the shitty past you've had and you can pretty much curl up and die, or you can move on with your life."

"Is there a third choice?"

I twisted the cap off my beer and took a sip. "Yeah, you can get off your lazy ex-hunter ass and show me how to beat your old friends up."

He laughed. "So you're saying I should just forget about my past."

"No, I'm not saying that at all. You were a hunter. Now you see that you were wrong. You have a chance to make a difference because your view on the subject is clearer than anybody else's could ever be. I have total faith that you're going to find the vamp responsible for the murders. There's no doubt in my mind about that. And no, you can't take back what you did . . . I'm not even saying that you should try to. Just use the rest of your life in a way that is positive." I stopped talking for a moment. "Do I sound a little bit like Anthony Robbins?"

"A little bit."

I shrugged. "I guess I must have bought some positive pants yesterday during my shopping spree."

"They suit you."

"Yeah. Well, I guess when the night is at its darkest, the sun starts to rise." I blinked. "Somebody stop me."

He eyed my neck. "So are you going to tell me what happened to your neck or should I just go ahead and guess?"

I touched the offending mark. "It was an accident."

"An accident," he repeated. "You just fell on his fangs, did you?"

"Don't you read romance novels? Biting is a sign of true love."

He shook his head. "What do you see in that guy?"

The question took me by surprise. "What?"

He stood up. "Thierry. What do you see in him, anyhow? I don't get it. Where is he? Why isn't he here right now? He should be teaching you how to look after yourself, not me."

"He's busy."

"Yeah, he's busy." He shook his head. "Even without

my suspicions, that guy is a self-righteous, overbearing, pompous dickhead."

I felt myself tense up. "You don't know him."

"And you do? Don't tell me that the two of you have a damn thing in common."

"We both enjoy *American Idol*. The man is a serious Clay Aiken fan."

He snorted. "I think I get it. You just *think* you're in love with him. He's this dark alpha jerk with his black cape and mysterious past. A romantic fantasy that you've convinced yourself is real."

"Alpha jerk?"

He swore under his breath. "You think you're supposed to fall for the tortured guy who lives in the shadows. But you've been with him for two months now, Sarah, has he come out of the shadows for you yet?"

"Quinn, I don't want to talk about this."

"No, of course not. You might actually start seeing the cold hard facts. Well, if you could look in a mirror, I think you'd see the cold hard facts staring at you from your neck. That is not a love bite, I don't care what you try to tell me. I may have killed vampires without knowing everything I should have, but I know that vamps as old as Thierry shouldn't be drinking blood."

I swallowed. "It's none of your business."

"Do you know what happens when they drink blood? Is that the reason he's off somewhere hiding his face right now? Is he embarrassed at showing you his dirty little secret? Or maybe he's off doing the same thing to another victim." He shook his head. "I admit I ended a lot of vamps that didn't deserve it, but some of them do. I'd forgotten. After everything that's happened to me, I'd forgotten that some vampires deserve to die. There is a reason there are vampire hunters, Sarah. To kill the bad ones. The ones we're at risk of becoming if we don't get enough blood. The ones the old ones become if they get too much. It's a fine line we walk now."

I stared at him. "Thierry's not like that."

"Maybe," he said, drawing closer to me. "Maybe not. I follow my gut, Sarah. And my gut tells me something is seriously wrong. You're at risk being involved with him. But I won't let that happen. I won't let him hurt you." He grabbed my hands and brought them to his lips.

My cheeks felt warm. "Quinn, what do you see in me? There are better girls out there for you. Trust me."

He managed to grin at that. "Well, for starters, most girls would have listened to my little tirade just now and then given me the finger and taken off."

I gave him the finger.

"You're still here," he said.

"Yeah, I am. Mostly because I still want to learn a few moves."

He drained his beer. "But you didn't let me tell you what I see in you. You want to hear?"

"Not particularly."

"Too bad. Okay, so what I like about Sarah Dearly, by Michael Quinn. You're funny."

"I do try."

"You're pretty. That dark hair you keep tucking behind your ears, and those big brown eyes with that glint of mischievousness. I like that."

I shook my head. "I'm no Veronique."

"No, you're not."

I frowned at him and he started to laugh.

"That's actually a compliment," he said. "Veronique's too . . . too *Veronique*. If that makes any sense at all."

"You barely know her."

"Now you're defending her?"

I shrugged. "She's not a bad person."

He leaned back against the edge of a table. "Do you know why we stopped seeing each other?"

My ears did their Barkley perk-up. "No, why?"

He pressed his lips together for a moment before he spoke. "Because I may have called her by your name at a very . . . *inappropriate* time."

I stared at him. "Please tell me you're kidding."

He shook his head. "She wasn't all that impressed."

"Why are you telling me this?"

"To prove a point. To show you that just because you mistakenly chose the other schmuck doesn't mean that this schmuck wasn't still thinking about you. *Inappropriately*."

I cleared my throat. "Let's move on, shall we?"

He grinned. "Fine. I like that you get embarrassed over small stuff, but all indignant over the big stuff. I like that you believe everything's going to be okay even when things look really bad. I like that you aren't afraid to ask for help. I like that you can handle your liquor—"

I shrugged and glanced over at the bar. "Vamps can't get drunk unless you're drinking blood at the same time. Believe me, tried, tested, and true."

"I like that you never stop talking even when some-body else is trying to speak."

"Some people might find that annoying."

"I'm not some people." He moved toward me and

reached up to catch a lock of my hair between his fingers. He smoothed it behind my ear.

"No, you're not some people," I agreed.

"And I'm not Thierry."

I broke away from him. "No, you're not."

"You never answered me. What do you see in that guy? He's dangerous. My gut tells me he's more than that. What makes him so damn special to you, anyhow?"

I stared at him but said nothing. What was I supposed to say? Rattle off a list of things I liked about Thierry? Depending on the hour of the day, that would be either a very short or very long list. But is that the proof of somebody's feelings for somebody else? The ability to list a bunch of qualities they admire in the other person? Maybe. Maybe not. I don't know.

Was I supposed to tell him that despite knowing everything about him, even the things that scared me and made my blood run cold, I still loved him so much it hurt? How can you explain something like that? Even to yourself?

"Teach me some moves," I said quietly. "Or I think we're finished here."

He looked at me for a long moment, then finally said, "Okay."

"Okay."

He moved back a few steps. "Attack me like you mean it."

Surprisingly, I wasn't as gentle this time. I threw punches, kicks; Quinn blocked them all. He showed me in slow motion how he managed to block them. How to break free of a chokehold. What parts of the body I should aim for that would do the most damage to my attacker.

We continued the lesson for a good half hour before I started to feel like I was getting it. Then he became the attacker, and I was the victim. It wasn't much of a stretch.

I realized that the more relaxed I was, the stronger I was. Along with my enhanced senses, my strength had definitely grown by leaps and bounds. I mean, I wasn't Wonder Woman or anything, but I could definitely throw somebody around.

Which I did by accident as Quinn came at me, and I deflected his attack with a push that knocked him head-first into a nearby table. He fell to the ground in a heap. I slapped a hand over my mouth in surprise and ran to his side.

"Oh, my God! I'm so sorry. Did I really hurt you?"

He wasn't moving.

"Quinn?" I got down on my knees next to him and tentatively touched his shoulder. Good God, did I knock him out? I was like *Xena: Warrior Vampire*.

Just as I was starting to get worried, he turned and grabbed me. "You always have to be on your guard."

He rolled me over so he had me pinned to the ground, his weight holding me down.

I looked up at him. "You totally cheated."

"Hunters cheat."

He moved my arms up above my head and looked down at me. "You're not trying to get away."

No I wasn't. That was very strange.

He grinned. "If I was the bad guy, you'd already be dead."

"Good thing you're not the bad guy, then, isn't it?"

"Yeah, good thing." He moved his face down closer to mine until our lips were almost touching. Until I could feel his warm breath against my mouth, his body pressed firmly against mine.

I heard the entrance door to Haven slam shut just as Quinn kissed me.

Chapter 12

I pushed Quinn back a few inches.

There was silence for a moment before Thierry spoke.

"I saw on my call display that you had phoned me from here, so I drove over to see you. I apologize if I'm interrupting."

He sounded very blasé, very cold, as if he hadn't just walked in on Quinn lying directly on top of me in the middle of his club. Oh, and the kissing thing. Yeah, couldn't have been better timing if I'd planned it.

And by "better" I, of course, mean "completely, incredibly horrible."

Quinn just grinned down at me with a self-satisfied smile on his face. Then, obviously not seeing the complete mortification in my expression, he winked, then pushed against the floor to stand up.

"Thierry," I began, propping myself up on my elbows. "Quinn was teaching me some self-defense."

His arms were crossed over his chest and he stood off

to the side by the entrance. His expression was tight. He nodded. "Ah. So that's what that was. I wasn't certain."

Quinn reached a hand out to me to help me up, but I ignored it and got to my feet by myself. I absently brushed off my jeans and wished suddenly that I was on a plane headed far, far away.

"My idea," Quinn offered after a long, uncomfortable moment of silence. "Sarah needs to learn how to protect herself, and I figure there were no other takers, so here I am, offering my assistance in the matter."

Thierry's jaw was tense. "That is very kind of you. So tell me, what kind of self-defense do you call that exactly?"

"That? Just straightforward street fighting."

"I see. And the kiss was just . . . for effect?"

I felt my cheeks blaze with heat.

Quinn didn't look the least bit embarrassed. "No, not for effect. That was just an added bonus. You know, when things get a little hot and sweaty, things tend to happen between two people. It's called chemistry. Sometimes you can't control that."

"Indeed." Thierry's gaze flicked to me for a moment.

I was busy searching for that hole in the floor I wanted to disappear into.

Quinn shrugged. "Maybe if you were around a little more, Sarah wouldn't have to find other people to help her with . . . *self-defense*. But that's cool. I enjoy . . . *teaching*."

A smile twitched at Thierry's lips. "Perhaps you're right. Sarah, I know I haven't been around very much lately and I apologize. I certainly understand the need for you to find your education from other sources. And as I said yesterday, it's so kind of you to be there for Quinn. You're very accommodating."

My lips thinned. "It's not like that."

Quinn frowned at me. "Not like that? Could have fooled me." He turned his attention on Thierry. "Listen, how about we all say what's really on our minds?"

"Yes, why don't we?"

He crossed his arms. "She trusted you and you bit her, you bloodsucking bastard."

I touched the bite marks on my neck. "Quinn, I don't want to talk about this."

"Why not? We're all friends here. What does your boyfriend here have to say about it? Was she tasty?" Quinn's eyes narrowed. "She hasn't healed up yet, like a good vampire should. With the marks still showing, I'd say you went a bit overboard, didn't you? I've done a little research on you . . . from what I found it wouldn't be the first time you showed your monster to a woman who trusted you. Luckily for Sarah, she's still breathing."

A trace of anguish played in Thierry's silver eyes. "You found that in your research, did you?"

"Yes. And a lot more, too. Want me to share it with the class? You want me to go chronologically or alphabetically for all the bad shit you've been involved in, old man? How about those murders I mentioned the other night? Got any inside information about that? I think you probably do."

"Quinn, just shut up," I said.

"No, I'm not shutting up. I've wanted to say this since the moment I met the 'master,' here." The two locked gazes.

"You mean the moment that I saved your life?"

Thierry replied softly. "When you were dying from being half-turned? When the vampire toxins were coursing through your body causing unbearable pain until I helped to ease it instead of allowing you to die in agony? Yes, I can see why that would elicit your hatred toward me."

Quinn snorted. "Whatever."

"Just the intelligent response I expected."

"Actually, I thank Sarah for saving my life that night. Don't you see, Thierry? She made a mistake when she picked you, she just won't admit it yet. If you are really all that concerned with her well-being, then I suggest you step aside and let a real man take care of her."

"Excuse me," I said, feeling that I had to nip this in the bud before things got out of hand. "I appreciate your concern, really, but I choose what's best for me. And frankly, right now I'm thinking it might be Lenny. He has that big knife, you know."

Quinn looked at me and shook his head. "You never answered me before. Just what do you see in him? I don't get it."

"In Lenny?" My eyes flicked to Thierry for a moment. He didn't smile. "No, in 'suicide watch' over there."

"I told you, we're both heavily into reality TV." I tried to smile, but found that my lips shook too much to pull it off believably.

Quinn scowled. "You need to stop being so stupid, Sarah, and open your eyes. Why can't you just admit that you made an idiotic mistake?"

He turned away only to realize that Thierry was now standing directly next to him.

"You can say what you like about me," Thierry said, his voice still steady and cool, but his expression betraying his anger. "But don't insult Sarah. Not in front of me. I won't allow it."

"I didn't insult her. I'm trying to make her see facts."

"You cannot make someone see facts by shoving them in her face."

Quinn grinned. "She didn't mind a minute ago when I was in her face, did she? Oh, and by the way, *not* the first time we've kissed."

Thierry glanced at me.

I bit my lip. "It was a long time ago."

"Look, asshole," Quinn grabbed Thierry's attention again. "Much as I'm enjoying this heart to heart, I've got places I need to be."

"Really? I was under the impression you were staying at a seedy motel, wasting your time as you figured out how to spend the rest of your worthless life."

Quinn's eyes narrowed. "I think you should give Sarah a little time to think things through. She's got a lot on her plate right now. You know, being a target? Which, in case you're not aware of it, is all your fault, you selfish bastard."

"You are trying my patience, hunter."

He laughed. "Am I? Am I carving into that oh-so-cool exterior of yours? Don't you see, Thierry? It's only a matter of time until she takes off her rose-colored glasses and realizes what a bloodthirsty monster you really are underneath the surface." He took a step closer to Thierry so they were chest to chest. "Now get the hell out of my way."

Thierry didn't budge. "Or what?"

Quinn smiled. "Get out of my way or I'll *make* you get out of my way."

I moved closer to them. "Come on, guys. Break it up. There's really no need for this."

"Sarah, stay back," Thierry advised.

Quinn shoved Thierry back a few feet. "Get out of my way."

Thierry cocked his head to one side. "No."

Quinn cracked his knuckles. "Oh, I have *so* been waiting for this."

"As have I."

Quinn's fist connected with Thierry's jaw, snapping his head back. Thierry reached up and touched the corner of his mouth, then looked at the blood on his fingertips, before his gaze locked with Quinn's again. "Do that again."

"With pleasure."

Quinn hit the other side of his jaw.

"Quinn, stop it!" I shouted.

I had to put a stop to this. Quinn was looking for any excuse to wipe the floor with Thierry. I didn't want anybody to get hurt.

"You know," Quinn said. "I find that since becoming a vampire, my strength has definitely increased. So you better watch yourself if you don't want to get seriously injured."

"I have been a vampire for much, much longer than you, hunter." Thierry licked his lips. "My injuries heal remarkably fast now."

"Fascinating." Quinn's fist came in for a third strike. Thierry caught it in midair, just before it made contact again.

"And after so many years—" Thierry grabbed Quinn's T-shirt "—can you imagine how strong I am?"

With a flick, he launched Quinn across the club to crash into a table, breaking it on contact.

My eyes widened. This was all happening too fast. Too fast. What was I supposed to do?

Frozen in place, I glanced at Thierry, but he didn't look at me. His attention was focused on the ex-hunter, who slowly got to his feet with a furious expression on his face and rushed the older vamp.

Thierry let Quinn punch him in the stomach, but he didn't make any sound, his face didn't reflect any pain. But when Thierry's fist connected with Quinn's left cheekbone, the blow was enough to knock him back and across the bar top and into the lined-up bottles of liquor, which shattered and flew in all directions. When Quinn emerged from behind the bar, he looked mad enough to spit.

Or kill.

He grabbed a chair from off the top of a nearby table and broke it over his knee, producing a crude, but sharp wooden stake.

"I think the world would be better off without you in it." Quinn's words were slightly slurred.

"Perhaps you're right," Thierry replied.

Quinn ran at Thierry with a yell that reminded me of men racing across the battlefield to meet the enemy. Thierry was still, so still, that for a moment I thought that he was going to let Quinn stake him without trying to defend himself.

"Thierry! No!" I screamed.

His attention flicked to me for the briefest second and our eyes met. Then he turned back to the charging Quinn and brought his hands up, moving so fast I could barely see him trip Quinn, snatching the stake out of his hand. Quinn fell to the floor, and in a flash, Thierry was on top of him, pinning him down, one hand clutched around his neck, the other with the stake pressed to his chest. Quinn grabbed at Thierry's wrist, but the look on his face was pure panic. And defeat.

"Kill me," Quinn managed. "Go ahead, asshole! Do it!"

There was a sheer sheen of sweat on Thierry's forehead. I approached, my entire body shaking and my mind reeling from what I'd just witnessed.

Thierry could see me out of the corner of his eye. "I would ask you what I should do with your hunter here, Sarah, but I have a feeling I already know what you'd say."

"Let him go," I said quietly. "Please."

"That's what I thought you'd say." He looked up at me, his eyes filled with the raw emotion that he'd been trying to hide. But it was still muted. Still controlled. "He would have killed me without a moment's hesitation."

"I know."

His gaze trailed to the bite marks on my neck and his expression grew pained. "I'm sorry about last night." His voice broke on the words.

"I know that, too. Let him go."

His grip on Quinn's neck tightened as he glared down at him. "Do not mess with me again." He let him go and stood up in one fluid motion and threw the makeshift stake away to the side where it clattered against the floor.

Then with a last look at me, Thierry turned away and left the club, slamming the door behind him.

I fell to my knees beside Quinn. "Are you okay?"

He touched his neck where Thierry's grip had left red marks behind. "Do you see *now*?"

I frowned. "What?"

He coughed, then slowly got to his feet. "That he's a goddamned monster?"

My frown deepened. "Why, because he managed to kick your ass?"

He snorted. "He didn't kick my ass."

"Shall we watch the slow-motion replay on that?"

He closed his eyes and let out a long shaky breath. "Well, maybe I was having an off day."

"You shouldn't have provoked him." I gingerly touched his cheekbone, which bore a cut from his introduction to twenty broken bottles. He caught my hand and kissed it.

"I will take an ass-kicking any day of the week if it proves to you that what I'm telling you about him is absolutely true."

I pulled my hand away from him. "I don't know what you're talking about."

He carefully sat up, wincing as he did so, then slowly got to his feet. "I need a drink."

"Help yourself."

He slowly walked behind the bar and grabbed a beer from the fridge. He cracked it open and took a long gulp from it.

I watched him warily. "Now continue. What were you saying?"

He wearily leaned against the bar top. "That everything I've told you about Thierry just got proven. You saw it for yourself."

"What I saw was two little boys getting into a scrap over hurt feelings."

"That guy doesn't have any feelings."

"He does."

"Yeah? Could have fooled me." He laughed wryly. "Like I said before, I'm willing to wait for you, Sarah, but I'm just not all that happy about it."

I stood up. "So you think that I should leave Thierry."

He shrugged, then winced at the movement. "Duh."

I glanced off in the direction that Thierry had gone. "Tell me why I should."

"I think I've given you many valid reasons, but okay." He took a deep breath and let it out slowly. "I originally didn't come back to Toronto just to see you again, but I'm here now. I think I might be a little bit in love with you. That's why you should leave him."

I swallowed hard. "You don't mean it, but I appreciate the thought."

He shook his head. "Why would I say it if I didn't mean it?"

I tried to choose my words carefully. "I love you, too."

A smile sprang to life on his super-serious face.

I held up my hand. "Not so fast. I think you're great, Quinn. I really do. And I do think you're sincere in wanting to change and be a better person now that you've seen the other side of things and remorseful for what happened when you were a hunter."

He nodded. "All that and a bag of chips."

I looked at him. A little beaten up but still really gorgeous. Any girl would be lucky to have Quinn say those words to her. He was a wonderful man. And he'd just succeeded in making things crystal clear to me.

"The problem is that you've morphed that remorseful feeling into this torch you're holding for me."

"What are you talking about?"

"I think that I'm the only person on earth who told you the truth from the first moment we met. I was real with you. Then I tried to help you when all you wanted to do was kill me. And you think that's true love."

"It is."

I shook my head. "No, Quinn. That's not love. That's gratitude."

His expression hardened. "No, that's not true."

"I helped ease you into your crappy new life as a vampire. And you've convinced yourself that there's more between us than there actually is."

"Sarah, just listen to me—"

"Just because you believe something is true, doesn't necessarily mean it is. Like thinking Thierry had anything to do with these murders. It's not true. If you just stand back and look at things objectively, you'd see it. The world is not as black and white as you'd like to think."

"It is true. It's all true. I love you."

I reached across the bar to touch his arm. "And I love you. But not the way you want me to. I want only the best for you. And it's not me."

"Don't say that."

"I'm sorry." My throat hurt. I felt tears burning my eyes.

He swallowed hard. "But when I kissed you, you kissed me back."

"I know."

"That meant nothing to you?"

"It meant that I'm confused. I'm trying to figure things out. It might take me a long time before I finally do."

"I'll wait."

I shook my head. "Please don't."

He looked away. "Then I guess we're done here."

"I guess so. I'm sorry."

"Yeah, me, too."

I reached up to touch his injured face again, but he pulled away from me, and with glistening eyes and a hurt expression he stormed out of the club without another word.

I was left alone. Again. Wondering if I should have just kept my mouth shut but knowing that would have been impossible.

Chapter 13

I didn't stick around the club for much longer after that. I cleaned up the place a bit, moved the broken furniture off to the side. Picked up the broken glass without injuring myself this time. Go me.

I got Lenny and Janie to drive me to Thierry's townhome, but he wasn't there.

No sign of Gideon Chase all day. Maybe he wasn't as interested in the Slayer of Slayers as Nicolai had been led to believe. Or maybe the news was already spreading that I was nobody to be afraid of.

I decided to think about it tomorrow.

Then, feeling like a big pile of crap who'd just destroyed everything she cared about in the world, I had them drop me back off at George's place to mope and feel sorry for myself.

Well, *our* place. I guess. It would only be a matter of time before he started charging me rent. Which, since I was broke, would probably end badly.

I didn't want to think about what had just happened. Quinn probably hated me now. I didn't even want to know what Thierry thought about the situation. I wanted to put it all out of my mind. Was that possible? Unlikely, but here's hoping.

I didn't have a key, so I knocked on the door. After a moment it swung open and Amy looked out at me with red-rimmed eyes.

"My marriage is over," she announced. "Want to get really, really drunk?"

I took a deep breath. "What the hell are you doing here?"

She held the door open and I brushed past her. Barkley came bounding over to me and I let him jump up and lick my face. If he really was a werewolf I was going to kick his butt someday, but if he was just a dog, it was a nice way to be greeted after a lousy day.

George emerged from the kitchen. "We're eating ice cream. Amy brought it over."

She nodded. "I did. Ben & Jerry's Chunky Monkey. Want some?"

I shook my head. "Remember I'm the one who can't eat solid food anymore? But thanks for rubbing it in."

She promptly burst into tears. "I'm sorry! I forgot!" She grabbed me and hugged me hard to sob against my shoulder. I patted her back.

"It's okay. So what's going on? Did you leave Barry?"

After a moment, she pulled away. "I know you've had a terrible week and I hate to unload on you like I have been. But yes. He doesn't know it yet, but I'm gone. I confronted him about my suspicions but he didn't say anything to make me think he's not cheating. In fact, I think the other woman was there this afternoon."

I raised an eyebrow. "Why do you think that?"

"Because he wouldn't let me go into the den. He has it barricaded. She was probably hiding in there like a cheap, hiding whore."

Or more likely it was all of the birthday party paraphernalia he was trying to hide. I didn't know why Barry insisted on throwing Amy a surprise birthday party. It was a nice idea and all, but now that she was all freaking out about thinking he was cheating on her, wouldn't this be a good opportunity to come clean? Maybe have a nice regular birthday party without the surprise, and therefore without the accusations of infidelity?

Then again, I was not exactly the right person to ask about her views on infidelity, or for that matter, surprises, so I was staying clear of this.

Besides, after our exchange earlier, I think if I let the proverbial cat out of the bag, Barry might stake me in my sleep.

Amy would be feeling her pain until tomorrow when it was revealed that her diminutive husband (aka Cranky Bastard) cared enough to throw a party for her. And then she'd be happy again. Till then, she was miserable. And since I was currently miserable—to say the very least—I figured that it was only fair.

"I never should have married him," she wailed.

I frowned. "What have you done to your teeth?"

She bared them for me. Her fangs, which she'd just developed last week, were gone.

"What happened to your fangs?"

"If I don't have Barry anymore, I don't want to be a vampire," she said very seriously.

I glanced over at George, then back at her. "I'm sorry to be the one to break it to you, but it's not as easy as just making the decision that it's not for you. It's kind of like getting a tattoo. Or a sex change."

"I know. But I don't want a constant reminder of what I am . . . what Barry is . . . so George gave me his dentist's number, and she managed to fit me in this afternoon. She specializes in fang reduction and porcelain veneers." She reached up and touched her teeth. "I feel normal again."

"Well, if that's all it takes."

"A hundred bucks. She says I have to come back every other month for fang reduction maintenance. Plus, apparently I have a couple of cavities. Which sucks." She started to cry again.

"So it's your big day tomorrow, isn't it?" I said, then looked over at George making the cut sign against his throat like "say no more." I guess he was in on Barry's big birthday surprise, too.

She sniffed. "Yeah. Happy stupid birthday to me."

"I still haven't bought your gift yet. Any suggestions?"

"The last two months of my life back."

I scratched the top of Barkley's head. His tail thwacked happily against the floor. "I'm already on the waiting list for that one. Other than that."

She shook her head. "I don't know. Maybe some cheap jewelry. I know you're on a budget. Plus, with what happened to your apartment, you have way more important things to think about than getting me a gift."

Understatement. Definitely. Just thinking about it made me cringe.

"More important? Me? Never. Now, I believe you said something about getting severely drunk?"

George came fully into the living room. "We're going out tonight to a club. I'm not working—*hallelujah*—Amy needs some cheering up. You . . . " he paused as he looked me up and down, "You look like you've seen better days."

I gave him a look, but then realized he was telling the truth.

His expression became more serious. "By the way, we were going to discuss your little love bite there? You were asleep last night when I got back. Still asleep when I left this morning. Maybe I should have been concerned, but I did have things to do."

I touched my neck and wished for the hundredth time today that I was wearing a scarf. "Nothing to discuss. The matter has been dealt with."

He looked unconvinced. "If you say so."

"So where are we going? And please don't tell me Haven, because I've seen enough of that place for one immortal lifetime."

George made a gagging sound. "No. I'm sick to death of vamp clubs. We're going to a human club. A new dance club in Queen's Quay called the Liar's Club. The plan is to dance like fools and drink ourselves stupid."

I sighed. "If only alcohol could do it anymore."

George grinned. "Well you're in luck. Because I managed to score a little contraband."

"What does that mean?"

He disappeared into the kitchen and emerged with a

small silver flask. "This is like gold, but I'm willing to share with my two favorite girls. Since they're not here, you two will have to do."

"Very funny. What is that?"

"It's called Moonshine. But it's not like regular home-made booze. It's . . . very special. And it works on vampires just like hard liquor works on humans."

I eyed the silver flask. "Moonshine, huh? Where did you get it?"

"If I told you I'd have to kill you. But then I'd have to get in line, wouldn't I? So are you in?"

I sighed and thought about it for a moment. Hunters of the world focused on finding me and killing me in a spectacular fashion. The leader of all hunters allegedly on his way to Toronto to have me all to himself before he refocused his attentions on hunting down Thierry. And I was planning on heading out for a night on the town of drinking and dancing?

Sounded like a plan. Bring it on.

Later that night I found myself in the dark, noisy interior of the Liar's Club. It was ten o'clock and I had spent a good chunk of time getting dressed in my new outfit, a short silver skirt and a flowy white blouse that rivaled last night's black dress for its plunging neckline. I wore enough makeup to make me look like a streetwalker. That is, if everyone around me, both women and some of the men, weren't wearing a similar amount. Amy had helped me apply it. Without my shard I'd been relying on pressed powder and lip gloss to see me through. Otherwise I might end up poking my eye out with a mascara wand.

I really had to save up for another shard.

Amy was dressed to kill, though considering her mood, I hoped not literally. Her skirt was even shorter than mine, and her top so low-cut that you could almost see her brand-new belly-button ring (a diamond-studded bat). Her hair was sleek and very blond and made her stand out in the crowd whenever she went under a light. She looked like a slutty angel.

"If only Barry could see me now!" she shouted above the techno thump of the dance music.

"Yeah, I think he might lose a few more inches in height."

"It would serve him right!"

Janie and Lenny were over in the middle of the throng of people crowding the bar keeping an eye on us party monsters. It was a lot different from Haven, mostly because it was very busy. Sweaty bodies were everywhere. And from the smell, I could tell that 99 percent of them were human. Humans just have a different smell than vampires, something I hadn't even realized before, since I didn't hang out with humans much—if at all—anymore, and especially not in these numbers. And it wasn't just sweat. It wasn't unpleasant. Just the opposite, in fact. It was slightly nutty, almost like a peanut butter smell. If I gave it any thought at all—which of course I hadn't—I'd say it was an appetizing smell that made my fangs ache slightly.

I'd always loved peanut butter.

But that would be a wrong thing to think. And extremely disturbing, given the week I'd had.

So, knowing that we were surrounded by regular Joes,

that pretty much left me, Amy, and George as the friendly neighborhood vampires in residence.

We secured drinks, and George tipped his flask into each of them, depositing a few drops of the Moonshine. And then we went to dance.

After a few loud, throbbing dance tunes, I was feeling a little more at ease. Not much, but a little. I used to go out clubbing a lot more before my vampification. It was fun. A good chance to forget your worries and dance your butt off after a hard week at the day job, knowing that nothing outside the dance floor mattered. The world came to a stop for fun, fun, fun.

Then again, I was much more of a bubblehead back then. Not being hunted helped my mind stay free of anything but the day-to-day issues of fashion, cute guys, and having a good time.

Aka the good old days. Sort of.

There *were* a few things about clubbing I'd never been particularly fond of, though.

Some guy had sidled up behind me and was now grinding his hips against me. "Hey, baby. Wanna dance?"

I glanced over my shoulder at him. He was your typical club rat . . . sweaty, yet peanut-butter-esque, dressed in the latest metrosexual fashion, about ten years older than he was trying to act. His eyes were fixed directly on my ass.

"I think that's what I'm doing already, thanks."

He put his hand on my hip. "*Yeah* you are. Shake that booty."

"Take a hike."

"Lemme buy you a drink."

"I already have a drink."

"You want me, baby, I can feel it."

"Feel this." I turned around and stomped my high heel into his instep. He howled in pain and hopped away.

If only all my problems could be handled so easily.

I turned back to George, who was grinning from ear to ear.

"That's so hot," he said.

I shrugged.

He grabbed my plastic cup and poured a little more Moonshine into it.

I frowned up at him. "Hey, how do I know this isn't poison or something?"

He poured some in his own cup, took a sip, then looked at me. "It is. And you've already had enough to kill you. We have about three hours to live."

I swung my arm over his shoulder. "Yeah, I wish."

"Is my little brunette buttercup depressed tonight?"

"George, we're totally soulmates. You and me. I'm going to leave Thierry, say goodbye to Quinn, and you and me can get together and live happily ever after. Maybe we'll raise a litter of Chihuahuas to keep Barkley company."

He grabbed my hand and spun me around in a circle, narrowly missing some other dancers on the crowded floor, a motion that made me a bit dizzy. "Honey, if you were male, ripped, and available, that sounds like a definite plan. It also sounds like the Moonshine is kicking in."

I looked up at his handsome face, with the music swirling around me, the strobe lights flickering in circles. He was absolutely right. I was drunk as a skunk.

I raised my glass. "Rock and roll, baby."

"Well said."

I frowned. "I kind of feel like something is missing."

George hugged me. "You're going to be just fine, my little chipmunk," he slurred. Obviously the Moonshine was working on him, too. "You just need to be more positive. Not that I'm an expert on positivity, but it beats feeling down in the dumps."

When he let me go, I shook my head, which made me even more dizzy. "No, I mean something specific is missing. Like, right now at this very minute. Where's Amy?"

"Amy who?"

"Amy, the blond chick we came here with? My friend? Remember? *Get Shorty*'s wife?"

He nodded slowly. "Oh, yeah, her. I remember now." He looked around. "She's not here."

"Obviously. But where is she?"

"Good question."

I tried to remember the last time I'd seen her. It was over by the bar when we got our drinks. What did she say? "*If only Barry could see me now*"?

Not good.

I pushed my way off the dance floor. George followed. I made my way through the sea of deliciously peanut-butter-scented clubbers and over to the ladies room where I opened up the door to poke my head inside.

"Amy, are you in here?" I called.

Two severely drunk girls looked over at me from the sinks where one had just vomited, the other holding her hair back off her face. "Who the hell is Amy?"

"Gross. Never mind." I closed the door and turned to George. "She's not in there."

"I'm sure she's fine. She's an adult, she can look after herself."

Which, in theory, should have been true. But this was Amy we were talking about. A few months ago she'd gotten lost at the Toronto Zoo, and I had to go and collect her in Lost and Found. Though they did let her hold a baby chimp who was in for a checkup to cheer her up a bit. She'd liked that.

But there were no chimps on site at the Liar's Club that I was aware of. No chimps at all.

Geez, I frowned. *What was I even thinking?* I was seriously drunk. Had to focus.

"What's the problem?" Janie approached me with Lenny hanging on behind her.

"I can't find my friend."

"Oh, is that all? I thought it was something hunter related. It's been a slow day."

I gave her a dirty look. "Yeah, sorry to disturb you."

Lenny grabbed Janie's arm. "C'mon, let's go dance."

She jerked her arm away. "I told you before, I'm not dancing. We're working right now, remember?"

"That doesn't mean we can't have any fun."

She spun around to face him. "Yes it does. Lenny, if you don't start acting more professional, I'm going to have to request a new partner. I'm sorry, but it's the truth."

His bottom lip wobbled. "But . . . I love you."

Her shoulders slumped. "Oh, my God."

He grabbed her hand. "I've always loved you. Can't you see that we're perfect together?"

She turned to look at me. "I'm going to need a minute here."

"Yeah. You take as much time as you need." I grabbed George's arm and moved us away from the little tableau of bodyguard love. I spotted a flash of blond hair on the dance floor. "Come on, I think I see her."

I approached close enough that I could see for sure it was Amy. She was dancing with her eyes closed, smiling a wide, currently fang-free smile, getting cozy with a cute guy who had his hands on her butt and was dancing so close to her that she might need a pregnancy test later.

And he looked awfully familiar.

Who had my best friend Amy just picked up in a human nightclub?

Oh, no.

It was Chad.

The vampire hunter with the stain-resistant Dockers. The one who'd informed me of my new little nickname.

He's going to kill her.

Just as the thought raced through my mind, he moved in, even closer to Amy, and . . .

Started making out with her?

I dug my fingernails into George's arm to a loud protest from him. That did not look like typical hunter behavior. Why wasn't he trying to kill her?

My eyes widened. Her fangs! She'd had them filed down. He didn't realize she was a vampire.

"Ouch." George pulled my claws out of his arm. "Watch it there, Wolverine."

"George," I turned to him. "Amy's dancing with a hunter."

He glanced over. "He's a hunter?"

"Yeah. He tried to kill me."

"Well, that's not good."

"You think? I can't go over or he'll recognize me." I looked over at the bar where we'd left Janie and Lenny. They'd disappeared. I turned back to George. "You need to go rescue Amy."

"Are you crazy? What about your hired muscle?"

"I don't know where they've gone. You won't get hurt. I don't think he'll automatically assume you're a vamp. Just go. Amy doesn't know how much trouble she's in."

He sighed, then nodded before he weeded his way onto the dance floor until he was standing next to Amy. He tapped her on her shoulder and she pried open her eyes. Chad's brow lowered and he said something to George I couldn't hear. Amy said something, too. George turned around and returned to me.

"She doesn't want to leave. She told me in no uncertain terms to go away. The girl needs her mouth washed out with soap. I am offended."

"Does she know who she's dancing with?"

"I didn't feel it was an appropriate time to let her know she was dancing with a potential murderer."

I looked at Amy, who glanced over at me. I waved my arm for her to come over. She shook her head.

"Stubborn little *bee-yotch*," I said.

Chad whispered something in Amy's ear and left the dance floor. I beelined over to her.

"What?" she said when I approached.

"We need to leave."

She shook her head. "But we just got here."

"Yeah, I know. But we have to leave. Right now."

"Why? I'm having fun. Plus, I feel drunk."

"That would be the Moonshine." I ignored the room, which had decided to begin spinning in leisurely circles around me. "Do you know you managed to pick up a vampire hunter?"

Her eyebrows went up. "Seriously? Too cool."

"No, it's not cool. It's very bad. And I'm not feeling sober enough to deal with this if we don't leave right now."

"He's buying me a drink."

"I don't particularly care if he's buying you a car. We're out of here." I grabbed her wrist and turned around. Chad was standing behind me with two blue-colored drinks in his hands. His eyes widened when he saw me, and the drinks slipped from his grasp and crashed to the floor.

"Slayer of Slayers," he breathed.

I smiled brightly. "Hey, how's it going?"

He took a step back. "Don't hurt me."

"Then get out of my way."

He stepped aside and let us pass. Well, that was easy.

George stepped in line with us and we headed for the nearest exit. In this case, it was the designated outdoor smoking area, roped off and crowded with people getting their nicotine fix.

"I don't want to leave," Amy protested, wrestling to pry her wrist away from me.

"Too bad."

"I really liked him. So what if he's a vampire hunter? You and Quinn managed to work past that, didn't you? He likes you even though he's a hunter."

"That's different. And I'm not sure how much he likes me anymore anyhow, since I believe I bruised his ego earlier. Also, he's not a hunter anymore."

"Quinn is hot," George commented.

"Besides, remember Peter?" I said. "You've dated a hunter before, and how did that turn out?"

She stuck her tongue out at me. Very mature.

I was examining the thick rope, which was like netting, that hung around the smoking area. They'd obviously set it up so people couldn't sneak into the club through this entrance without paying the hefty cover. Or, in our case, sneak out.

Some of the smokers were heading back inside. Actually, most of them, steadily moving back into the club until there was nobody left out in the cold, smog-clogged air but the three of us. Amy was pouting and had her arms crossed.

"Some birthday. This totally blows."

"Your birthday isn't even till tomorrow. Listen, we need to go out the same way we came in," I said. And we turned to the entrance.

A pale-faced Chad the vampire hunter was staring at me.

"I thought I told you to get out of my face?" I said, thrilled that I managed to sound adequately brave.

"That's her." He pointed at me. "The Slayer of Slayers."

"That's right, jerk. And I'm going to—" I looked past Chad to see that he was flanked by several other guys who all had their arms crossed and their eyes narrowed. They were all wearing University of Toronto jackets. Tall, young, all very cute. Fraternity guys, maybe.

Chad was pushed to the side and the huge frat boy behind him grinned at me. "Well, isn't this our lucky night? I've heard all about you. This is an honor."

I blinked at him. "Gee, thanks."

"It will be an honor to end a celebrity vamp like your-self." He felt at his belt and pulled out a wooden stake. "The other guys will be so jealous."

I took a step back. "You have the wrong person."

Where the hell were Lenny and Janie? Wasn't this ex-actly the kind of situation they were being paid to protect me from? I strained to look past him and into the club but couldn't see anything.

He shook his head. "I don't think so. Chad here's my boy. And if my boy says that you're the Slayer of Slayers, then that's just who you are."

My stomach dropped. I suddenly wished I hadn't drunk so much Moonshine. My lack of foresight, not to mention lack of bodyguards, was seriously going to be the death of me.

Which, according to the look in Frat-boy's eyes, was going to be in T minus ten seconds.

Chapter 14

"My goodness, that was an excellent cigarette I just inhaled into my very human lungs," George said loudly. "I guess my human friends and I should head back inside now."

I eyed him. "Really?"

He shrugged. "It was worth a shot."

Frat-boy shifted his stake to his other hand. "Somebody get the camera. This is worth documenting."

My eyes widened. The camera?

Come on, Janie, I thought. *Time for you and your lovestruck partner to save my ass.*

I waited.

Any time now. That would be super.

"Here it is," one of the other guys said, after fishing a digital camera out of his pocket. "The card's almost full and the batteries are running low, so let's make this quick."

"No problem," Frat-boy said, and took a step closer to me.

Janie?

Lenny?

Did they get in a fight and leave? Did they quit? Was that necklace guy right when he said that Janie was not to be trusted? If that was the case then we were completely screwed.

I braced myself. I was going to have to put my self-defense lesson, such as it was, to immediate use. I only hoped I'd learned enough to . . . disable five fully grown men with weapons.

It could happen. Sure.

I glanced at George and Amy, hoping one of them had a plan to get us out of this.

They looked back at me blankly.

Self-defense. I wracked my brain. What had I learned?

Frankly, not a whole hell of a lot.

I jumped as the flash went off. Frat-boy handed the camera to his buddy, and they produced wooden stakes out of nowhere.

"Who takes a wooden stake to a dance club?" I said aloud.

He smiled at me. "I just like the way it makes me feel."

Great. *Think, Sarah, think.*

"All right, let's do this." He took a step toward me. "The Slayer of Slayers and her evil minions."

"Minions?" George repeated, sounding vaguely offended through his fear.

I held a hand up. "Just one second."

"What?" Frat-boy stopped in his tracks.

"So you know who I am, right?"

He glanced at his friends, then back to me. "Sure."

"I'm the Slayer of Slayers. That means that I'm extremely dangerous."

He laughed. "You don't look so tough. I think I can handle you."

"That's what the others said. And now they're six feet under."

I saw Chad visibly flinch at my words. "She's right. Maybe we should just clear out."

Frat-boy shook his head. "She's bluffing."

I shrugged. "Do you know who Gideon Chase is?"

He hesitated for a split second. "Of course. Everybody does."

I nodded. "He's on his way to Toronto right this very minute. Why? Because of me. Because of who I am. He wants to meet the Slayer of Slayers himself."

"So what?"

"So if you kill me, kill us, I think he's going to be majorly pissed off. It'll be the ultimate insult. Spoiling his fun. And you know Gideon. He likes his fun, doesn't he?"

Well, I hoped he did, anyhow.

Frat-boy pressed his lips together. "Gideon Chase is coming *here*."

I nodded. "That's right. So this can go one of three ways, boys. You can try to kill us and succeed, and when Gideon gets here and finds out what happened he'll probably kill you for taking his fun away. Number two, you can try to kill us, but being that we're incredibly dangerous vampires, we'll kill you instead. Horribly and painfully." I bared my fangs for full effect. I hoped I didn't have any lipstick on them. "Or number three, you can turn around and leave us the hell alone and live to see another day. I strongly suggest you go for number three. Then again, number two's fine also. I am a little hungry and you boys do smell delicious."

I glanced at George and he nodded in agreement. "They do. They really do."

Frat-boy appeared to think about it for a moment, a range of emotions going through his expression: doubt, fear, and finally anger. He didn't like me telling him what to do. He gripped his stake tighter and took another step toward me. I forced myself not to move back.

"I guess I'm a bit of a gambler, then," he said. "Because I was sort of looking for another kill under my belt. Right, guys?"

He was met with silence.

The other guys had taken off around the time I mentioned the "kill you horribly and painfully" part.

He glanced over his shoulder, and then back at me.

I took a step forward.

He nodded and tucked his stake into his belt loop. "Say hi to Gideon for me."

Then he turned around and left the smoking area. Quickly.

"I seriously think I just peed myself," Amy said. "That guy who bought me a drink was going to totally let us die."

I gave her a look and tried to tell my churning stomach to relax. "Didn't I try to tell you that?"

"Well, I couldn't visualize it. Now I can. That was terrible."

"Yes," George agreed. "Terrible. Who chose this stupid club, anyhow?"

"You did."

"And it's a great club, if it wasn't for all the hunters. They should put a warning on the sign out front. And what's the story with that Gideon guy you were talking about?"

I swallowed hard, but just shrugged. They didn't know. They didn't need to know. It would just make them worry more than they already did. "I was just making it up as I went along. Luckily it worked. All I know is I seriously want to get the hell out of here right now."

He looked around. "Where did the bodyguards go?"

"No idea."

"I think I need some more Moonshine," he said.

I realized my buzz was almost gone, replaced by three layers of stress. "Yeah, let's have it back at the house. I hope you bought a gallon of that stuff."

So, without any further protestation from Amy, we left the Liar's Club, on guard, on edge, and still a little tipsy. I was fuming that Janie and Lenny had basically abandoned me to my own devices. At least until I saw Lenny pounding his head against the wall of a nearby alley.

"Lenny?" I said. "Where the hell did you two go? I needed you in there."

"Sorry. I was coming back. I just needed to get some fresh air."

I frowned at him. "What are you doing?"

"Pounding my stupid head."

"That's what I thought you were doing. And why are you doing that?"

"Because I'm a big, fat dummy, that's why."

I glanced at Amy and George, who stayed back a bit so I could approach the masochistic bodyguard. "Can you be a little more specific?"

He stopped pounding and looked at me. "Janie hates me."

"She doesn't hate you."

"Oh yeah? Are you sure about that?"

"Well, actually, no. But I can't imagine that she'd hate you. You seem very . . . uh . . . nice."

He swallowed hard, and I could see his large Adam's apple move up and down. "Okay, she might not hate me, but she . . . she doesn't love me."

"Is this what you guys were talking about earlier? Your crush on Janie?"

He let out a shuddery sigh. "It's not a crush. It's a deep, passionate love that fills my soul and keeps me from thinking about anything or anyone else."

"Okay. If you say so."

"I write her poems all the time. But she doesn't seem to care."

I nodded slowly. "I got to read one of them yesterday. It was . . . lovely."

He took a deep breath of the cold night air and braced a hand against the wall he'd just bashed his head against. "Thank you. They're from the heart. My heart tells me what I should write."

"Well, maybe she just needs more time."

He sniffed loudly and shook his head. "No. It's over. She'll never love me. I may as well throw myself off a bridge."

"Trust me, not the way to go. Listen, sometimes people just don't connect. Sometimes one feels something when the other doesn't, and that's just the way it is." I thought about Thierry and a lump formed in my throat. "You can't force something unless both people want it to happen. You need to realize that, accept it, and move on, because I'm sure the perfect girl for you is just waiting."

He blinked at me. "Look, I'm not into vampires."

I stared at him for a second and then sighed. "Why does everybody think I'm coming on to them this week?"

He shrugged his big shoulders. "I would understand if you're attracted to me. I mean, I am your protector. Chicks think that's kind of hot."

"Protector. Right. Except for five minutes ago when I almost died because you needed some fresh air. But I'm over it." I pressed my lips together. "Yeah, so very attracted. But shucks, you're not into vamps. I guess I'll have to accept that."

"Tell Janie if you see her, that I . . . I had to go."

"Where are you going now?" I asked his now-turned back, quickly moving away from me down the street. My voice sounded a bit pitchy. "Hey, aren't you on the clock? We need a ride home!"

He didn't turn around. I could have sworn I saw a Kleenex tucked up his sleeve.

I walked out of the alley to meet George and Amy, but heard a voice from the shadows.

"We messed up," Janie said. "Sorry."

I turned to face her.

"What?"

"I said we messed up. I'll understand if you want to fire us."

I crossed my arms. "Let's not get carried away. I don't want to fire you. It's just that it wasn't only me tonight. My friends were in danger. This is serious."

"I know." She looked away, then after a moment

turned back to me. "By the way, you don't need to give Lenny relationship advice, you know."

"He was upset. I figured that since I'm still breathing, I'd give him a few words of dubious wisdom."

She shrugged. "He'll get over it."

"I just want to go to sleep," I said. "Are you going to give us a ride home?"

She nodded. "Let's go."

I studied her for a moment. "Can I trust you, Janie?"

She tensed. "Of course you can, Sarah. Completely."

I smiled at her, then walked toward Amy and George, our lives in the hands of somebody who my gut was telling me was a big fat liar.

Amy insisted that she be dropped off at her house, which was fine, and then George and I went home. I didn't invite Janie inside. We got severely drunk on Moonshine. It didn't help me forget my problems. But it did make the room spin around long enough that I finally fell onto my mattress and into blissful unconsciousness.

I woke up with a mouth full of cotton. Literally. It seemed that I had chewed into my pillow during the night and was now surrounded by feathers. Oral fixation. Now with more dangerous teeth. Not a good combination.

I glanced at the clock. It was almost noon. Ugh.

Moonshine not only got vampires drunk without the necessity of being a chaser to blood, but it seemed that it also gave vampires hangovers. Big hangovers. My head felt about the size of a hot-air balloon. On fire.

I needed water. I crawled out of bed, noticing that I was wearing George's old, oversized Duran Duran

"Simon Forever!" T-shirt as nightwear, and opened the door to my room.

I heard knocking. I stopped in place and listened. Yes, definitely knocking.

"Oh, for the love of all that is holy!" I heard George cry out from his bedroom. "Would somebody make it stop! The noise! Make it stop!"

Good to know I wasn't alone on the Moonshine pain experience.

I grabbed the handle and slowly opened the door, looking blearily out into the bright sunshine.

At Thierry.

He frowned. "Sarah? Are you all right?"

I rubbed my eyes, suddenly realizing how lousy I must look. I felt my hair, which had turned into one large brown tangle.

"Thierry," I managed. My mouth had the oh-so-pleasant taste of a chemical toilet. "Hi."

"I . . . tried phoning, but no one was answering. I was concerned."

I ran my fingers through my hair until they got caught on the demon tangle. "Oh, right. Slept in. George, Amy, and I went out for a few drinks."

He nodded. "I wanted to stop by. I had to see you to make sure you were all right. And I really want to talk to you." His gaze moved to my neck and he frowned.

I touched the bite marks. "I want to talk to you, too. About what happened yesterday with Qu . . . well, you know. I'm glad you're here . . . even though it would have been nice if I'd heard the phone ring. I could have found something better to wear. I think George has a Depeche

Mode shirt I could borrow that is much more stylish." I smiled.

"You look just fine to me." His gaze moved up to lock with mine. He reached toward me and ran a warm hand down my bare arm. I took a step closer to him.

My smile widened. "So do you." I noticed his gaze leave my probably shiny and feather-encrusted face to glance over my shoulder. His eyes narrowed.

"Just the three of you went out last night, you said?"

I nodded. "Yeah. I needed to let go of some pent-up energy. And dancing's great for that."

"Dancing," he repeated. "Is that all?"

"Of course." *And almost getting killed*, I thought. But really, that's a given.

His expression darkened even further and he didn't meet my eyes again. "Yes, it looks like you had an excellent time, Sarah, relieving your excess energy. I apologize for any intrusion. Should you find the time to speak to me in your very busy schedule, I'll be at the club all afternoon."

He turned around and walked away without even looking at me again.

I felt seriously confused. What just happened? What was his problem? Was my morning breath that bad? I breathed against the back of my hand and grimaced.

Yeah. It really was.

But it was the Quinn thing. Must be. He was pissed off. I couldn't say I blamed him, but why wouldn't he even let me explain? Just storm off after he'd come all the way over here. It just didn't make any damn sense.

I closed the door and turned around.

A naked man stood behind me, casually drinking from a coffee mug.

"Hi there," he said with a smile.

He was about six feet tall, with shaggy black hair, piercing blue eyes, and a lean languid line to his body.

His aforementioned *naked* body.

When I didn't say anything due to my jaw being on the floor, he approached me, ignoring my wide eyes and stunned gaze, and . . . enthusiastically licked up the side of my cheek.

I smacked him in the mouth.

He held a hand up to his face. "Hey! What was that for?"

"What was that for?" I sputtered. "Get away from me! Who the hell are you? I'm going to call the police. George! George!"

I heard a bang, and a couple of crashes, before George emerged from his bedroom with a salmon-colored towel wrapped around his waist, gingerly holding his head. "You don't have to scream. What is it?" He eyed Mr. Naked. "Um . . . first of all, *hello there*. And secondly, who the hell are you?"

"It's *me*," the man replied.

George glanced at me. "Sarah, you naughty little minx. Did you—"

"No!" I looked at the guy again, shielding my view of his nether regions with a strategically placed hand. "Explain. Right now. Or you're in big trouble, mister!"

"First of all, don't freak out," Mr. Naked said. "It's me. *Barkley.*"

"Barkley?" My eyes widened. "The dog?"

"*Werewolf*," he corrected, and absently scratched behind his ear.

I gaped at him. "You have *got* to be kidding."

"No, not kidding. Thought I was stuck that way forever . . . but boom, here I am. What do you know?"

"Yeah," I glanced at George half naked in his towel, then at Barkley, completely naked in his . . . nothing. A vampire and a werewolf.

I shook my head. It was obvious. I was having one of my Anita Blake dreams again.

George pinched me. "Ow!" I frowned, and rubbed my arm. Okay. Not a dream. "This is obviously why Thierry just took off all pissed off. He thinks I've been having hot monkey love in here."

Barkley took another sip of the coffee. "You know, I've always enjoyed the way you scratch my tummy. My tail's wagging just thinking about it. So I'm game if you are."

I grimaced. "For the love of God, would you put some clothes on? I am traumatized enough already this week."

He looked down at himself. "I don't have any. Besides, nudity is natural. I didn't wear clothes in my wolf form."

"That was very different. There was fur involved." I took a deep breath and let it out slowly. "Why are you human now when you've been stuck as a wolf for so long, anyhow?"

George had gone to fetch another towel, and he handed it silently to Barkley.

"Well . . . actually, I have no damn idea." He shrugged. "You guys left last night. I ate some of my food. Drank some water. I was still hungry so I may have eaten one of George's leather moccasins."

"My moccasins!" George moaned. "Not the moc-casins."

"Sorry." He shrugged again. "Then I got kind of tired so I curled up in my bed over there and went to sleep. When I woke up this morning, I was like this."

His bed.

I looked over at it and frowned. Couldn't be.

I walked over to the pile of blankets George and I had set up for Barkley in the corner. My hand suddenly felt clammy as I felt around underneath. I closed my fingers around the chain and pulled it out where the gold caught the sunlight streaming in through the side window.

I glanced at Barkley.

He shrugged. "Found that in your room last night. What can I say? I'm drawn to shiny things. It's not like I ate it. Remember last week when I ate that pair of tweez-ers? I still can't sit down right."

I eyed the necklace without saying anything. What was it? Obviously not just for decorative purposes if it had anything to do with Barkley's transformation. And I had a funny feeling that it did. I left it under the blankets. As good a place as any to keep it hidden.

I shook my head. "This is ridiculous."

He finally put the towel in place. "Hey, you don't have any of those steak-flavored biscuits lying around, do you? I think they would be awesome dipped in this coffee."

I bought Barkley those biscuits for being instrumental in getting me to go outside before my apartment blew up. I looked at him with a frown.

"That night. My apartment. How did you know? Do you remember?"

"Of course I remember. I was stuck as a werewolf, not

a werewolf with amnesia." He appeared to think about it
for a moment. "Yeah, I had a sense that something bad
was going to happen. I'm a little bit psychic. That's one
of the reasons I left my pack two years ago. I sensed that
somebody was going to kill me since I was next in line to
be alpha. Since I didn't want that to happen, I took off
and after a while traveling in wolf form, I got stuck that
way. You ever see the TV show *The Littlest Hobo*? The
one with the German shepherd who travels around helping families and then leaves when he's done to help
somebody else?"

"I used to love that show," George breathed. "I always
wanted him to stay with the family. They would have
been good to him! He wouldn't have been cold or alone
anymore. Why, is that like you? You travel from town to
town helping people, but never find a home of your
own?"

"No, I was just going to say that that wasn't a German
shepherd at all. It was a werewolf stuck in that form just
like I was. Real jerk, too." He shook his head. "*Actors*."

The doorbell rang.

George clutched his head. "Ahhh!"

My brain was working overtime trying to figure everything out, and I absently walked over and opened it up. It
was a guy in a brown uniform. A courier van was pulled
up at the curb.

"Got a delivery here for a Sarah Darling?"

"Sarah *Dearly*?"

"Yeah, that's it. Sign here." He pointed at the bottom
of his clipboard and I signed my name, eyeing him nervously. Then he wheeled a large flat box inside the house
and placed it up against the wall.

"Have a nice day," he said, without much enthusiasm behind the words, and left.

I looked at the box. "I didn't order anything."

"You must have," George said. "They were here yesterday trying to drop whatever that is off, but nobody was here, remember?"

I shook my head. "It's a bomb. I just know it."

"But you sound so calm."

"I know. It's a little eerie." I took a deep breath. "It's the hangover."

"It's a little flat to be a bomb," Barkley said. "And I don't smell any . . . bomblike materials being used."

"You can smell that?"

"My sense of smell is very acute."

"So's mine. Sort of." I sniffed the box. It smelled like cardboard. So much for my superpowers.

"So open it."

I looked at the courier form on the front. Whatever it was came from New York City.

It was a little too flat to be anything all that scary. I hoped. With my luck it was just one very large piece of junk mail. Or a huge bill.

I tore the strip down the side. There were a few layers of bubble wrap I waded through before I got to an envelope.

"There's an envelope," George pointed out.

"I see that."

I grabbed it, tore it open, and saw that it was the shipping receipt. Whatever it was had been ordered personally by Thierry.

I looked at the box again and removed the last scrap of bubble wrap.

George gasped.

"It's me," I said.

And it was. My reflection, anyhow. Reflected in a full-length, oval shard, as tall as I was.

"You are so lucky!" George said. "Holy crap, I hope somebody bombs my place so I can get one, too. So worth it."

I could only imagine how much something like this cost, or how hard it would have been to find a shard of this size and have it delivered so quickly after I lost the first one in my apartment.

I was completely speechless. Other than the first shard Thierry gave me, it was the most generous, thoughtful gift I'd ever received in my entire life.

And it did officially confirm that I looked like hell today.

"What an amazing gift," George said, after no sound came out of me for a moment. "The man is obviously crazy about you."

Barkley nodded. "It's true. Werewolves are very perceptive about love."

I felt sick to my stomach. What must Thierry think of me? This was supposed to have been delivered yesterday, according to the papers. Did he think I had gotten it and just didn't mention it? That I wasn't grateful?

"He must have sent this right after my apartment blew up. After yesterday, I can't imagine that he'd still feel that way about me. If he ever did at all."

Barkley hitched his towel up a bit. "What are you talking about?"

I swallowed hard. "He caught me kissing Quinn yesterday. Well, Quinn kissed me, but it's not like I was trying to stop him or anything."

"Quinn is hot." George sighed. "Have I said that before? And hold on a minute, you kissed him?"

"It doesn't mean anything. Thierry's the one I want to be with."

George's expression turned serious. "And what about your little accident there on your neck?"

I touched it, then inspected the fang marks in the shard, a fading bruise with two darker red marks. It was quite ugly, but it didn't hurt at all. The only thing that hurt was the memory of what had happened. The look in Thierry's eyes when he'd realized what he'd done. "This was an accident. And it scared the crap out of me at the time. But until this happened, I thought that Thierry was perfect and flawless and basically untouchable, but he's not. He's got problems, just like me. Is it wrong for me to say this makes me love him even more than I already did?"

"Not wrong," George said. "Crazy, yes. But not wrong."

"Sorry to interject," Barkley said. "But Thierry looked pretty pissed when he left here. I'm thinking he's not going to want to take me on any more walks."

I frowned. "He took you on walks? Really?"

"Not so much, but he opened the door for me like a pro."

"So what should I do now?"

George blinked at me. "What do you want to do?"

I looked at my horrendous appearance in the mirror. "Well, I need to have a shower."

"An excellent start."

"Put on some makeup."

"Without a doubt."

"And then . . . " I yanked the Duran Duran T-shirt down a bit. "And then I'm going to go see Thierry."

"And then?"

I grinned. "And then what I do is none of your business."

"That's not very nice."

"Wait a minute," Barkley said. "What about me? Who's going to take me out for a walk later?"

I glanced at him. "Seriously?"

He shrugged. "It's okay. George is here. He'll take care of me."

George looked at him. "You're not gay, are you?"

"Not the last time I checked."

"I hate my life."

The phone rang. George screamed in pain before grabbing it off the hook. "What?" he snapped, paused for a second, and then held it out to me. "It's your favorite."

My breath caught and I took the phone from George and held it to my ear. "Thierry?"

"It's Barry."

"Well, it rhymes. Sort of." I twisted the phone cord around my finger. Talk about a lunch bag letdown. "What do you want?"

"Amy isn't speaking to me."

"Well, that would be because she thinks you're cheating on her."

"You need to bring her to the party later."

I sighed and shifted the phone so I could rub my throbbing temples. "What time do you need her there?"

"Six-thirty. And remember, this is a *surprise*."

"Yeah, I figured that out due to it being a surprise party. Where is she?"

"She's getting her hair done. You can find her at Style V."

Style V was a vampire salon. Two birds with one stone. I could make an appointment for my nails while I was there. Excellent.

There was a long pause and for a moment I thought he'd hung up on me. "Why doesn't Amy trust me?"

He sounded . . . upset. Dismayed. And frankly, a little heartbroken.

I shook my head. "I don't know."

"But you're her best friend. You know her. What have I done to make her think that I'd cheat on her at the first opportunity I get?"

I sighed. I couldn't stand Barry and the feeling was obviously mutual, but I hated hearing that somebody else was in pain when I could help a little. "Amy's been burned a lot in the past. She's got that sunny personality and her heart has always been wide open to the thought of being in love. I guess she's built up more scar tissue than she even realizes. She assumes up front, probably subconsciously, that whoever she's with is going to break her heart sooner or later. It's a defense mechanism."

"What can I do about it?"

"You're asking me? I thought I was on your shit list this week."

He paused. "Your dealings with the master have nothing to do with this. It still angers me that you have yet to remove your selfish, chaotic presence from his life, but I am asking you purely out of my love for Amy."

"Well, gee. Don't go sugarcoat it or anything." I sighed again. "Just be patient with her. Prove yourself enough to her and she'll come around."

"That's not terribly comforting."

"You want comfort? Crochet an afghan. See you at six-thirty."

"Don't be late."

The phone clicked as he hung up.

I left the half-naked werewolf and vampire and went to get ready, using my cool new, less portable but much more practical shard to make myself look as good as vampirically possible given that I had a hangover the size of Texas to deal with. From my new wardrobe, I picked a simple pair of black pants and a warm, slightly fuzzy white sweater.

And then I went to Haven to tell Thierry that I was still crazy. About him.

Chapter 15

*H*aven was empty and silent when I got there, but I expected that. It was only midafternoon and usually nobody would be there at all. But I knew Thierry was. My vampire nose could smell his cologne, light on the air. I followed the scent to his office, the door open a crack. I knocked lightly before I pushed it all the way open.

He sat behind his desk, fingers curled around a glass of light-colored liquid. I frowned. Not cranberry juice. I inhaled slightly. Whiskey. Hmm. I'd never seen Thierry drink alcohol before. Strange.

Just seeing him made me smile. "Hi there."

"Sarah," he responded.

I bit my bottom lip, feeling suddenly shy. I reached up to twist the gold necklace I'd decided at the last minute to now wear for safekeeping around my neck. I hoped it wouldn't turn me into a werewolf or anything. I wanted to show it to Thierry, to see what he thought about it, but there were other things to take care of first.

"Just for the record, the naked guy? Was Barkley. He changed back to human before finding a pair of jeans."

He nodded. "The werewolf."

"Right."

"I see." He took a sip of his drink, his gaze steady on me. "Did you come here to tell me that?"

"Yes. And I wanted to see you."

"Me specifically."

"Of course."

His small smile was enough to give me courage to continue. "I got the shard. It was delivered earlier. Thierry . . . you shouldn't have. It must have cost so much."

"You were so distraught about losing your other one. It was the least I could do. Especially after putting you through additional stress with Nicolai in town."

I approached him as he rose to his feet and threw my arms around him. "Thank you so much. I love it."

"You're very welcome." He leaned into my embrace. I felt his warm lips brush sensuously against my neck before he tensed and pulled away from me. "Sarah, I think we need to have a talk."

He looked mega serious. I didn't think I wanted to have a "talk" with Thierry when he looked that serious.

"So is everything set for the party later?" I asked, stabbing blindly at an innocuous subject that might lead us away from dangerous territory.

He looked at me blankly for a moment, then rubbed his forehead. "Yes. I believe so. Barry has been here a few times already today setting things up."

Another question. Right now. Think, Sarah.

"Have you known Barry for a long time?"

"A very long time."

"How long?"

He pressed his lips together. "Is this the continuation of our question-and-answer session from the other night?"

I shrugged. "Maybe it is. I didn't get to ask you too much then."

He took a deep breath and let it out slowly. "No, you didn't. I . . . Sarah, I . . . "

I waved my hand before he had a chance to say anything else. "So why don't we continue?"

His gaze turned soft as he looked at me for a moment. "Very well."

"Do you want to go to Mexico again?"

"Your question is not what I would have expected." He blinked. "I'd never been to Mexico before. It was an experience."

"A good experience?"

I thought about our trip. I was originally supposed to have taken the trip with Amy. It had been something we'd both been incredibly excited about. A little sun, a little sand. A lot of fun. All-inclusive. Bottomless Raspberry Margaritas. The brochures had looked so good I'd tacked them up on my fridge at home and in my cubicle at work. Then the shit had hit the fan.

After I was vampified, my whole world turned upside down. But after everything settled down and I was actually sitting on a beach with Thierry at my side, it seemed like a dream come true. And it was. We'd had a wonderful time. Even after the sunburn from hell. I'd never managed to convince him to wear a bathing suit and frolic in the ocean, but you can't have everything. Besides, Thierry wasn't really a frolicking kind of guy.

"Mexico was . . . " He hesitated before continuing. "Unusual."

"Unusual?"

He gestured as if he was having a difficult time finding the right words to describe our fun in the hot, blistering sun. He finally came up empty and met my gaze. "I was out of sorts there, Sarah. I don't know if I'd return."

I felt a heavy thud of disappointment. "There are other places we can go."

He shook his head. "Being there . . . with you . . . " he pressed his lips together for a moment. "Made me forget myself."

I frowned at that. "What is that supposed to mean?"

"It was wrong of me to go, for us to go to such a place potentially filled with danger. You have the ability to make me forget—to want to forget—but the past few days have been the reminder I've needed. Such distractions can only do harm."

It was like he was speaking Latin to me. All I could hear him saying was that he didn't enjoy himself with me in Mexico. His jaw was tense and when he looked at me his gaze was guarded—as guarded as it had ever been.

I forced a smile to my lips. "Well, just try to say that after we've gone to Disney World."

"Sarah—"

"It's the happiest place on earth, you know."

He shook his head, his eyes stern, but a smile played at his lips. "You are incorrigible."

"I actually have a T-shirt that says that. It has sparkles."

"After all this time, you have yet to embrace the uniqueness of your situation. You have spent the last two months living life as you always have. Going out at any time during the day or night with barely any heed to your own safety, despite the dangerous situations you've found yourself in time and time again. You told me just last week that your parents expect you to come and visit them soon."

I put a hand on my hip, feeling awkward at the direction of this conversation. "I'm going to tell them I'm a vampire. Eventually. My mother is a huge Buffy fan. She might be excited for me."

He sighed. "You shouldn't tell them anything. You should simply not see them. It is safer that way. For them and for you."

"There's no such thing as safe, Thierry. I'm seeing that more and more every day."

"There is. I have survived for nearly seven centuries by paying attention to my surroundings. To make certain I am in no immediate danger."

I faked a yawn. "Sounds really exciting."

"It's *not* exciting. But it is necessary for survival. Have you not witnessed this for yourself? The danger you've faced in the last few days? Hunters will never give up, whether or not they think you are a great threat to their safety. Nicolai's malevolent presence in town has only increased the level of risk."

"Nicolai isn't that bad. I think you two just don't like each other."

I immediately cringed as I remembered what Nicolai had told me about his wife. About Thierry. An accident so long ago.

His expression softened. "You're so young."

I moved toward him and put my hands on his chest, then moved them up to tangle in his dark hair. Enough with this interrogation. I didn't care about hunters, or bodyguards, or necklaces, or old mistakes, or vampire elders other than the one in front of me right that moment. I just wanted Thierry to kiss me. Nothing else mattered.

He took my hand in his and, as if he'd read my thoughts, pressed his lips against it. My heart did a little cartwheel and I smiled at him.

"I'm not that young." I paused. "You know, my high school reunion is coming up soon. I got an invitation last week. Ten years. I can't believe it."

He shook his head. "See? You jump from one subject to the next like a hummingbird trying to find the sweetest flower. Your life is in constant danger, yet you speak of silly things that would only matter to a human."

"High school reunions are not silly. Stressful? Yes. And somewhat nausea-inducing since I don't have anything to wear." I caught his look and shrugged at him. "I am an enigma."

He squeezed my hand and let it go. "And I am caught up in your enthusiasm for life. You make me forget myself, Sarah. In Mexico. And here."

I took a deep breath and studied him. So guarded and yet so uncertain as he looked at me.

"All right, so Mexico as a yearly destination is out. I get that." I looked at him directly and raised an eyebrow. "Though they did have that nice hot tub in our room, remember?"

His gaze grew more intense, but then he looked away. "Yes, it did have that."

That hot tub was a definite highlight of the week. Several highlights, in fact. I smiled at the memory.

Then the smile vanished as I remembered that the only highlights since we returned were the ones in my hair. And even those were fading.

I absently brushed my fingers against my neck, feeling the fang marks from the other night. They felt rough against my fingers. My eyes flicked to him. He stared at my neck with a pained look on his face. I removed my hand from my neck and my hair fell back into place.

"You were going to tell me how you met Barry."

"I was?"

"Sure. Did you pick him up at a flea market? Was he on sale?"

His expression shadowed. "You mustn't joke about buying slaves. It is something I have witnessed personally over the years in many places and is a cruel, barbaric practice."

I blanched. "I didn't mean to. I . . . Barry just makes me always want to say mean things about him. I know I shouldn't."

"He can be difficult. I understand that. And I haven't seen him extend you any courtesies, either, so don't be alarmed. He is no innocent."

"No, he's not. But I shouldn't be such a bitch to him. I know that. And he really does love Amy. I can't figure out their relationship at all, but if she would stop being so paranoid and he would stop being so secretive, I actually think they might be perfect for each other."

Hint, hint.

"Two people so vastly different from each other?" he said. "You truly believe they have a chance for future happiness?"

"If they want it enough, then yes. I believe it. But their problems are pretty tall. Much, much taller than Barry." I frowned. "See? I can't help myself. I'm such a bitch."

"No. You are simply fiercely protective of your friend's happiness."

"You're just saying that."

"Perhaps." That smile played again on his lips. "And perhaps I reacted so quickly to your flippant comment about how Barry and I met because it comes so close to the truth. I met him at a traveling fair in England two centuries ago where he was held against his will and forced to show himself in a humiliating spectacle."

The color drained from my face. "A freak show?"

"You could say that. A vampire kept in a cage and displayed as something to be laughed at instead of feared. He was beaten mercilessly if he refused to tear apart the animal they would throw into his cage as part of the entertainment."

A knife twisted in my stomach and I tried to push the mental images away. Barry. Poor Barry. I had no idea. "So you saved him."

He shook his head. "I was so disgusted by what I'd witnessed that I couldn't help but go to see him, to try to speak with him. He barely spoke, huddled in the corner wearing dirty rags for clothes. His masters arrived, decided that I was a lone aristocrat in the wrong place at the wrong time, with a wallet thick with money they decided to relieve me of. After I had finished with them, I allowed all of their prisoners to escape, including Barry."

A chill went down my spine. "After you'd *finished with them?*"

He held my gaze. "Yes."

I nodded, slowly, imagining low-life scum torturing other human beings for a profit, then thinking they'd found another victim only to find Thierry.

Touch me again and my boyfriend is going to rip your lungs out.

Maybe not such an empty threat after all.

Thierry continued after a moment. "Barry followed me that night. He pledged himself to help me out in whatever I needed, said that he owed me his life. I tried to brush him off, tell him to find his own life, but he'd never known that before. He'd been sold to the fair as a child. Given to a vampire as a snack for a fee when he reached manhood. Used mercilessly after that. He knew no life other than what he'd had."

"So you helped him."

"I had no choice."

"Of course you did. You could have turned your back on him. Just like you could have turned your back on me on the bridge that night when we met. But you didn't. You're a good man, Thierry."

He shook his head and looked away. "I'm not."

"Veronique told me once about how the two of you met."

"I know." His expression shadowed. "I'm not sure how much she told you."

"During the black plague? She was alone and in hiding. You were—" I stopped talking. Thierry's life had contained a whole heap of pain. Is that what happened when you lived for so long? The bad times outweighed the good? Or was he just really, really unlucky? "You were stabbed, thrown on a pile of burning corpses." I shivered, then met his uncertain gaze. I reached out and stroked his cheek, moving till my fingers tangled in his dark hair. "Is that true?"

"It was long ago."

I frowned and touched his tense arm. "If she hadn't turned you, you'd be dead. I can thank her for that."

He laughed and finally pulled away from me. "Yes, thanks so much to Veronique. So selfless she is. Saving my life in such a noble way."

"Do I detect a small amount of sarcasm?"

"No, you detect a great deal of sarcasm."

"She saved your life."

"That she did. Only because it suited her needs at the time. Why did she save me? Because she was hungry." His grin twisted into something darker. "Why did she turn me into an immortal vampire? Because she was lonely."

"You've stayed with her all these years."

"The years we've spent exclusively in each other's company are fewer than you would believe, Sarah. Veronique has been a good friend to me, but . . . "

"But what?"

He met my gaze directly. "But she's never made me forget myself."

I blinked. "What does that mean?"

He smiled, but it was cold. "You don't know what kind of man I truly am, Sarah. Or perhaps you do now." He looked at my neck again, his expression pained.

The look he was giving me was so frustrating. He

looked so dejected and despondent, it was starting to piss me off.

"You just told me what kind of man you are, didn't you? Don't you even see it yourself? You're *wonderful*. You're generous. You're selfless. You care about other people even if you won't admit it. You'll extend yourself to ensure somebody else's happiness even if it's complicated. How can you not see that?"

He shook his head. "You don't know me at all. You've known me for less than two months."

The words cut. "That's true. But I *want* to know everything about you."

His gaze hardened. "You know who you can ask? Who, I believe, knows me better than anyone else?"

"Who?"

"Quinn." He met my eyes, and his were steely gray, cold, but his lips twisted into a humorless smile. "Your ex-hunter isn't fooled by any of my outward pretense. He can see me for what I truly am. You're trying to avoid speaking about this, but it doesn't make any of it go away." His chest rose with a deep breath. "I hurt you the other night."

I frowned and touched my neck. "This? This little scratch?"

His jaw tensed. "I nearly drained you. One taste of your blood was enough to send me over the edge of sanity."

"Thierry—"

He shook his head, his face tense. "Another minute and it would have been the end. And even then? Even after your heart ceased to beat I might not have stopped. There is such darkness inside me, such thirst . . . Sarah—

I fear it. I've tried to hide from it all these years. That is the true reason I wished to meet my own end when we first met, Sarah. Not out of some deep-seated boredom with a long, empty life, but so I wouldn't hurt anyone. Never again."

My throat closed up. Tears burned my eyes. Every word he said was filled with anguish. How could I tell him that it would be okay? That I loved him regardless? That whatever he was dealing with I wanted to help him?

But he didn't let me find my voice to say anything before he continued, every word filled with self-hatred.

"The worst thing of it all, even after all I'd done to you, is that when I saw in your eyes that you were weakened, drained, I didn't stay to help you. To give you back some of what I had taken. No. I ran. Like a coward. Like a damned coward." His jaw clenched closed, his Adam's apple shifting in his throat, his chest heaving with labored breathing.

"Thierry—" I moved around to the other side of his desk and wrapped my arms around him, hugging him tightly against me. He pulled back a little and took my face in his hands.

"So, you can speak of fun trips to Mexico, you can ask me to tell you stories of my past, you can talk hopefully of the future, but all I can think about when I am with you, Sarah, is how sweet you tasted. There is a monster inside me that is much more dangerous than any hunter you've ever faced. And it wants more of you. Even now, at this very moment."

There was a heavy silence for a moment until I finally found my voice.

"Then you're wrong," I said.

He blinked. "What?"

"You're wrong. You don't know what you want. And that monster inside you? He's an asshole. You need to tell him to shut the hell up. You can't let him rule you."

"The older I get, the less I am able to argue."

"Then you need to make your argument louder. And shorter. Look Thierry, you can beat yourself up for what happened the other night if you want to. But I'm still here." I shifted on my somewhat sensible high heels. "See? Right in front of you. And do I look scared of you?"

"A little bit."

I crossed my arms. "Well, okay. Granted. That speech was a little Bela Lugosi. But I'm still here."

He studied me for a moment. "Your sense of self-preservation is severely lacking."

"If you're trying to tell me that I'm fabulous and wonderful, then I accept the compliment."

He took a deep breath in and let it out slowly. "You are standing before me, open to me, like a gazelle facing a lion, and you do so willingly."

I blinked. "Yeah, even when you say weird shit like that."

"We are too different, Sarah."

"Vive la différence."

He nodded slowly. "And what of Quinn?"

The blood suddenly pounded in my ears. "Quinn?"

"Yesterday you were kissing him. Passionately and of your own free will. He was not forcing you."

I crossed my arms. "No, he wasn't."

"Are you in love with him?"

Silence. My face flushed red. "No. I'm in love with you."

"Why would you kiss him, then, if you are not in love with him?"

I bit my bottom lip, feeling suddenly as if I was being cross-examined in court. "I kissed him because he wanted to kiss me. Because he makes me feel like I'm important. Like I'm somebody who shouldn't be ignored."

His mouth was a thin line. "Then perhaps you should be with him."

"That's not what I'm trying to say."

"No. But perhaps that is what *I* am trying to say." He wouldn't meet my gaze.

My chest hurt. "You're saying you want me to be with Quinn?"

"You will need someone to protect you when I am gone."

I frowned at him. "What are you talking about? Where are you going?"

"This is what I wanted to tell you." He took a deep breath and let it out slowly. "I've sold Haven. Just today. I plan to leave Toronto indefinitely."

"You *what*?"

His gaze again touched lightly on my neck. "I've fooled myself into believing that I can be a regular man. That is not possible. When I leave, I want you to be taken care of. Quinn cares for you. I have faith that he will not let you come to any harm."

I shook my head. "Things are rough right now, but not anything we can't work out if we want to. It's going to be okay. You don't have to go anywhere. You belong right here with me."

"What I said earlier is the truth, Sarah." His voice was quiet. "You don't fit in my life. I don't fit in yours. To believe otherwise would be foolish and potentially deadly to both of us. You should be with Quinn."

I felt myself grow cold at his words. "No, Thierry. Didn't you hear me? We can work through this. All of this."

"My decision to leave the city is final." His jaw tensed and he looked down at the top of his desk covered with papers and envelopes. "I'm sorry, Sarah, but it's over between us."

He walked past me to the door and left his office without another word.

Chapter 16

I wasn't watching where I was going when I left the club shortly after Thierry dumped my sorry ass. I was in shock. At that very moment, all I wanted to do was crawl into a corner somewhere and die. Alone. Pathetic and alone. *Hello there*, I'd say. *I'm pathetic and alone and I'm dying in a corner. Look away.*

Even though I knew his decision on the subject had been an ever-present possibility that loomed over my head. Even though everyone I knew had told me it was only a matter of time before this would happen . . . it was still the worst feeling in the world. And he was leaving? Sold the club and leaving just like that?

I'd never felt so alone. My heart ached. My throat felt tight. My eyes burned with tears of frustration. Every word he'd said hurt like nothing I'd ever experienced before.

"You don't fit in my life. I don't fit in yours. It's over between us."

And then he was gone. Had to have the last word, didn't he? I gritted my teeth at the vivid replay in my head. What was I supposed to say after that? He'd been very clear. Crystal-freaking-clear.

If I'd been seeing straight at the time, if I'd been able to focus on anything except his parting words, I'm sure that I'd have seen that he was right. We were totally wrong for each other. It was only a matter of time before this happened. I'd been fooling myself that things would work out with so many strikes against us.

It sounded rational enough.

Besides, it wasn't the first time I'd ever been dumped in my life. I'd been dumped. I'd been the dumpee.

But this felt different. Worse.

I took in a painfully ragged gasp of cold air and stopped walking, hugging my arms to me, letting the pain sweep over me.

It felt like somebody had just stabbed me in the heart with a two-by-four.

I'd seen a TV show recently where somebody had been impaled by a wooden fence post. A huge, blunt, full-sized wooden fence post. Right through his chest and out the other side. Rusty nails and all.

He'd lived.

He *had* looked a little pale, though. And the scar would have been a real bitch to cover up. But he'd lived.

Distracted, with my heart currently wooden-fence-post-free, but still broken in a thousand pieces, and feeling majorly sorry for myself in the middle of the street a block away from Haven—I didn't even hear the bus coming.

I felt a rough shove against my back, which made me

stumble to the ground, narrowly missing the bus's front tire, which zoomed by about two inches from my face.

"What are you, on crack or something?" Janie gestured at me and at the passing bus. A Greyhound, I noted without much interest, as I lay on my back in the gutter. "You need to watch where the hell you're going."

My cheeks were wet with "I've just gotten my ass dumped" tears. I blinked at her from behind my dark shades, now askew. "Where did you come from? I thought you were in the car waiting."

She looked at me like I was a complete idiot. "When you ignore the car and wander off down the street I follow. I'm your damn bodyguard, remember? Though it's supposed to be hunters I'm protecting you against, not public transit."

"I didn't even see you."

She rolled her eyes. "When you see me, I'm not doing my job properly. I'm like a ninja. Only better dressed. Are you going to get out of that gutter or what?"

I closed my eyes. "I like it here. Just leave me. Leave me to die."

"Wow, somebody took their drama pill this morning. Come on." She reached out a hand to me. "Let's go."

I opened my eyes and looked at her skeptically for a moment. Then I grabbed her hand and let her help me to my feet. I adjusted my sunglasses.

"Where's Lenny? Did you two talk things through?"

Her shoulders slumped. "He's around. I think he's a little peeved at me."

"He likes you."

"Yeah, don't ask me why."

I sniffed. "Thank you for saving me from the evil bus.

That's a few times now that you've saved me. Except for last night, of course. But I'm still breathing, so all is well."

"You're welcome. And I've saved you a lot more than that, you just don't know it. Some hunters are very interested in seeing you on the wrong side of a wooden stake. I've taken care of them." She looked at me for a moment. "I'm surprised you haven't even noticed. Distracted much?"

It chilled me to think that she'd been protecting me from getting killed when I hadn't even been aware of it. "On a scale of one to ten, one being totally okay and ten reflecting that I'm having the worst day of my life and am mega distracted, I'm hovering at about a thousand."

"Want to talk about it?"

"Not particularly."

A grin twigged at her lips. "This got anything to do with your boyfriend? What did you say about him? He's really old, and married, and he has a drinking problem? Haven't personally met him yet, but that still sounds hot, by the way."

I frowned and shot her a look.

Her grin widened. "Frankly, from what I've heard about him, if it's over between you two, I'd say that's a good thing. He's nothing but trouble."

I turned away from her, trying to ignore the big lump in my throat. "I think I'm going to go. Can you drive me back to George's?"

"Getting ready for the surprise party?"

I swiveled back around to look at her. "How do you know about that?"

"As your bodyguard, I *need* to know these things. If I

don't know everything about everybody I'm involved with personally or professionally, it could probably kill me. Although, since I didn't retrieve that necklace yesterday, I'm as good as dead, so I hope I get an invite to the party. Consider it a last request."

I felt a twinge of guilt about keeping the necklace from her. But my gut still told me to wait and see what happened.

"Sure, you can come. You should see the cake. It's huge."

"I love a good surprise party. It's for your friend Amy, right? The one who's married to the short guy?"

"That's right. She's thirty." I thought about her for a moment. "Totally over the hill. Might make us feel better about our own problems."

She laughed. "You're such a bitch. No wonder your boyfriend dumped you."

I felt my stomach turn. Her words felt like a slap, even though I'm sure she didn't mean them that way. I started to cry, right there on the street with warmly dressed, peanut-butter-smelling people pressing past me on all sides.

Janie's face lost its amused expression. "Sarah . . . he dumped you? I'm sorry. I was just guessing."

I nodded. "It's over. It just happened."

"Honestly, after everything you told me about him, this is probably a good thing. It might not feel like it right now, but it's for the best."

I started crying harder and without thinking, stumbled forward and hugged her. "It's not. He's an idiot. I love him so much and he's too damn stupid and stubborn to see that. I don't know what to do."

She awkwardly patted me on my back. "Seriously? You love him? The old married guy with the drinking problem?"

I nodded against her shoulder.

"Okay," she said. "Enough. Get a hold of yourself before I have to slap you." She stepped back, leaving me with nothing to cling to. I blinked wetly. She dug into her purse and pulled out a Kleenex and handed it to me. "Here. Suck it up. Geez."

I gave her a look. "Your compassion leaves a lot to be desired."

"I haven't cried over a guy since I was a kid. It was an unrequited love thing. I was madly in love with a friend of my brother's, but he didn't even notice me. Tears didn't do much to change the situation. Soon after, my life got so that I couldn't be soft. It was either toughen up or die."

"What a beautiful story."

"I know. Nora Roberts should be calling me any day."

"So you're telling me I should toughen up."

She snorted. "When I first heard about you, Sarah, I would have predicted that you were harder than nails. I mean, the Slayer of Slayers, right? You're a *vampire*. You should be all . . . *grrr*." She held her hands up like Nosferatu claws and snapped her teeth at me.

I blinked at her. "Right. Well, sorry to have disappointed you."

She shrugged. "Not a disappointment as much as a surprise. You know, I like you. You seem fairly sincere."

"I am sincere. I am the epitome of sincere."

"You wear your emotions on your sleeve." She shook

her head. "Pretty dangerous to do that in your situation. But good for you, I guess. I can't do that."

"Why not?"

"Because of what I do. If I let my guard down and turn my back I'll probably find a knife in it." Her eyes narrowed. "My brother let his guard down and he's dead."

"I'm so sorry about that. Any leads on who did it?"

Her expression grew cold. "Yes. As soon as I finish up my other business, I'm going to take care of that little matter."

I felt a chill at her words. *Take care of that little matter?*

After a moment she spoke again. "Is it hard being a vampire?"

I took a deep breath. "Yes, it is. But it's hard being human, too. It's the same thing with different rules. I mean, I still need a place to live."

"You seem to have recovered pretty quickly considering you lost everything the other night."

My stomach lurched just thinking about it. "I haven't recovered, but I try to dwell on it as little as possible. It almost killed me. Who knows, maybe it did. Maybe I'm dead and heaven is exactly like my everyday life. Only worse. Or maybe this is hell."

"Maybe you can get a nice new coffin. Lined in satin."

I rolled my eyes. "No thank you. Besides, I'm seriously claustrophobic. I need space. I don't know how much longer I can live with George."

She smiled. "George is hot. He doesn't swing both ways, does he?"

"Not that I'm aware of. Besides, I don't think you want to get mixed up with a vampire. The drinking-blood thing is a serious turn-off."

She grimaced. "Maybe you're right. That is disgusting."

"I only drink it because I have to. I needed it more when I was first turned. Now I can go a bit longer."

"Before you turn all . . . grrr?" Nosferatu claws again.

"I get stomach cramps from hell." I shivered at the memory. Hadn't happened lately, but the flashback was enough to remind me how bad it could be if I didn't watch my diet.

She studied me for a moment. "I've heard some rumors about dead bodies discovered lately in Toronto with puncture marks on their necks. Are you talking about a pain that would prompt you to attack a human?"

I crossed my arms. "I heard about that, too, and absolutely not. I can't ever see myself biting anybody no matter how much pain I'm in."

I thought about black-eyed Thierry and how he'd lost control the other night. Would that ever happen to me? It seemed so unlikely that I didn't even want to give it a thought.

"I've seen the dark side," Janie said. "I've seen out-of-control vamps, and there's nothing fun or friendly about them."

"Lucky you."

"But you're different. I can see that. That's what makes things so difficult."

"Makes what difficult?"

She shook her head. "So you're in love with this Thierry guy, huh?"

I nodded.

"Love is an emotion for fools," she said.

"Gee, what a lovely sentiment."

She laughed. "Sweetie, you're a mystery. That's for

damn sure. Listen, I know you probably don't give a shit what my opinion is on your messed-up love life, but I'm going to give it to you anyhow."

"Let me guess. I should forget about Thierry since he's wrong for me and will only bring me pain? Take a number on that piece of advice."

She shook her head. "If you're seriously into this Thierry guy, you need to forget about what anybody else says, because who the hell cares what anybody else thinks? They're not you. You're the only one who knows what you want. And you're the only one who can get it. Don't even listen to Thierry himself, because he's obviously just trying to protect you from him, which is probably not such a bad idea. If after all these warnings and red lights, you're still convinced that you're in love with this freak, then start fighting for him."

"He doesn't want to hear what I have to say. He always finds a way to walk away from uncomfortable discussions."

She sighed. "Stop being such a spineless coward. If you want to fight for your man, you need to force him to listen to you. Force him to hear how much you love him. You know, silver handcuffs do work wonders on vamps. Even old ones."

I raised my eyebrows at that. "And you're speaking from personal experience?"

She grinned. "I'll never tell. But I do keep a pair on me at all times just in case."

"I don't know."

"Then if you don't know, that's your answer. It doesn't matter. If it does matter, then you know what to do."

"He sounded very convinced that it was over between us. He even sold the club and is planning to leave town."

"Then it's over."

My throat tightened. "No."

She shrugged. "Then fight your ass off for him."

I looked at Janie for a moment. Did she really care one way or the other about my future happiness? She seemed so trustworthy, seemed to be somebody I could tell absolutely anything to and she'd give me her honest opinion. Like we could become really good friends.

If we wanted to.

Just like me and Thierry. We were different. There was no debating that fact. But from the moment he entered my life, I knew that he filled that empty part of me—the part I didn't even know was missing something. I fell head over heels for him. And even when he'd gone all thirsty vampire on me, I hadn't stopped loving him. I wanted to help him, not run away from him. That had to count for something, didn't it? Other than my total lack of self-preservation. I didn't care. I wanted Thierry. Even though I now knew he wasn't perfect. *Especially* now that I knew he wasn't perfect. He was Thierry. And I loved him.

Now if only the jerk could see that.

Honestly. *Men*.

I smiled at Janie. She returned the expression.

"By the way," she said, "do you know who Gideon Chase is?"

My smile flew away. "What?"

"Gideon Chase." She pressed a finger against her earpiece, then grinned at me. "He's the leader of the hunters. Big bucks. Apparently really hot, too. He's in town. Might make things a little more exciting around here."

"I am going to be sick."

"We'll protect you. Don't worry. Remember, the ninja thing? Why do you look so freaked out?"

I decided to tell her everything. Well, almost everything. About Nicolai and his plan to trap Gideon when he made a move to kill me. About how I hadn't told Thierry.

Still didn't mention that I was wearing the necklace right at that very moment. Later. I'd give it to her later.

My mouth felt dry when I finished. "So I guess I shouldn't go to the party. Amy will be mad, but she'll understand. Man. I think I'm going to throw up."

She waved her hand. "Relax. I won't let anything bad happen to you unless I do it myself. So just go about your regularly scheduled activities." She grinned. "Do you trust me?"

I nodded. "Yeah, I trust you."

Her grin widened. "Now, go about your day as you normally would. I'll be watching. Don't even think about the fact that you are now at constant risk of death. With any luck, you won't even notice if Gideon tries to attack you. I'll take him down first."

"If you say so."

"So let's get you back to George's so you can get ready for your friend's party."

I nodded, anxiety filling every cell of my body. As we headed for the car, I almost expected to see a swarm of hunters coming directly for me, but there was nothing but the normal swell of oblivious people on the sidewalk.

Gideon was in town to kill me. And I was putting my life in the hands of somebody I didn't quite trust 100 percent.

I wondered what I should wear to the party.

*   *   *

"It's pink."

"Yeah, don't you just love it?"

I stood behind Amy at Studio V, the vampire hair salon, and gazed in the shard mirror at her newly made-over reflection. She'd dyed her platinum-blond hair a vibrant shade of pink and cut it super short. The stylist—a tall, skinny vamp with hollow cheekbones and black eyeliner—raised an eyebrow at her.

"It's *fabulous*," he proclaimed. "Honey, you are fanged and fabulous."

Amy grinned and pointed at her sanded-down teeth. "Well, you're half right, Bernardo!"

"It's pink," I said again.

"And you can't do it, too, this is all me."

"Why pink?" I asked.

"Why not?"

"Do you want an alphabetical list or just off the top of my head?"

She pouted. "It's my birthday, I can dye if I want to. This is the new me. I'm wild and free and don't care about anyone's opinion but my own." She looked in the shard in front of her and blinked. "Are you saying you don't like it? Because I can change it back."

"No, I'm not saying that. It's . . . different. What will Barry think?"

She rolled her eyes. "Do I care?"

"I don't know. Do you?"

"He loved my blond hair."

"And?"

"It serves him right." She took a deep breath and looked in the shard again, at me. "I'm leaving him."

"So you've been saying. And that is happening when?"

"As soon as I find another place to stay. Hey, you're looking for a new apartment, right? We should be roommates."

While I adored Amy and she was my best friend, there was no way I was going to room with her. A vacation is one thing, constantly being in each other's presence without the respite of your own home is something entirely different. But she was fragile. And it was her birthday, so I wasn't going to shoot her down when she was in such a fragile mood. She might go and get a tattoo or something.

I forced a smile. "Let's talk about it later."

"Cool."

I'd made the decision to not tell her about the surprise party. It was very tempting, but I'd managed to hold my tongue. I figured as soon as she saw what Barry had done for her, she'd snap out of this melancholy, "let's dye our hair pink," kind of mood. It was a theory. Besides, after hearing about Barry's backstory I was feeling a little warmer toward her diminutive husband. Just a tiny bit. No pun intended.

"So what now?" Amy asked as she paid Bernardo and made an appointment for next month to have her roots touched up.

I looked at her innocently. "What, you think I have something planned?"

"It's my birthday."

"Yeah, so how does it feel being one of the ancient?"

She slid her wallet back into her big black leather purse. "It feels epic. In a very small way."

"Okay, so what do you want to do?"

She looked disappointed. "You mean you don't have anything planned? You did that stripper thing for my last birthday."

Ah, the memories. I took her to a club called Precious Illusions with a couple of other girls from the office. We'd drunk ourselves senseless and shoved five-dollar bills in the general G-string direction of oily muscle-bound men with names like Shadow, Ace, and Diego. Good times.

I shrugged. "We could go there again."

That earned me a look of shock. "But I'm a married woman!"

"Would you make up your mind, already?"

"And you're also spoken for, young lady. What would Thierry say if he saw you canoodling with male exotic dancers?"

"Well, first of all I don't canoodle." I swallowed hard. "Second, I wasn't going to bring this up, but I may as well. Thierry and me . . . we're over."

"What?"

"Yeah, we had a nice heart to heart this afternoon, which he ended by breaking mine. He doesn't think we're right for each other."

Half shrug. "Well . . ."

I sighed and gave her a dirty look.

Another half shrug, other shoulder. "Like I was saying the other day—"

"I don't want to talk about this, Amy."

She nodded. "We should definitely go see the strippers. That'll cheer both of us up."

"Fine. We'll see the strippers." I glanced at my watch.

It was six-fifteen. *Showtime*. Time to get Amy to her surprise party. "But first I want to stop by Haven. I have to pick something up."

"Okay." She turned and glanced at herself in the reflection of a shop window that didn't reflect me. She touched her hair. "What have I done?"

"It will grow out."

She turned to face me with tears in her eyes. "Why doesn't Barry love me?"

"He *does* love you."

She sniffed loudly, and ran her hand under her nose. "Being a vampire sucks."

"Can you say that a little louder? I don't think the people over by the bus stop heard you." I paused. "Look, Janie's here and she'll give us a ride."

"I think I just want to go home. I don't feel so good."

I closed my eyes. I didn't feel all that hot either. But I had to suck it up. There was a party to go to. A party that would contain Thierry.

"If you don't feel like doing anything, that's fine. But we have to stop by Haven."

"Okay," she said, wiping a last tear away. "The sooner we get there, the sooner we can leave."

Let the good times roll.

Chapter 17

It was dark out when I knocked on the door to Haven at six-thirty. The little window shuttered open.

"Yeah?" Angel the bouncer barked.

"It's me."

"Me *who*?"

I took a step back so he could see me. "Um. Sarah?"

"What's the password?"

Right, the password. An extra security feature implemented just today to help keep the club even safer, giving it a rather Harry Potter dorm room feel.

I wished I'd paid attention earlier when George had told me what the password was. I glanced at Amy, then back at the beady eyes of the bouncer. "Is it . . . *Open Sesame*?"

"Nope."

"How about *Red Rover*?"

"Not even close." Amusement flashed behind his gaze.

My eyes narrowed. "How about, *Let us the hell in or I'll have you fired*?"

The door swung open. "That's the one."

I grinned at him. "Thanks so much."

"Enjoy yourselves."

"Oh, we're not staying long," Amy said. "But thanks!"

Janie had chosen to stay outside for the time being. Lenny was still missing in action. So Amy and I moved along the hallway and I started to feel very apprehensive. What was I going to say to Thierry? How could I convince him that we were supposed to be together? I wondered if anybody had a pair of those silver handcuffs Janie had mentioned on them.

"Maybe I'll just wait out here," Amy said when we got to the second door that led into the club itself.

"No, I'm going to buy you a birthday drink. Just a quick one." I opened the door. It was quiet inside. *Very* quiet.

"Okay." Amy nodded and brushed past me into the club.

Five-four-three-two-one.

"*SURPRISE!*" A dozen vamps—most I recognized, a few I didn't—came out of the woodwork. Not literally, because that would have been very strange. Figuratively. They swarmed around Amy giving her hugs and kisses and birthday wishes, wearing silly hats that looked very out of place on their vampire heads. George was nearby and he blew on a birthday buzzer thing, making the streamers fly out in all directions. He looked at me and rolled his eyes.

"What . . . what's going on?" Amy asked, stunned.

"Amy, my angel," Barry approached her. "It's a surprise party. Happy birthday!"

"A . . . a surprise party?" she said. "For me?"

"Of course."

She started smiling. "But why, and when . . . and how?"

"Because I love you, I've been planning it for weeks, and there is no *how*. Just enjoy it. I'm sorry you thought I was up to no good. I wasn't. I was just being secretive about this. I wanted you to have a birthday party you'd always remember." He eyed her with trepidation at her reaction.

"So you're . . . you're not cheating on me?"

"Of course not, my silly Amy."

She blinked back tears. "I'm so sorry." She leaned over to hug him hard. "I'm such an idiot."

"No you're not. You're beautiful. And wonderful."

"I love you, snooky."

"I love you too." He kissed her, then pulled away. "What on earth have you done to your hair?"

She straightened up and tentatively touched her fuchsia locks. "Do you hate it?"

"No, it's you. I love it."

She smiled widely and leaned over to embrace him again. He looked over her shoulder at me and shot me a very dirty look that clearly blamed me for what she'd done to her hair. I shrugged at him. Didn't matter. I was fighting off the big lump in my throat from their little scene. They were so different from each other, but they would work things out between them. They *wanted* to.

George came over to stand next to me. "That was so sweet I think I need a shot of insulin."

256 Michelle Rowen

"Yeah, me, too."

"Want a hat?"

"I think I'll pass. Hey, George," I turned to look at him. "Did you hear that Thierry sold the club?"

He nodded and looked away. "I just heard. Haven won't be around for much longer. I guess I'm going to have to look for another job. Maybe it's a sign. I should expand my horizons wider than being a waiter. What do you think I could do?"

I frowned. "Well, I know Precious Illusions is always looking for new dancers."

He smiled. "It's like we have the same brain. A brain of brilliance."

I swallowed. "Where is Thierry right now?"

"Around. Probably holed up in his office as usual. I tried to get him to wear a hat too, but he was all 'get that hat away from me right now or else.' Total club-selling party pooper."

"I . . . I need to talk to him." I looked around, feeling tense. Janie had told me I should fight for him. I'd fight for him.

George frowned. "You look upset. Is everything okay?"

"No, everything's not okay. I . . . just need to talk to him."

He nodded, then rubbed my shoulder. "I'm here for you, gorgeous. Whenever you need to talk."

"Thanks, George."

"But you're still moving out of my place soon, right?"

I managed to laugh at that. "You don't want me to be your roommate anymore?"

"I love you as much as I could possibly love somebody with breasts, but I need my space."

"What about Barkley?"

He nodded over at the bar. Barkley waved at me. He was dressed in George's clothes, a very metrosexual outfit of a tight white shirt and tight brown leather pants. He looked pretty damn good for somebody I'd recently taken on leashed walks. He was drinking from a highball glass. Well, maybe *lapping* was a better description.

I frowned. "He's very . . . *doglike*, isn't he?"

"He was looking at my leg a little funny earlier."

I raised an eyebrow at him. "Well, you said your love life was sucking lately."

"He only had eyes for my leg. Unfortunately."

"You'll find somebody, don't worry. Who could resist an amazing guy like you?"

He smiled. "Right back at you, babe."

"I'm an amazing guy?"

"You are. You really are."

Everyone at the party got drinks, mingled, and started having fun. Except for me. I observed the fun taking place. There was a buffet of all of Amy's favorite finger foods: chicken fingers, quesadillas, fried mushrooms, nachos, brownies, tiny cheesecakes. I eyed it all with equal parts envy, since I couldn't partake without throwing up, and disinterest, since my stomach didn't growl at the sight of food I couldn't have anymore.

The sound system kicked it, the lights dimmed, and the strobe light started spinning. The first song started belting out and Amy led everyone onto the dance floor. She dragged me up next to her. I went up for one dance. Then I had to focus on everything else.

"You should have told me," she scolded.

"Then it wouldn't have been a surprise."

Her expression wilted. "I shouldn't have doubted my Barry. He's so wonderful. We're lucky to have found each other."

She looked at me expectantly. Like I was going to make a jab at her husband. An insult.

I just nodded. "You're right. You're lucky. Both of you. Now remember that the next time Mr. Doubt comes a-knocking."

She beamed at me. "I will. I promise."

"Good."

"Now you need to find *your* perfect man. I know he's out there somewhere for you, Sarah. You can't let yourself give up hope. Don't let all the other drama in your life get you down. Just go after what you want, and you'll get it. I have faith."

I nodded and stopped dancing and turned away from her. "You're right."

"Where are you going?"

"I need to take care of something."

Without waiting for a reply, I left the dance floor and walked slowly across the club, past the bar, to the hallway leading to Thierry's office. His door was closed.

I took a deep breath and knocked on it tentatively.

"George?" his deep voice said after a moment. "I already told you I don't want to wear the hat. I wish to be alone."

I pushed the door open. "It's not George. And the hat would look cute on you. Are you sure?"

He sat behind his desk surrounded with computer

printouts and other papers. He looked up at me but didn't say anything for a moment.

I raised my hands. "Surprise!"

He regarded me for a moment longer. "I am surprised. I would have thought you wouldn't wish to speak with me again after . . . earlier."

"I didn't, but I changed my mind." I smiled at him. "I wanted to see if you were okay. Let you know there were no hard feelings."

"I'm very glad you feel that way."

"So you didn't tell me where you were going when you leave the city."

"To France."

I nodded and had to force my voice to remain light and carefree. "Wow. So you're not just leaving the city, you're leaving the whole country. When are you going?"

He looked down at his papers and I saw his throat muscles work as he swallowed before speaking. "I'm leaving tomorrow."

The warmth left my body in a rush. "Tomorrow?"

"Yes."

"You're leaving tomorrow. For France."

"That's correct." He looked up when I didn't respond. "Nicolai has left town."

"He has?"

He nodded. "This morning. So the threat he presented to you has also left. I wanted to wait until he was gone before I, too, made my departure."

Nicolai had left town already with Gideon just arriving? What the hell?

He broke the silence after a moment. "Was there anything else, Sarah?"

"I . . . " My chest felt like an elephant was sitting on it. A fatter-than-normal elephant. What was I going to say? He'd obviously made his decision. "Will you be coming back?"

His face held no discernible expression. "I have no plans to."

I nodded. "I see. Is that why you're here in your office while the party's going on out there? Because you didn't want to see me before you left?"

He moved closer to me. "I wouldn't have gone without saying good-bye to you first."

I laughed. "I'm such an idiot. I actually came in here because I wanted to convince you that, despite what everybody else says, we're right for each other. That we can work things out if you just give me a chance. But now I see that I was mistaken."

He let out a long breath, which hissed between his teeth. "Sarah—"

I shook my head. "Maybe you're right. I'll go find Quinn, who by the way has been keeping far away from me because I told him that I wanted to be with you. But maybe I need to find him and beg his forgiveness and hope he's still interested in me. Then he and I can be together. That's what you want, isn't it?"

"I think it would be for the best."

I slapped him. Right across his left cheek. My eyes widened. I hadn't planned to do that.

He didn't flinch. "I'm sorry that I've hurt you, Sarah."

"I didn't mean to hit you."

He smiled. "Yes you did. And an excellent blow, too. Your strength is increasing."

"I'm sorry."

"I am, too. For everything. I never should have given the idea of a relationship between the two of us room to grow. It was very wrong of me."

I felt utterly empty inside. "I know I can't make you love me. I understand that now."

"Is that why you think I'm doing this—?" He clenched his teeth shut and his brow furrowed. Then he looked away and nodded. "Of course. Yes. I think it is best that we say our good-byes now."

"Fine." I pressed my lips together and nodded. "But will you answer one last question from me before I go?"

He studied me for a moment and turned away. "Anything."

I took a deep breath. "I want to know what really happened with Nicolai's wife."

He froze in place. "Who told you of that?"

"Does it matter?"

"Nicolai spoke to you alone before he left. I should have known this." He turned back to face me, his expression cold. "The fact that you would ask me about this makes me believe you already know all too well."

"Hearsay. People tell me lots of things about you, Thierry. Ever since we met. Am I supposed to believe their stories, or get it from the subject himself?"

"How would you know whom to believe?"

"I would make that decision once I have all the facts."

"What did Nicolai tell you of Elizabeth?"

"That she was wonderful, that he loved her more than life itself, and when he turned his back you ripped out her throat. In a nutshell."

He let out a bark of laughter. "My, that is the short version. And did you believe him?"

I swallowed. "Being that it was right after this," I touched my neck, "I wasn't sure what to believe."

"And now?"

"I'm still not sure."

"Then you're a very foolish woman. Because it's true. I was responsible for Elizabeth's unfortunate end. To believe otherwise would be naïve."

I suddenly had to struggle to breathe. "You drained her."

His gaze rested briefly on my neck before he looked away. "Yes."

"But you couldn't control it. It's not like you did it on purpose."

He shook his head and looked at me as if I were a five-year-old who wouldn't learn her lesson. "The extenuating circumstances mean nothing. It is my fault that Elizabeth died so long ago. It haunts me to this very day. The moment I feel that I am free of it I am reminded—" his gaze flicked to my neck again "—reminded that there is a monster inside me capable of something heinous and uncontrollable."

"But you were able to stop with me."

"Barely. And it was the same with Elizabeth. When I tore myself away from her, she ran from me into the clutches of hunters waiting outside the inn where I stayed. She had no chance. All I could do was stand by and watch her die."

I frowned. "Hunters killed her?"

Thierry's expression was tense and haunted. "No. I killed her. It is my fault. Had I not attacked her she never would have needed to run."

Nicolai didn't know this version of the story. I was

positive he thought that Thierry had ended Elizabeth himself. God, this was too much to take. But Thierry *hadn't* killed her. Hunters had. Why couldn't he see that himself?

"Were you in love with her? With Elizabeth?"

He frowned at me with an expression of confusion. "Of course not. She was Nicolai's wife. At the time he was my closest friend. While he was away on business I had promised to keep an eye on her, make sure she was all right. Elizabeth was only a fledgling, having a difficult time with the transition from human to vampire. The nights proved long for her and her love for Nicolai was unfortunately not as deep as her love for his thick wallet. When he was gone for many months on Ring business, she became lonely."

"She threw herself at you."

"In a manner of speaking."

"Where was Veronique?"

He shrugged. "I don't recall. In Europe somewhere."

"So you had an affair with this woman."

He seemed uncomfortable with my continual questions. "She was my friend's wife. I respected that. But that was her goal. One night when I was alone, she . . . attempted to seduce me."

I felt a sharp twinge of jealousy. "Oh."

"I had not had blood for some time. I was old enough by then that I could go without it entirely if I chose to, but I was still hungry. She wanted me to bite her. And . . . it happened. And I lost control. I took too much and she is now dead because of me."

"Why didn't you tell Nicolai the whole story?"

He sat down behind his desk. "The whole story is not

much better than what he has believed for all these years."

"That his best friend killed his wife?"

"It doesn't matter now."

"So that's why you quit the Ring?"

"Yes. It was best that I removed myself from his presence. From everyone's presence. I have kept to myself since then. It has been a century since I have tasted another vampire's blood."

"Till the other night with me."

"And now I see that I can never taste it again." Our eyes met and I watched as his darkened a shade. "And that will be very difficult."

I felt a moment of fear from that look in his eyes, but it quickly faded into concern for him. "But not impossible."

"You should leave now, Sarah. We've already said our good-byes, have we not?"

"Yes." I swallowed. "But I want one last thing."

"What is that?"

I waited for a moment until I knew my voice wouldn't go all shaky. "A kiss?"

He almost smiled. "First you slap me, now you want a kiss? You are of two minds, Sarah."

"I know. But . . . just a good-bye kiss." I took a deep breath. "You don't have to if you don't want to."

He shook his head. "No, it is fine. One last kiss between us."

He hesitated for a moment, then slowly pulled me to him, staring down at me with his silvery eyes. I was about to say something else, I don't even know what, but I didn't have a chance. He touched his lips to mine, just soft like a feather. Hardly touching. And I thought that's all it would be. Just a tease. A reminder of what it was like to touch him. He seemed to pull back a bit, but then stopped.

"Thierry—" I managed, but my words were cut off as he crushed his mouth against mine, his grip tight on my upper arms, then slowing trailing down my back, against my waist, and he crushed me against him as if he never wanted to let me go.

The kiss deepened and I opened my mouth to him. He staggered back a few feet until he hit the edge of his desk and my hands were under his jacket, under his shirt, and against his warm skin. I couldn't stop touching him. I wanted him so much. Despite everything. All the harsh words, all the fighting, all the uncertainty. This was real. I could feel it. This wasn't good-bye. It couldn't be.

The kiss made my head spin, my heart ache, and then it was over. My lips felt bruised. He turned away and made for the door.

He stopped in the open doorway. "I wish you the best of everything for your future."

"Thierry . . . " I said, shakily, the pain a living, breathing thing in my throat as I spoke.

He didn't turn around. "Good-bye, Sarah."

And that was that. He was gone. Back to make a brief appearance at the party before he disappeared forever. Somewhere I'd probably never be able to find him even if I wanted to.

And why would I want to? Why would I want somebody who didn't want me back? Who'd made it painfully obvious?

My legs gave way and I sat down heavily in his chair

behind the desk. I just stared at the door, feeling like my heart had turned into a paperweight in the center of my chest. Heavy and easy to shatter. But I didn't cry. I just felt numb.

I didn't want to go back out there. Not yet. After a few minutes, and without thinking much about it, I opened my purse and searched through the contents for a moment before I found what I was looking for. Then I grabbed the phone and pecked in the number on the card.

It rang four times.

"Oui?" A beautiful voice sang out.

"Veronique?"

"Oui, c'est ça."

"It's . . . it's Sarah."

There was a pause.

"Sarah Dearly," I clarified. "From Toronto."

"Of course! Sarah, my dear, how are you?"

I cleared my throat. "You were right."

"I am right about so many things. Can you be more specific?"

"Thierry. He dumped me. He's sold the club and he's moving back to France. Tomorrow."

"He's coming here?"

"That's what he said. Maybe you two can work out your problems and have another thousand years together. Whatever." My vision blurred but I sucked it up. Focused on the letters on the phone pad. My lips still tingled from the kiss.

"Oh, no, no. That won't do. If he's coming here I'm sure we will not see much of each other. I have my own life." She covered the receiver, but I could hear her say, "Yes, yes, I'm coming, Jean-Luc. Just a moment."

My throat felt tight. "I'm sorry if I'm interrupting."

"No, you are a friend in need. And I am here with the advice to help mend your broken heart."

"I'm listening. Help me mend."

"He wasn't right for you. Not from the beginning. You are—too different. He is so old, you are so young. He is so serious and rigid, you are so goofy and whimsical."

"Goofy?"

"He is a very important man of business, you are essentially a glorified waitress. You see? It is best it ends now to avoid any unnecessary pain."

I nodded. "We *are* very different."

"See? My advice is already helping. It was such a short relationship that it really is no great loss."

"But, I *love* him." And I did. I still did. Damn it.

She tsked with her tongue. "The fantasy a schoolgirl might have of her handsome teacher. That's all it was."

I shook my head even though she couldn't see it. "No, that's not true."

"Do not worry, your feelings will fade with time. Then you will see them to be nothing more than romantic illusions, like those silly books they sell at the drugstore."

I twisted the cord around my finger. "I don't know what to do."

"What you do, my dear, is to move on. You will find the strength within yourself. Time is a great healer. Also, I find that buying a new shade of lipstick is an excellent distraction."

"I don't know. Veronique—"

"I do hate to cut this off so soon, but I am rather busy. I certainly hope you are feeling better soon. Call again

whenever you wish. I am always here to help. *Au revoir*."
The line clicked dead as she hung up on me.

My back straightened and I let the phone slip back
onto the receiver.

Maybe she was right. Maybe I was just a silly schoolgirl with a crush on an unattainable dark hero.

Maybe I needed to give myself some time before I
could see this situation clearly.

Maybe I just needed a good stiff shot of Moonshine.

Yeah. That sounded like a plan.

I stood up from the desk and then sat down hard
again. No. She wasn't right. Why did I even call her? Did
I really think she was going to make anything better?
She didn't know Thierry any better than I did.

I wished I could hate him. It would make things so
much easier. Why didn't I? After everything I'd learned
about him. After seeing his dark side, why was I having
such a difficult time with this?

Why did he have to kiss me like that? It wasn't fair.

It might not be fair. But it was over. It was clear to me.
He didn't love me. He never did and he never would.

I absently searched the top of Thierry's desk for some
Kleenex. I needed to blow my nose, wipe my tears, pull
it the hell together, and get back out to the party. I didn't
want anyone seeing me like this.

No tissues. Great.

Just a lot of stupid papers. Faxes. Photocopies. Phone
records.

I frowned. Some of the papers were from the sale of
Haven. Some weren't. Some had my name on them.
That's what caught my attention. I picked one up and
stared at it, trying to make sense of it.

It was an agreement. The address of George's house. A picture of me.

I flipped the stapled page over. It was for a bodyguard service different from the one I had now. Not Janie and Lenny this time. Thierry had hired an agency to keep an eye on me starting tomorrow. And he was paying a very hefty fee. Indefinitely.

There was a notation at the bottom:

A bonus if Ms. Dearly remains unaware of your presence to ensure her continued safety.

Thierry had hired bodyguards to keep me safe. Even after he left town.

First the shard. Now this. Everything Thierry did seemed to be in my best interest, whether or not I ever found out he was responsible for it. What did it mean? Did he feel guilty that he was leaving? Or was it something else?

I gripped the side of the desk. It wasn't hopeless. It *wasn't*. I clung to this small sliver of light.

I had taken one shaky step toward the door when the phone rang. I glanced at it apprehensively. Was that Veronique calling back?

I grabbed the phone and swallowed hard before speaking. "Haven. Can I help you?"

"I need to talk to Sarah." It was Quinn. I could hear a lot of background noise and voices. Music.

"Quinn? It's me. Where are you?"

"I'm at Clancy's."

My eyes widened. Clancy's was a bar widely known to be a hangout for vampire hunters. After a big day of busting vampire heads, they'd go there and shoot some pool, yap about their conquests, throw some darts, and drink some beers. A real classy joint.

"What are you doing there? Are you insane? If they find out who you are do you know what they'll do to you?"

He laughed, but it wasn't a pleasant sound. "Why do you think I'm here?"

"Quinn—"

"Listen, Sarah. I'm not in a good place right now."

"No, obviously. You have to get out of there right now."

"No, I don't mean here. I mean, in my head. I don't know what I'm doing with my life. I'm all messed up."

"So you've gone all kamikaze on me? I'm sorry, I'm so sorry about the other day, but this is no way to handle things."

He laughed again. "I guess I'll have to handle things the way I have to handle them."

"Yeah, that makes a lot of sense. As in, not at all. Are you drunk?"

"If I could be, I would be. But unfortunately no. I'm here trying to get more info on the vampire killer. Three more victims died last night. But I . . . I called for a reason. Are you going to listen to me or what?"

"Yes, of course. What is it?"

"I overhead some hunters here talking. They were discussing that female bodyguard of yours."

"Janie?" The cord was twisted so tightly around my finger that it was cutting off circulation.

"That's right. She and her partner aren't just bodyguards. They're also Mercs."

"A Merc? What's a Merc?"

"A mercenary. Usually ex-hunters, who now sell their services as bodyguards or assassins to vampire or hunter . . . or even regular humans. They don't give a shit who they work for or what the job is as long as there is a great deal of money involved. They're scum, Sarah." He paused while I was trying to find my voice. "Where are they right now?"

I licked my suddenly dry lips. "She's waiting outside the club. I don't know where Lenny is. But, Quinn, she's not bad. We've talked lots of times. Even if she is one of these Mercs, she's probably just got a lot on her plate. She says she's working a bunch of different jobs."

"Yeah, I bet she is."

"I like her. And I think she likes me, too."

He snorted. "Then you're in more trouble than I thought. When I saw her yesterday, outside Haven, she seemed familiar to me. I couldn't place it at the time. I thought she just had one of those faces, you know? But I was a little distracted and wasn't looking at other women at the time so I didn't pay much attention."

I twisted the phone cord more tightly around my finger. "Quinn . . . "

"But listening to the hunters tonight talking about her it finally hit me just a minute ago. Who she is."

"Who is she?"

"Her last name is Parker, isn't it?"

I tensed. "Yeah. Janelle Parker. How did you know that?"

"Because I already know her. Because I . . . I knew her older brother."

"Her brother," I repeated. "She told me her brother was murdered. That that's one of the reasons she's in

Toronto, because she wants to avenge his murder. She seemed really broken up about it."

He swore under his breath. "She *knew*. This whole time. I know it. That must have been why she targeted you. I can't imagine that Thierry would have known when he hired her. He couldn't have. Probably got her through an agency. But *she* knew. She's wily. I haven't seen her since she was a kid. Probably when she was no more than twelve or thirteen years old."

"What are you talking about? Who is she?"

"Sarah," Quinn paused, his tone a little strangled. "Janie is Peter's sister."

"*Peter?*" My stomach dropped. "Don't kid about something like that. It's not funny."

"No, it's not. And I'm not kidding."

My mind flashed to the horrible dream about Peter I'd had the other day when I fell asleep in Starbucks.

"Oh, I'll get my revenge, darlin'. And you won't even see it coming."

"She's the one who bombed your apartment," Quinn continued. "That's what the hunters here were saying."

I felt the color drain from my face and I sat down heavily in the chair again. "No."

"You're in danger. I don't know why she hasn't done anything yet. She must be waiting for the right time."

I shook my head slowly. This was crazy. It was. It couldn't be true. But . . . but it was. I felt it. It made a sudden awful sense. And I'd liked her, too. Even though the necklace guy said she wasn't to be trusted. I hadn't completely trusted my gut.

She must hate me.

Of course she did, I thought. *I killed her brother.*

Self-defense. It was self-defense.

But it must have looked as if her brother Peter, the brave vampire hunter idolized by his little sister, had been killed by an evil vampire. And the rumors about me being the Slayer of Slayers definitely didn't help to clear my name.

She blew up my apartment.

Because I killed her brother.

"Sarah? Are you still there?"

My mouth was dry. "Yeah. I'm here. I don't understand. We've been alone a few times. She's saved my life. Why wouldn't she just kill me?"

"I don't know. Maybe she wants to finish the job of being your bodyguard. Get paid. Before she . . . " he trailed off.

"Before she really finishes the job her brother started." I rubbed my forehead hard, frowning, then looked up. "Wait a minute. Her name is Janie *Parker*."

"That's right."

"So that means that Peter . . ." I swallowed. "That his full name was *Peter Parker*?"

"Yeah."

I burst into tears. "Oh, my God! I killed Spiderman!"

"Sarah, get a grip."

"I need to go. I need to tell—"

"Thierry?" he said it with a generous helping of bitterness.

"No. I don't know. I don't know who to tell. I just need to go now. Quinn?"

"Yeah."

"Get out of there. Don't get yourself killed."

"Yeah, you, too. I'm just going to try to get some more information before I take off."

He hung up.

Chapter 18

Janie was Peter's sister.

There were no words to describe how I felt about that.

Wait a minute. *Flabbergasted*. That was a word.

A couple more words would be *stunned* and *bewildered*. Right.

Scared and *shitless*? Yeah. That pretty much summed it up.

I killed her brother.

A shiver shot down my spine. It was true. I *killed* him. And now she'd come for a little dose of revenge.

All this time I'd been scared of the hunters, hell, even of this Gideon guy I'd never heard of before. And all the time I should have been the most afraid of the well-dressed blond bodyguard lurking in the shadows.

My grip tightened on the door handle of Thierry's office and I felt hot fury start to creep up inside my chest.

I might have killed her brother, an act that filled me with major daily guilt, but it had been self-defense.

She'd tried to kill me when I was asleep—in the middle of the night. All she ended up doing was destroying all my worldly belongings including my irreplaceable DVD collection.

Somebody had to pay for that.

So what was that outside today? Our little heart to heart? Her advice on my troubled love life? She must have been laughing at how unbelievably stupid I was.

Real freaking funny.

I just wondered what the hell she was waiting for. She and I had been alone a couple of times. She'd saved me from hunters and from a dangerous bus. Why hadn't she tried to kill me?

It just didn't make any damn sense.

It didn't have to make sense. It was true. Janie was Peter's sister. No matter what else she was here in Toronto for, even if it included being my bodyguard, hired by Thierry of all people, it didn't change what her real purpose was. What she really wanted.

Me dead.

And since I didn't particularly want to die any time soon, I took issue with that.

But what was I supposed to do?

Thierry would know.

My heart twisted at the thought.

Could this night get any worse?

Probably.

I finally, uneasily, entered the bar area to rejoin the party. I scanned the crowd to see if Janie had come in for that piece of cake she wanted. I didn't see her.

Amy bounded toward me with a drink in her hand— pink to match her new hairdo—smiling merrily.

"The new bartender made it for me." She raised her glass. "It's called *The Amy.* You want?"

"I think I'll pass." I glanced over at the bartender, who gave me an enthusiastic thumbs-up. Ah, yes. My loyal fan from the other night.

"This is a super party," Amy said. "Don't you think?"

"Yeah, it's fantastic." I took a deep breath and let it out slowly. "Have you seen"— *oh, kill me now*—"Thierry anywhere? I need to talk to him. And then I may need a few dozen of those drinks, preferably made with Moonshine and razor blades."

She frowned. "Hmm. I saw him a minute ago. George tried to get him to wear a party hat and I think Thierry punched him in the nose."

I scanned the room for George. He was over at the bar holding a wet cloth to his face. I walked directly toward him.

"My nose is broken," he said. "He's damn lucky he's so old or I might just take him down one of these days."

My eyes widened. "Thierry did that?"

"I get it. Okay? He doesn't want to wear the hat. A firm and repetitive no would have been more than sufficient."

"Where is he now?"

"Gone. Took off. I don't know and I don't care." He pulled the cloth away and looked at the blood. "If this place wasn't closing down I would quit. Or I'd go all Sally Field in *Norma Rae* and demand we start a vamp union. What did you say to him to put him in an even fouler mood than normal, anyhow?"

I crossed my arms and looked away. "Nothing. I didn't say anything."

"Yeah, sure." He studied me for a moment and his brow furrowed. "What's wrong?"

I told him everything Quinn had just told me on the phone about Janie. "She knows I killed him and she wants to kill me back. She's the one who blew up my apartment."

His eyes widened. "You're kidding! And what about her megacute partner?"

"Lenny?" I said. "He's probably in on it, too. He's just as corrupt and devious and secretive as she—"

"Excuse me." I felt a tap on my shoulder. I turned to see Lenny standing behind me. "Did you just say Janie is trying to kill you?"

I took a step back and pressed up against George. "Get away from me."

Lenny raised a finger and took a swig from his glass before speaking again. "Janie didn't know what she had. She didn't until it's gone. I'm gone. Gone, gone, gone." He hiccupped. "Excuse me." He looked at George. "And did I just hear you call me cute?"

"Well . . . " George glanced at me. "That was before I found out that you're in cahoots to kill Sarah. But yeah. Megacute. I'm a sucker for big and brawny. And you can take that sentence any way you want to."

"Why would I want to kill you?" Lenny said, then drained the rest of his glass. "I was hired to protect you. I'm here because I wanted to wish Amy a happy birthday. Janie told me about the party. I thought I'd come in for a few free drinks." His bottom lip wobbled.

I opened my mouth to speak, but he didn't give me a chance.

He smashed the glass down on the bar top. "You know

what? I'm sick of it. SICK OF IT! I give and give and give, and what do I get? I get trampled on. Like I'm dirt under her designer stupid dumb shoe. I would have treated her like a queen. But *noooo*."

"I'm thinking you might be a little bit drunk," George commented.

"You're wrong, buddy. I'm a whole lotta drunk."

"Listen, Lenny," I grabbed his wrist. "Janie wants to kill me."

He frowned. "Well, that blows."

"You need to help me. She told me earlier that Gideon Chase is in town now. Is it true? Maybe she was lying. What should I do?"

"I'll tell you a little something about Janie Parker," he slurred. "She's *evil*. The woman is an evil vixen who has stolen my heart and locked it away. Do you know what she does with the poetry I've written her? Do you?"

I shook my head.

"She throws it away. In the garbage can. Like it means nothing to her. Nothing!"

"I'm sorry to hear that."

"Would you like to hear some of my poetry?" He felt around in his pockets.

"Can I take a rain check on that? Look, Lenny . . . is Janie still outside?"

He shook his head and signaled for another drink, which the bartender quickly made for him. "She came in here a minute ago. Where she is now? Anybody's guess."

I froze. "She was here a minute ago? Here. As in . . . here?"

"Yeah. I turned my back for one moment and she was gone. Poof. She's like Houdini." He pouted. "A beautiful, untouchable Houdini angel. I saw her talking to your friend just before she disappeared."

I glanced around, feeling extremely uneasy. "Who was she talking to?"

"The birthday girl. Pink hair and the big piece of cake." He took the new drink and downed it in one big gulp, then sniffed and rubbed a big mitt of a hand under his nose. "Janie loves cake."

I strained to look around the club, feeling panic rising in my chest. But then I saw Amy, who'd obviously just requested a country song and was currently "Boot Scootin' Boogie"-ing it on the dance floor with Barry.

I waved at her until she spotted me. She gave Barry a big kiss that made me only a little queasy to witness, and came over to stand in front of me.

She frowned. "You don't look happy. Are you mad at me?"

"You? No. Not at all. Was Janie here?"

She smiled and nodded. "Yes, a few minutes ago. She's super nice."

"She's not. She's evil incarnate. Did she hurt you?"

"Of course not. She told me she liked my hair."

"That lying bitch."

"What?"

I bit my lip. "I mean . . . your hair is great. Really. So she was here and she left?" I let out a long sigh of relief. "Well, that gives me a little time to figure out what the hell I'm going to do now, I guess."

She shoved a forkful of cake into her pink-lipsticked mouth and chewed thoughtfully. "Yeah. She took off right after Thierry did. Said she wanted to take care of him. What does that mean?"

I blinked. "What did you just say?"

Another mouthful of cake disappeared. "Oh, come to think of it, she was looking for you, but I had no idea where you were. She wrote a note that she wanted me to give to you." She reached down the front of her shirt and pulled out a small envelope.

I took it from her with shaking hands.

"Is everything okay?" Amy said.

"Yeah. Fine." I tore my eyes away from the innocuous-looking envelope. I forced a smile. "Barry looks lonely. Better go back to him."

She grinned and grabbed me to give a quick kiss on the cheek. "I think my thirties are going to be great. It's like a whole new start."

She turned away to join her husband on the dance floor.

George touched my shoulder. "What's going on?"

I shook my head, then, with shaking hands, opened the envelope to pull out a piece of lined paper, holding it so both of us could read it at the same time.

Your ex-boyfriend is really hot. I might play with him a bit before I kill him. Would that hurt? If I ripped his heart out? Kind of an eye for an eye after what you did to my brother, Peter. Remember him? The vampire hunter whose eye you gored out before you murdered him? You may have fooled everyone else with your innocent act, sweetie. But I'm not everyone. And I guess I've fooled you up till now, haven't I? Want your boyfriend? Come see the show. I'm waiting for you.

She hadn't signed it. I guess she figured that I'd know who it was from.

"Her penmanship is atrocious," George commented.

"She has Thierry." I was surprised I was able to talk, the lump of panic in my throat was so big. "She's going to kill him."

He looked worried. "What should we do?"

I glanced around the club. The music throbbed. The lights swirled. The alcohol and various on-tap blood types flowed. Nobody had any idea what had just happened.

"I'll help you get your friend back." Lenny approached and threw an arm around George's shoulders. "I know Janie. I know how she thinks. And we'd better hurry if you want a chance to save him." He gulped back another drink.

I exhaled deeply. "Thanks, Lenny. You have no idea how much this means—"

"I jess wish"—he hiccupped and swayed on his feet—"that I wasn't so drunk."

I watched as his arm slipped off George's shoulders. Then the glass hit the floor and shattered, closely followed by Lenny's entire tall, muscle-bound body. On the ground. Unconscious.

"Now what?" George asked.

This was bad. Very bad. I felt a wave of anxiety sweep over me and almost knock me over. What was I going to do? Who was I supposed to ask?

It didn't matter who I asked. I knew what I had to do. Without question. I didn't care that it was over between us, even though the thought still twisted like knives in my gut. I had to save Thierry. Janie wasn't bluffing. If I didn't get wherever she was and give her something else to focus on, she was going to kill Thierry.

How the hell had she grabbed him, anyhow? He wasn't exactly helpless.

I frowned deeply. Maybe she was lying. Maybe the note was just meant to get me to expose myself tonight on a wild-goose chase.

I ran over to the bar phone and dialed Thierry's cell phone. It rang. Two times. Three. Four.

My throat felt tight. *Answer, Thierry*, I thought. *Please answer. Even if you immediately hang up on me, I just need to hear your voice.*

On the sixth ring, just before it went into voicemail, someone picked up.

"Thierry?" I said breathlessly. "Is that you?"

"This is a nice phone," Janie said. "Really. I've been meaning to upgrade. But do you know how much it costs? Ridiculous, really."

"If you hurt him I'm going to . . . to . . . " I trailed off, frowning hard, my whole body trembling.

"What are you going to do? Tell me. I'm fascinated."

My jaw clenched. "Thierry hired you to be my bodyguard."

She laughed. "What the hell do I care? So it's one job I won't get paid for. This is personal, babe. God, you know what? Thierry is *really* hot. When you said old, married and a heavy drinker, I had my doubts. But, hello, cowboy! When he wakes up, he and I are going to have some fun."

Every muscle in my body tensed up. "You touch him and I'll . . . I'll . . . "

"Again. Still waiting for this master plan of yours. You

know, I think I finally may have you figured out. I bet you didn't even mean to kill my brother, did you?"—pain twisted her words into harsh sounds—"but you did. You made your choice. And now I have something you love. Even if he doesn't give a shit about you. Isn't that what you said? Well, you've got a choice now. Let me make your breakup a permanent thing, or come and get him. And then we'll settle things just between the two of us once and for all. How does that sound?"

I tried to ignore the tight feeling in my throat. "Where are you?"

"It's in the note. If you can't follow simple instructions I think you've already made your decision. Bye, bitch." She hung up.

When I hung up the phone my palms were sweating.

Simple instructions. I glanced at the note again.

Come see the show. I'll be waiting.

See the show.

I shook my head, trying to concentrate with my mind racing in a million different directions. She said it was an easy clue.

Where would I go to see a show?

After another moment it clicked.

"We have to go to the Paragon Theater," I told George.

"Where's that? And what's this 'we' thing you're talking about?"

"That's where Janie's taken Thierry."

"Bully for her. I don't think this is a very good idea. Thierry can look after himself." He gingerly rubbed his injured nose.

"She must have knocked him out. Maybe he was distracted or something." I thought back to our last words.

Our last kiss and how he'd stormed away. How he'd over-reacted to George's obsession with party hats. This was all my fault.

I had to fix this.

"There's no time to debate the issue. Will you come with me? I'm going. With or without you, but I'd really appreciate the company."

"The boss is really in danger?"

I nodded.

He looked over at the dance floor, at all the people having fun at Amy's surprise party. Then he nodded, too. "I don't think we should tell anyone. They'll just panic. Make things worse than they already are."

"I agree."

He tucked his shoulder-length sandy blond hair behind his ears. "We're going to do this. We're going to rescue Thierry. Even though he punched me in the face."

"Yeah."

"Just you and me. The two of us." He nodded firmly, his handsome jaw set in a square line. "We're like war-riors. I like that. We don't need anybody else." He looked down at Lenny. "We are a power to be reckoned with. And when people mess with the people we care about, they'd better prepare to have their asses handed to them on a platter."

"That's right. Well, almost right."

He blinked at me. "What?"

"The part about you and me going alone. *So* not the way it's going to go. Janie is dangerous. She'd mop the floor with us."

"Really? She's that tough?"

I nodded.

"Then maybe we should give this more thought." He touched his nose again. "The boss did step over the line."

I grabbed his arm. "No, we're still going. But we're making a quick stop for reinforcements."

"What are we taking?"

"Not what. Who." I swallowed. "We need to get Quinn to help us."

He looked at me sternly. "Sarah, this isn't a double date."

"He's trained. Just like Janie is. He'll know what to do. Now come on. We can't waste any more time. We have to go to Clancy's."

"*Clancy's?* Are you talking about the hunter bar?"

I didn't reply, just stared at him for a moment before I turned away. I didn't think he needed the confirmation. I wasn't going to force him to come and potentially get hurt. But I was going. All alone if I had to.

I walked through the club, headed for the exit without a backward glance. Breezed past Angel the bouncer, who held the door open for me, and then I was outside. The cold wind whipped my dark hair over my face, covering my eyes for a moment until I tucked it back where it belonged.

George stood in front of me. I raised my eyebrows at him.

"Well, come on, then," he said. "What are you waiting for? There are butts that need to be kicked."

I couldn't have said it better myself.

Chapter 19

Less than fifteen minutes later, George and I stood, currently bodyguard-free, on the curb outside Clancy's, looking at the hunter bar with a large serving of uneasiness. I nervously twisted the gold necklace around my neck.

"How do you even know he's still in there?" George whispered.

"I just know." I had my arms crossed in front of me. Strangely enough, my feet had stopped working. Completely. They were a lot smarter than me, I guess, and didn't want to go any closer to the pub than we already were.

"Why don't we just shout his name? Maybe he'll come out."

"No, we're going to have to go in." Odds were that by now these hunters knew what I looked like. I'd be risking my life going into Clancy's tonight.

But I needed Quinn.

I had to save Thierry. Nothing else mattered.

My feet, however, were still having their doubts about the whole situation.

"There's a phone booth across the road," George said. "Why don't I call Clancy's and ask to speak to Quinn?"

I glanced at him. "You can wait out here if you're scared."

"Scared? I resent the accusation. I'm not scared. I'm simply trying to be practical. And this is a new shirt. I'd rather not get it dirty. Or get a huge hole from a stake in it. Call me crazy."

"You're not crazy. Okay, let's just go. It'll be like pulling off a Band-Aid, do it quickly and it doesn't hurt."

"Pulling off a Band-Aid, getting a wooden stake through the heart. Potato, Po-tah-to."

I tried to smile but failed. I looked down at my feet. *Come on boots. Start walkin'.*

And they did. It was a miracle.

I pushed the door open and got a big whiff of cigarette smoke. Despite the city's going completely smoke-free, Clancy's had obviously deemed itself to be the exception to the rule.

Trying to latch on to any good sign, I noticed that the club was fairly empty. Must have been an off night. There were a few hulks playing pool off to the right. A hulking woman was yelling at her hulking boyfriend by the dart board. The hulking bartender was counting cash up in the till with a cigarette dangling from his hulking lips.

Nobody even looked at us.

George dug his fingers into my arm. "There he is."

I looked over at the bar, through the smoky haze. There was Quinn. Sitting hunched over at the bar. In fact, it was the exact same bar stool he'd been seated at when we'd first met. He had a bottle of beer in front of him and was playing with the label he'd peeled off. He wore dark blue jeans and a long-sleeved black T-shirt. I could almost see the little black rain cloud hovering over his head. Then again, it was pretty smoky in there. He didn't particularly look like he was investigating a series of murders, but maybe looks were deceiving.

I glanced apprehensively at the other hunters and quickly walked over to him. George didn't loosen his tight grip on my arm. I swung onto the stool next to Quinn. He didn't look at me.

"What do you want, Sarah?" he asked as he studied the shredded beer label.

"World peace." I sighed. "I'd also really love one of those tiny teacup Chihuahuas, you know, like Paris Hilton has? And . . . I don't know, maybe longer hair. It gets a little limp if I grow it too far past my shoulders, but it would be a nice change."

That earned me a sideways glance. "You shouldn't be here."

"Neither should you."

"You're going to get yourself killed."

"You're probably right. Listen, Quinn, I don't have much time here. I need you."

He frowned. Then he looked up at George, hovering behind me.

George nodded. "I need you, too. Group hug?"

Quinn returned his attention to his beer label. "Why are you here?"

"How can you even ask that? You're the one who

called to let me know Janie wants me dead. Or was that somebody who just sounded like you?"

"I just wanted to give you a heads-up. But I'm sure your boyfriend can keep you safe."

I tensed. "Maybe it was a mistake coming here."

"Maybe it was. Now why don't you take your little buddy and get out of here before my friends over there—" he nodded in the general direction of Hulk Central "—notice that public enemy number one is in the house."

I let out a long sigh of exasperation and looked at George. "Could you give us a moment?"

"A moment?"

"Yeah, I need to say a few things to Quinn in private."

George glanced around the bar. "Um. Okay, I'll just be over by the coat rack, trying not to die."

He shuffled off to the side, trying to stick to the shadows, which there were plenty of in Clancy's.

I looked at Quinn. "Listen, I don't mean to sound unfeeling. I get that you're in a 'bad place' right now. I do. I know you've been through hell the last couple of months and I haven't exactly lightened your burden. But you know what, Quinn?"

"What?"

"Suck it the hell up."

He blinked at me. "Pardon me?"

"I said suck it up. You say you're here investigating the murders? Looks more like you're indulging in self-pity and tempting fate by dangling yourself in front of a bunch of hunters. I'm worried about you."

He frowned. "I thought you said you didn't want to see

me again? That you didn't care what happened to me anymore."

I sniffed, and found that I was starting to cry. *Again.*
Alert the media. "I care. *Of course* I care. How can you
think I don't?"

"But Thierry—"

"Stop it. Just stop it, would you? He dumped me.
Today. He says it's over between us. Does that make you
happy? That now I feel like a pile of discarded crap?"

He blinked. "Well, actually, it doesn't hurt."

"Glad to help." I wiped my tears away with the back of
my hand. "Janie has taken Thierry and plans on killing
him if I don't show up and take his place."

His eyebrows went up at that. "She kidnapped
Thierry?"

"She has him at an abandoned theater and if I don't get
there soon it's over. I need you to help me because without you, I have no chance against her. Sure, George has
those muscles, but they're really just for show."

"So let me get this straight. If I don't help you rescue
your ex, Janie will probably kill him."

"That's right."

"Not exactly seeing the problem." Then he sighed. "By
the way, not that it'll be any surprise to you, but I've ruled
him out as a suspect in the murders. Too many similar
murders in too many cities. Not just Toronto. It's not
him."

"I already told you that."

He took another gulp of his beer. "So let me get this
straight. He broke up with you, and you still want to rescue him? You're a lot more noble than I'd be."

My jaw clenched. "So you're saying you're not going to help me."

"I'm saying that you need to think about things before you go off running haphazardly all over the city. Janie wants to kill you. From what I've overheard around here tonight, Gideon Chase is really interested in finding you, too."

"Oh, yeah. Didn't I already tell you that? Old news."

"No, the subject didn't come up. You already knew this?" His jaw tensed. "Honestly Sarah. Gideon is an asshole of the first order. Usually funds everything and doesn't get his hands dirty. His father was way more hands-on, but maybe he's trying something new."

I tried to shake off the reminder about Gideon, which was nothing but a distraction now. "I don't care about that right now. I can't let Thierry die."

"Why not?"

"How can you even ask that?" I stared at him for a moment. How could I convince him to help me? "Listen, Thierry told me something . . . he . . . he thinks you and I should be together."

"What?"

"You and me. He doesn't like you, and I know you don't like him. But he knows you're a good man. At least, when you're not being a total pain in the ass like right now."

His lips twitched. "Compliments will get you anywhere, Sarah."

I tried to pick my words carefully. "So maybe he's right. Maybe I did make the wrong choice. Maybe I *should* be with you. Because you're wonderful, Quinn. You are. And even if you don't see it, it's the absolute

truth. I know that you'll do the right thing, even if it's difficult. I know you feel guilt about what you did in the
past. Thierry saw all that. And he saw how much you
wanted to protect me from him."

"It's true."

I crossed my arms. "So, maybe . . . maybe we can
make this work. If you want to. I know I've been a total
bitch and I wouldn't blame you for telling me to go
straight to hell, but I don't know. It's totally up to you
now, I guess."

He stared at me for a moment. Then he took a swig of
his beer. "Let me get this straight. Thierry has given his
permission for you to be with me. And you're okay with
that."

I swallowed hard and nodded.

"And you want me to help save his life. After that, you
and I can be together. Is that what you're saying?"

I nodded again.

He studied me for another moment, then stood up from
his stool and walked close to me so we were only inches
apart. He looked down the length of me and ran his hand
lightly along the side of my neck, along the light marks
that still remained from Thierry's bite. Then Quinn pulled
me against him and he kissed me long and hard.

When we parted he looked at me for another moment
and a small grin pulled at the side of his mouth.

"I never believed you were actually in love with that
asshole."

I blinked up at him, a little stunned. "What?"

"I though you were just imagining it. Because he was
such a mystery man. Women like that. I know it. But I

didn't know it was real, thought it was just a passing fancy. Until now."

"Quinn, what are you—?"

He held up a hand. "This is difficult enough as it is without being interrupted every three seconds."

I frowned.

"I've been giving a lot of thought to what you said to me yesterday. About how I've taken my situation, my shitty life, and morphed it into this big torch I'm carrying for you? That what I was really feeling was just gratitude because you gave me the time of day when everybody else turned their backs on me? I thought you were just saying that because you wanted me to leave you the hell alone. That you still resented me for trying to . . . to kill you. For my shitty mistakes I've made in my life. But now I see . . . you were right."

"I was?"

"Yeah. I convinced myself that I had a thing for you because it made things so much easier. Gave me something to focus on. A goal. But now I see that it's never going to happen. Sure, I could take you up on your offer. We could be together . . . " He cocked his head to the side and grinned. "And I would do my damnedest to make you very happy. Every night. Maybe several times a night."

I felt my face flush. "Quinn—"

"But it wouldn't be real. It wouldn't be like what you feel for Thierry. And when I'm with a woman I want it to be real. If I can't have all of you, Sarah, I don't want anything."

I nodded after a moment. "I'm . . . I'm sorry, Quinn. Really. I am."

"Just answer me one thing, Sarah. Are you really, seriously in love with Thierry? Even knowing what he is and what he's capable of? Even knowing it's not going to be a smooth road for you?"

I felt my eyes well up again. "Yes."

He nodded, but there was no smile to back it up. "Then that settles it."

A hulk approached to stand between us. He had a wooden stake in one hand. "Hey, I know who you are. You're Sarah Dearly. The Slayer of—"

Quinn grabbed the guy by the neck and whacked his head on the side of the bar. The hulk fell to the ground in an unconscious heap. Then Quinn took a deep breath and looked at me. "Okay, so let's go rescue your boyfriend."

All I could do was stare at my would-be assassin with a gaping open mouth, and nod in agreement.

We arrived at the Paragon Theater quickly and parked George's car—a twenty-year-old red Mustang—out in front. I hadn't realized the other day that the theater wasn't the only thing that was abandoned. The whole damn neighborhood seemed to be.

"Do you think they miss us from the party yet?" George asked.

"I don't know."

"You're sure they're here?" Quinn led the way to the back of the theater, where, I'd told him, there was a way to get in.

"Almost positive. But I sure as hell hope so. Just follow me. And try to be quiet."

I walked along the sidewalk, feeling the chill of the night cut through to my skin. Being a vampire meant that regular cold didn't bug me too much, but this felt colder than normal. It was mid-January and the theater was located near a side road that led directly to the lake. When the wind picked up it was positively frigid.

I knew this was where Janie would take Thierry. If I was a psycho, crazy assassin who wanted to extract her revenge in a dramatic fashion in front of an audience, then a stage would definitely be my choice.

We entered through the broken back door. It was dark inside. Really dark. Quinn lit a Zippo lighter that didn't help much, but I could see the hallway we had taken yesterday. I felt along the wall as we walked until I could see something up ahead. We'd made our way around to the front. Where the ticket booth was an empty ghost of what once was. A few small lights that resembled candles were on, set into the walls. I wondered when was the last time this theater had been open. Why hadn't anyone bought the property? It had just been left, as it was, for at least fifty years. Sad.

Quinn pushed open a door that led to the main theater. I caught a quick glimpse at the stage and took in a quick breath. There was a spotlight on and it was aimed at the stage.

And I was right. This was the place.

George and I stopped walking and looked at Quinn, who'd already seen what was down there.

Thierry was sitting on a chair in the middle of the stage. I squinted and focused my sharper vampire vision to see that his hands were restrained behind him, his head slumped forward to indicate that he was unconscious. I clenched my teeth. Janie was going to pay for this.

"There he is," George whispered. "Let's go down there and get him."

"Wait," Quinn said. "This is too easy. It's obviously a trap."

I nodded. "I agree."

"Wow," a voice said from behind us. "Three vampires to figure that out. How many vamps does it take to change a light bulb?"

I turned around slowly. Janie stood ten feet away, alone, with her hand on her hip, looking surprisingly relaxed. She grinned at me.

"This was your plan?" I said. "Get me out here and then insult me? Good plan. Fantastic."

"Thanks so much."

I chanced another look over in Thierry's direction.

"He's not dead, if that's what you're wondering," she commented. "Vamps his age, you know, they just disintegrate. Not much left behind, but it's so hard to get out of cashmere, you have no idea. You'll notice that I'm wearing jeans tonight."

I turned back to face her. "Okay, you've made your point."

"Oh, and what point is that?"

"I only wish you could have talked to me. We could have resolved this issue just between the two of us. It didn't have to come to this."

"What issue? You mean the one about you killing my brother?"

"It was self-defense. He was trying to kill me."

She nodded. "Whatever helps you sleep at night."

My eyes narrowed. "Having a hard time with that since you blew up my apartment."

She smirked at me. "Much as I'd like to lay claim to that little event, I didn't do it. If I had, you wouldn't be talking to me right now, since when I do something, I do it right. That was just some hunters into pyrotechnics."

"What Sarah said about Peter is true," Quinn said. "She didn't have any other choice."

Janie shot him a look. "Well, Michael, long time no see."

"Michael?" George said.

"That's his first name," I told him.

"Learn something new every day."

Quinn took a step forward. "Janie, why don't you just stand down? You don't have a chance here. You're a smart girl, you must be able to see that, right?"

She rolled her eyes. "I'll get to you in a second, handsome. Now, Sarah, honey, what were you saying about my brother and it being self-defense? I'm certainly willing to listen to any and all arguments before I pass final judgment."

"When was the last time you saw your brother?" I asked.

Her expression tensed. "It was a few years ago, actually. He was excited about going on the tour with the other hunters. Get to see the world, and all that."

I nodded. "I'm guessing he was probably a really nice guy once upon a time. And I know you're his little sister and you guys were probably close back then, but those few years must have changed him, Janie. The Peter I got to meet wasn't nice. He wasn't somebody you could reason with. He was a cold-blooded murderer."

Her lips thinned. "Takes one to know one."

"Do you think I wanted to do what I did? If he'd given me any other choice, I would have taken it. But at that moment, it was him or me, and I chose me."

She nodded stiffly. "How did you do it?"

I licked my dry lips. "A gun."

She continued to nod. "I see. Well, I promise when I gut your boyfriend, I'll be as gentle as possible. You're more than welcome to watch."

Anger rose to heat my cheeks. I stepped forward, but Quinn put his arm out to stop me.

"Janie, she's telling the truth. Peter was all messed up. He didn't know what he was doing anymore. He'd started looking at vampire hunting as a game, not as a service."

She snorted at that. "Yeah, and I'd believe you because? Last time I checked you were one of the bloodsuckers now, *Michael*. So save your breath, if you have any. I don't know, do vampires need to breathe? Do they have heartbeats? I'm not up on all this new age vampire stuff. Last time I checked, vamps were evil and needed to be snuffed out, not treated like equals and given free passes when it comes to murder."

"I'm not asking for a free pass," I said. "I'm just trying to tell you what happened. Peter tried to kill me. Several times. He failed. When he tried again I happened to have a weapon and I fought back. He lost. End of story."

She laughed. "End of story. Yeah, I guess it is, isn't it?"

"Janie," Quinn said. "I know you've had a hard life. It was just you, your little sister, and Peter after your parents died, right? I remember you used to play with your dolls while Peter and I hung out. You were a cute kid."

She frowned at him. "I'm not a kid anymore, in case you haven't noticed."

"No, you're definitely not. But I don't think you've changed that much. Just stop being difficult. We're not going to let you get away with this. We're going down there to get Thierry and we're leaving. Now you can either let us or you can stand in the way."

"And what if I stand in the way?" She put her hands on her hips.

"Then we're going to have a problem."

She studied him for a moment, her brow creased with a frown. Then she glanced at me and raised an eyebrow. "You're helping Sarah get the other man? That's so noble of you."

He shrugged but didn't say anything.

"You used to be so in control. Have to say I'm a little disappointed that you've turned into a sloppy-seconds-loving wimp who lets the world walk all over him. Too bad, really."

His expression darkened. "You've got a big mouth, Janie."

She laughed, a short staccato sound. "Is Sarah the one who made you into a vampire?"

"No."

"That's a rather short answer. No long, entertaining anecdote of how you became a monster?"

Quinn visibly grimaced. "Most vampires aren't monsters."

She nodded. "Right. Keep telling yourself that, handsome. And maybe you'll believe it some day."

His expression darkened even more. "Janie, just step aside, would you? I'm running out of patience here."

She grinned at me. "You know, when we were talking the other day and I told you I used to have a big crush on one of my brother's friends? Three guesses who it was and the first two don't count. Small world." She fixed him with an appraising look, up and down his frame. "You were a little skinnier then. You've been working out. Is being a vamp really hard work?"

Quinn glanced at me, then back to her. "Janie—"

"Yeah, I was head over heels with you, Quinn. You prefer to go by your last name now, huh? When I saw you again the other day I have to admit it freaked me out. Made me remember how I used to feel when I was just a kid. Dorky and awkward. Just Peter's kid sister. Every time you'd come over and spar with my brother, I was lurking about. Watching. Learning." She sighed wistfully.

"Janie, we can talk about this—"

"I had the hugest crush on you back then." She raised her hand from her waist. I noted with horror that it now held a gun. "But I'm over it now."

She shot him in the chest.

Chapter 20

Then Janie shifted her aim and shot George.

"No!" I screamed.

Both the guys' eyes bugged and they looked down at their chests in unison. But there was no blood that I could see. My heart beat so loudly that I could barely hear anything except its thundering sound, as I watched Quinn pull the small dart out of his chest and stare at it with confusion before he looked at Janie.

She slipped the gun back into her shoulder holster. "Geez, don't look at me like that, handsome. It's just a garlic dart. I wouldn't kill you. Not today, anyhow. I'm not that much of a bitch. My issue isn't with you, but I can't have you spoiling all the fun."

He frowned. "Garlic . . . garlic dart . . . "

"That's right. Works like a tranquilizer on vampires. You should remember that, silly. Night, night."

I watched George and Quinn keel over, as if in slow motion, and hit the ground, before I ran over to check on them. Check their pulses. They seemed fine other than the fact that they were both unconscious. I picked up the dart on the ground and looked at it.

Garlic dart?

I was so happy it wasn't a real gun that I felt like crying. That would have been it. I'd learned that silver bullets are enough to kill not only werewolves, but vampires, too. If she'd had a gun filled with silver bullets that would have been it. I would have just lost two of the most important people in my life. Just like that. The thought made me feel physically ill.

I turned around expecting to see her grinning at me, but Janie was gone.

I didn't take the time to think things through. I turned, pushed open the door that led to the main theater, and started down the aisle, keeping my focus directly on Thierry's still form. It was so dark everywhere but on the stage itself that even with my new and improved vampire vision, I stumbled a few times on the steps, but I didn't slow down. When I was down on the floor I grabbed hold of the edge of the stage and pulled myself up, breathing hard, and then I was there. I was right next to Thierry. I touched his shoulder. Shook him.

"Thierry. Wake up."

I looked at the back of the chair where his hands were restrained.

Silver handcuffs. What a surprise.

I pulled at them, hoping to use my Vampire Strength, and then realized I really didn't have any and gave up. Plus, the silver hurt if I pressed against it too hard—as if it was sharp even though it wasn't. If Thierry struggled too much against the cuffs, he might succeed in cutting his hands off trying to get loose. I shuddered at the thought.

"Thierry, please, please wake up!"

I gently pushed his head back from the slumped-on-his-chest position it was in. I ran my fingers through his dark hair.

Nothing.

Then I slapped him hard against the side of his face.

"Sorry! But wake the hell up!"

His chest rose and fell as he took a deep breath and slowly opened his eyes, staring at me for a moment before confusion set in.

"Sarah? What's going on?"

I felt a wave of relief and I kissed him hard on his lips, holding his face between my hands. He blinked at me with surprise.

"I'm rescuing you."

"Rescuing me?" He looked around the stage. "Where are we?"

"Let me nutshell it for you. Janie, one of the bodyguards you so kindly hired to keep an eye on me? Is Peter's sister."

"What?" He looked so shocked by this I knew without a doubt he'd had no idea.

I nodded. "She wants revenge on me and she grabbed you coming out of the club. Must have shot you with a garlic dart to . . . incapacitate you or something. If I'd known that's all it took, I might have invested in a few myself." I tried to smile as I stroked his face. "Are you okay?"

He looked around the stage, taking it all in for a moment, then looked at me, a frown creasing his forehead into deep lines. "You shouldn't have come. It isn't safe."

"No, it sure the hell isn't. But she was planning on killing you if I didn't come."

"Then you should have let her. Sarah, you must leave immediately." He shifted in his seat and tensed up as he felt the silver bite into his wrists.

I ignored him and fiddled again with the handcuffs. They weren't going to open without the keys. Or a locksmith. Were there vampire locksmiths? I'd have to consult the Yellow Pages.

"I got Quinn and George to come with me."

"They have restrained Janie, have they?"

"Actually no. She shot them with those garlic darts. You know, I had garlic bread at my cousin's wedding rehearsal. I couldn't keep it down but if I had, would I have passed out?"

"Sarah, please. Please. You need to leave me here."

"Don't make me smack you again."

"Sarah—"

I frowned at him. "I'm not leaving you here. Get it through your head right now so we can move on."

"You're in danger."

I stood straight up and looked down at him. Even after everything that had been said and done between the two of us, all I wanted to do was to hug him. Or throttle him. One or the other. "Thierry, I'm always in danger. Even when I was a human I was in danger, I just didn't know it. From a mugger, from a speeding bus, from anything. Life isn't safe. It's never been safe."

He shook his head. "This is a little different than that. You can choose to be safe."

"I can choose to gag you in a minute if you don't stop arguing with me."

He frowned at me. "With what will you gag me?"

"I'll find something."

"You're rescuing me." He said it like he didn't believe it.

"Yes I am. Well, trying to, anyhow."

He stared into my eyes for a moment. "Even though you must hate me for how we left things earlier, you would risk your life to help me?"

"I don't hate you."

"You should."

"I don't. Now shut up, okay? I have no idea where Janie went and I have to figure out how to get these handcuffs off you fast."

"Oh," Janie said from stage right. "You would use this."

I glanced over at her. She held up a tiny silver key that shone under the spotlight. She grinned.

I got a sinking feeling. Which, considering my stomach had already dropped through the floor, was difficult but not impossible. This was a setup—and not just Janie's doing. I hadn't known why, or who, but now I had a pretty good idea.

"You're working for Gideon Chase, aren't you?" I said.

"He would pay really good. The man has bucks." She smirked at me. "But it's not him. My real boss wanted me to get you here." She looked around the stage. "I feel like singing something from *Spamalot*. Is that wrong?"

I felt so tense I thought I might shatter. "So what now?"

"Before or after my encore?"

"This isn't funny, Janie."

Her eyes narrowed and her smile dropped away. "Oh, I know that. Believe me, I'd rather have you all to myself, but the boss has other plans. And he does pay well. Not as well as Gideon would, but still. Not too shabby."

"And what boss would that be?"

"That would be me."

I turned at the sound of a familiar voice. Nicolai stepped out from the wings and onto the stage.

My stomach fell yet another three feet. "I thought you were gone."

He shrugged. "I changed my mind."

"Nicolai . . . what are you doing?" My voice sounded strangled as he came further into the light. I realized his eyes weren't normal. They were darkening, slowly bleeding to black. Shivers ran down my arms.

"Stay the hell away from her," Thierry snarled behind his back.

Nicolai raised an eyebrow at me and turned. "Thierry, my old friend. Given your current position, I don't think you should be telling anyone what to do."

I was very confused. "Nicolai . . . what's wrong? What's going on here?"

"What's wrong?" He laughed. "Where do I even begin?"

"What about Gideon?" I managed. "I thought he was in town. Or was that a lie, too?" I glanced at Janie, who now held a wooden stake in her hand.

"Oops." She grinned. "Is my nose getting longer?"

I watched as Nicolai ran the tip of his tongue along his sharper-than-normal fangs, studying me as if I were prey.

Not a good feeling, to put it mildly. What was wrong with him? What was he up to?

"I must admit, Sarah, that when I arrived in town my intentions were honorable. My plan was to assassinate Gideon Chase when he made a move on you. It would have been my greatest achievement."

"Assassinate him?" I repeated as my eyes widened. "You didn't say anything about assassinating him. I thought you just wanted to capture him."

He shook his head. "And hide him away from the world? Perhaps reason with him and let him go? So young and stupid, you are. I truly am surprised that Thierry would give you any attention whatsoever. When I arrived, I expected great things from the Slayer of Slayers. I put so much hope into it. You have been the ultimate disappointment." He looked over at Thierry. "Granted, she is young and attractive, but what else is there? Don't tell me you truly care what happens to this girl."

Thierry's expression darkened and he strained against his bindings. "Touch her and you will die a horrific death."

With a look from Nicolai, Janie moved to stand behind Thierry, running the tip of the wooden stake along the edge of his black shirt.

"I'd put a sock in it if I were you," Janie advised. "Nicolai isn't in a very good mood. Frankly, neither am I. Nicolai, I thought you said that if I got them here, you'd handle Thierry and I could have bitch face over there."

Bitch face? That's the best she could come up with? If I hadn't been scared out of my wits, I'd have been seriously insulted.

He gave her a cold smile. "My plans have changed."

"Oh, and when did that happen?" Her jaw clenched.

"Some time ago." Nicolai turned to survey me again. I instinctively took a step backward. The look in his black eyes was predatory. What was his problem with me? What had I done to piss him off so much?

"So . . ." I tried to breathe normally. This wasn't as bad as I thought. No. Keep telling myself that and maybe everything would be okay. Nicolai was one of the good guys. He'd given me his blood after Thierry bit me. He was the leader of the Ring, for Pete's sake. "I'm thinking we have some issues we need to hash out. Why don't we all go for a coffee somewhere and chat? There's no reason we can't all be friends."

Yeah. Didn't sound terribly convincing to me, either. But it was worth a shot.

A cruel smile twisted his lips. "Passably attractive. Not terribly bright. Slightly endearing in her naïve attempts at humor." He turned to Thierry. "I still don't understand. But so be it. You want to know when I changed the plans, Janie?"

She shrugged. "Actually, I'd rather just get this over with."

"It was when I arrived at the nightclub the other night. To find Sarah unconscious and bleeding. I knew at once what had happened. That Thierry had nearly drained her and left her for dead."

I saw Thierry visibly flinch at his words.

"I also knew right then that the rumors about the Slayer of Slayers were false, for this wouldn't have happened to one with an ounce of strength or common sense," Nicolai continued, "and it was as if the last hundred years had never passed. It was as if I was seeing my Elizabeth, dead in front of me. Murdered by someone I trusted. Someone I considered to be my friend. My first thought was to help. And I revived her. Didn't I?"

I nodded. "You did. And I appreciate it. But why are you—"

He waved me off. "I should have felt good about my sacrifice. I was the better man. I wanted to help save her. But as she drank from me, as she was revived, my feelings began to change. I saw the bite marks fresh on her neck. They were the bite marks that Elizabeth would have worn. And all became clear to me once again, after so, so very long. All I wanted to do was to finish what Thierry began. To finish you, Sarah, and find some closure to my own tragedy." His eyes narrowed at me. "Perhaps then I would have learned what he sees in you. Do you taste sweeter than the rest?" He took a step closer to me.

"Nicolai—" Thierry's voice was edged with violence.

He turned to Thierry. "I told her that Gideon Chase wanted to kill the Slayer of Slayers. That he also wanted to kill you. She was willing to put herself at risk in order to ensure your future safety. Isn't that foolish of her?"

I didn't look at Thierry, but he was silent.

Nicolai sighed. "However, he is not here. His plans changed, as mine have. So now there is only us."

"What does that mean?" I said, my voice now shaky.

"Revenge," he said simply. "It is finally time for me to seek my revenge. I have tried to put it behind me. But seeing Thierry after so long. Seeing you with Thierry, with your eyes filled with romantic stars. Realizing that he cares for you. That he would care what happens *to* you. It was well worth the wait. He murdered the woman I loved more than anything else." He looked around the theater. "That's why I wanted to come here. After Janie told me of your little adventure yesterday, I knew this was the perfect place. My Elizabeth was an actress. Thousands saw her perform in her short life. I gave her immortality and she should have shone onstage for millennia. But that was cut short when she was murdered." He turned to stare daggers into Thierry. "Do you have anything to say to that?"

Thierry looked down, his chest heaving. Then he raised his gaze. "Do what you wish to me. I deserve it. But Sarah . . . let her go. As one whom you once considered your friend, I beg you."

Nicolai regarded him for a moment. "You beg me." He started to laugh. "Oh, this is too, too wonderful. He begs me to spare her life."

Obviously, Nicolai was the only one who seemed to get this side-splittingly not-funny joke.

"Thierry de Bennicoeur begs me to spare the life of the woman he loves. Don't you see? This makes what I'm about to do so much sweeter. For I never had the chance to beg for the life of Elizabeth, did I?"

Silence fell on the stage as his laughter ceased.

"Nicolai," I said after a moment. "I don't know you very well, but I know that you aren't a bad guy. Listen to me. Listen to reason for a second, would you?"

He turned to me and cocked his head. "I am nothing if not a reasonable man."

"Thierry didn't kill Elizabeth."

His expression darkened to match his haunted, and as I realized now, insane eyes. "He did."

I shook my head and tried to keep my voice steady and

panic-free. "He may have bitten her—which I'm not trying to justify—but when she ran, she was attacked by hunters. *They're* the ones who killed her. *They're* the ones to blame."

He stared at me for a long moment.

"And why did she run?" he asked softly. "What did my Elizabeth run from?"

My mouth went dry.

"Me," Thierry said. "She ran from me."

Nicolai nodded. "So you see, my dear Sarah, that is all the proof I require." He turned to Thierry again. "So you do accept the punishment that has taken me a century to deliver?"

Thierry didn't look at me. "Release Sarah first."

Nicolai smiled. "But Thierry, my old friend, Sarah is part of your punishment."

Thierry's eyes widened and he struggled with his bindings as Janie stood like a statue behind him. "Sarah . . . run!"

But I didn't have a chance. With a speed I'd never witnessed from either human or vampire, Nicolai had closed the distance between us and was behind me, an arm around my neck that I grabbed, searching my brain for a suitable self-defense tactic. I came up blank.

"Yes," Nicolai hissed into my ear. "Before I kill you, Thierry, I will drain the woman you love. So the last thing you see will be the life slipping from her eyes, knowing there was nothing you could do to save her." He moved his face down my neck where the faint bite marks from the other night still remained. He pulled the collar of my shirt down to expose more skin.

"Hey," Janie said. "Is that the necklace I've been looking for? Around your vampire neck? What the hell?"

I ignored her, as a sick realization hit me. "Nicolai . . . are you . . . are you the one responsible for the recent vampire attacks in the city? The murders? I hoped it wasn't true. That a vampire . . . that a vampire wouldn't—"

"Wouldn't kill?" I felt him smile against my ear. "Wouldn't hurt another soul? That they were innocent creatures unjustly accused of centuries of monstrous crimes? That hunters are completely and totally wrong in what they do? After what happened to you the other night I would have thought that your naïve opinion of your kind would have changed. And perhaps that your doubts would be with Thierry. But they weren't, were they? Not for one moment."

I managed to shake my head at that. "Thierry wouldn't do something like that."

He inhaled and pushed the hair off my neck. "Loyal to the end. Just like my Elizabeth."

I struggled, but the guy was just as strong as he looked. He held my head in such a way that I couldn't even bite him. "Just an FYI, Nic, your Elizabeth was a bit of a tramp. She tried to seduce Thierry. Real loyal. I guess absence made the heart go yonder, didn't it?"

"Shut up." His words were accompanied by the tightening of his arm around my neck. I choked against the intense pressure.

"It is true," Thierry said, his eyes glittering like diamonds under the stage's spotlight. "And I was not the first."

"Liars."

Janie shifted the stake to her other hand and pressed it against Thierry's neck to stop him from saying anything else, but her attention was on me and Nicolai.

"Is it true?" she asked. "Are you responsible for the murders?"

I felt his lips against my neck and I shuddered. "A man has his appetites. And sometimes they can't be denied. Isn't that right, Thierry?"

She frowned. "So, is that a yes?"

He snorted. "Oh, Janie. Always so inquisitive. That's what I like about you. Yes. I take what I want when I want it and have done so since I was a fledgling. Hunters, other vampires, humans. I do not care whose blood I enjoy. I am bound by no human rules. If more vampires thought as I did, we would have no need to fear the hunters. They would fear us. Remember that, Thierry, for the moments you have yet to live. That only the strong survive."

"Nicolai . . . no!" Thierry shouted.

I felt a searing pain as Nicolai sank his fangs into my neck. I couldn't move. I couldn't think. I should have fought harder against him. I should have learned more self-defense. I shouldn't follow my heart instead of my head. It only led me into trouble.

I couldn't get out of this one. And there was nobody left to help me. To help *us*.

Suddenly Nicolai's body jerked and I yelped as he pulled his fangs out of my neck. I staggered back from him a few feet. He looked down at himself, then pulled a dart out of his shoulder and looked up at Janie.

She had the garlic dart gun in hand. "Sorry, Nicolai. But you just weren't playing fair."

"What do you care?" he snapped at her. "You hate her. She killed your brother."

She flinched. "I'm beginning to learn that there are no easy answers in life. To anything, I'm afraid. And I guess I'm not too happy that I've been working for a serial killer. Just couldn't let that slide. Not even for a little revenge."

"Morals? For a mercenary?"

"Well, she also has my necklace." She shrugged, and then frowned at him. "Uh, shouldn't you be unconscious by now?"

He nodded. "It is good that I trust no one. Including you. I took an antidote for the darts before arriving here."

"Well, *shit*."

I looked across the floor as I clamped my hand against my neck. Things were a bit blurry. I didn't know how much blood he'd taken. Couldn't be much. It hadn't been that long. But I'd felt better, that was for sure.

A small silver key sparkled about six feet away from me. The key to Thierry's handcuffs. Janie must have dropped it.

I looked at Thierry. His face was filled with concern for me. He followed my line of sight to the key. He shook his head and mouthed "run" to me.

"Bad girl, Janie. I'm very disappointed. You came highly recommended."

"What can I say?"

"Nothing at all." He flew at her, grabbing her as he had me, and bit her neck. She screamed with surprise and pain, clawing frantically against him. But he had her at a disadvantage. He'd done this before. It was obvious. She didn't have a chance.

I could grab the key. I could free Thierry and we could both get the hell out of there before he finished with her and started looking for dessert.

But that wasn't going to happen.

I pulled my hand away from my neck and crawled across the stage as quickly as I could, and grabbed the gun to point it and pull the trigger.

Nicolai jerked again and pulled away from Janie. He looked down at the dart I'd just shot into his other shoulder before he pulled it out and threw it away from him.

"Really?" he said incredulously. "Didn't you hear about the antidote? Truly, I have never witnessed such stupidity from a woman."

I stood on shaky legs and threw the dart gun away from me. It clattered to the ground. "Okay, jerk. First off, I'm not that stupid. Got it?"

He raised an eyebrow.

"Because," I continued, "I wasn't trying to knock you out. I was simply trying to distract you. Who's stupid now, asshole?"

He turned just as Janie sank her wooden stake into his chest and stepped back, holding a hand to her wounded neck. He looked at her with surprise.

"Now I do realize that this probably means I'm not going to be paid for this job, too," she said. "But I'm okay with that if you are."

He opened his mouth to respond, but the rest of his body was too busy turning into a puddle of goo to let him.

"Gross." I stepped away from his remains. Luckily, I wasn't wearing my new good shoes. I wanted to feel bad about what had to happen, but I found that I simply couldn't. Nicolai was dead and all I felt was relief.

Janie stared at what was left of Nicolai for a moment, clearly shaken by what had just occurred, then she turned away.

"Where are you going?" I asked. "Don't you want the necklace?"

She turned back to look at the gold chain hanging around my neck. "To tell you the truth, I'm a little sick of following orders. I'm going to tell my boss I didn't get it. Whatever happens, happens."

"What is it, anyhow?" The metal felt cold against my skin as I thought about how it might have helped transform Barkley back into his human form. "What does it do?"

"No idea. I just retrieve them, I don't write the instruction manuals."

I tucked it back under my shirt. "You didn't let me thank you for saving my life."

She shrugged. "I guess we're even. That doesn't mean we have to hug, does it?"

I shook my head.

"Look," she said. "I'm not okay with what happened to my brother. I get that he was different than I remember. I know in the end that he was a bad guy. But still. It hurts. So we're *not* friends."

"I know that."

"I'm out of here."

"What about Lenny?"

She smiled at that. "While he should devote his attention to someone who deserves it, I'm afraid he's stuck with me as his partner for a while. I'll catch up with him."

"Enjoy the poetry."

"Yeah, I'll do that. And tell Quinn . . . " she paused,

and then smirked before turning away again. "Tell him I'm sorry I kicked his ass."

"I'm sure he'll love that. Oh, and by the way, Janie?"

She turned again. "Yeah?"

"Great shoes."

She looked down at her feet. "Yeah, I know. Would you believe these were on sale?"

"Lucky bitch."

She shrugged at me and then smiled, just a little one, and vanished into the shadows offstage.

Chapter 21

I turned to Thierry.

He stared at me and shook his head.

I shrugged. "I don't even get a thank-you for saving you?"

"What you just did was incredibly foolish."

"And what's your point?"

"It could have gone very differently. You could have died. You are lucky."

I touched my neck and flinched. "I guess I am. I didn't even check my horoscope this morning to make sure that all my stars were in alignment or anything."

"Don't make light of this, Sarah. Nicolai would have killed you. And I would have been able to do nothing to prevent it. It was all my fault that he felt that way."

I shook my head. "Nicolai was insane. Get it? And no matter how you try to rewrite what happened with Elizabeth, you weren't responsible for her death. Hunters were. End of story."

He took a deep breath. "You're so very innocent."

"No, I'm practical. You're just addicted to guilt. Gets you through the day like caffeine used to with me. But you have to let go of it. It's over. Permanently over now. Nicolai was the true murderer who definitely deserved what he got. If he didn't, we wouldn't be having this conversation about guilt and caffeine."

He looked away. "We shall agree to disagree, then."

I studied his handcuffs again. "We probably shouldn't stay here. We need to leave."

"I agree."

"See? We don't disagree about everything." I paused. "Besides, you wouldn't want to miss your flight to France tomorrow."

His expression tensed. "No, I wouldn't want that."

"I saw the papers in your office. You don't have to hire anybody to look after me, you know. I'll manage."

"You weren't meant to see that."

Time to be brave and put on a good face. After everything that had happened, it was the least I could do.

"But I did. Look, I want you to know that I'm okay with it. Whatever you decide to do, even if it's leaving the country. I just hope that it's not just to get away from me. I have enough of a complex as it is."

He pulled at his bindings. "It's not just because of you, Sarah. Now, please, we need to leave this place."

I studied him for a moment, all tied up with no place to go. "Well, isn't this interesting. Can't escape now, can you?"

He stopped struggling and looked at me. He cocked an eyebrow. "Escape?"

"Yeah, every time we start to talk about something uncomfortable you turn around and leave."

"I leave when there is nothing left to say."

"No, you leave when there's nothing left for *you* to say."

"It is the same thing."

I crossed my arms. "Fine. So it's over between us. You made your point loud and clear earlier. But now that I have your undivided attention I have a few last things I want to say to you before you go ahead and leave the country."

He sighed. "Sarah—"

"Please, Thierry. Just listen to me, okay?"

His jaw tensed. "Very well."

I swallowed hard. "I went to see Quinn tonight. I told him that you said that we should be together. I told him that if he helped me rescue you then we could be. Together. Him and me."

Thierry's expression hardened. He nodded. "It is the right thing."

I clenched my fists. "No it's not. And you know why? Because after everything that's happened, after knowing you all these weeks, I've found out a few things about you. You're kind of a jerk. A little bit self-involved, to say the least. Very private. Secretive." I touched my neck. "And you bit me. You almost killed me. I tried to sugarcoat it, but that's what happened. There is a monster inside you, Thierry, and not one I'm particularly fond of."

He nodded and turned his gaze away.

"You haven't even touched me since we were in Mexico," I continued, "other than a few kisses. I tried to tell myself it was because you've been so busy with the new club, but I don't think it was just that, was it? You've been avoiding me on purpose. Maybe you were hoping that I'd end things before you had to?"

He looked at me. "Perhaps."

"Everybody. Absolutely everybody has been telling me over and over and over that you and I have no chance of making things work between the two of us."

I walked over to him and crouched next to him.

"And then you go and break up with me. Tell me that you're leaving the country. It hurt so bad. Even though I always knew that it was only a matter of time. And when you told me that I should go after Quinn, the guy who on paper is totally right for me, who has always put me up on a pedestal and makes me feel like I mean something in the grand scheme of things, do you know what I wanted to do?"

He shook his head stiffly. "You wanted to go to him."

"No. It made me want to scream. Because you are so damn stupid."

His eyebrows went up and he looked at me. "Stupid?"

"Yes. You're too stupid to see how in love with you I am. And after finding out about your dark side, after learning everyone else's opinion about us, after everything, all I want to do is be with you. Finding out you're completely messed up doesn't make me love you any less, it makes me love you even more. And maybe that makes me foolish. Maybe that makes me stupid, but I don't really give a shit what anybody else thinks. All I care about is what I think. And what you think." I sniffed. "And unfortunately, you don't feel the same way about me. Or even a fraction. I get that. But it doesn't make me love you any less. I wish it did, but it doesn't."

"Sarah—"

"I know this was just a quick fling for you. I'm too young, too naïve, too . . . as Veronique put it . . . *goofy*. I think she could have picked a less Disney word, but it's the truth, I guess. I know I don't fit into your life. And I . . . I don't care. None of it changes how much I love you. I tried listening to everyone else tell me what I was feeling wasn't real. And I almost believed them. But they're wrong. My heart wouldn't feel like it does if they were right. But I'm not going to force myself into your life if you don't want me. And I know I'm not . . . not a lot of things. Nicolai just said that there's nothing special about me. I know that. You deserve more that I just can't give you."

He swallowed. "You are a fool, Sarah."

I laughed. "Gee, thanks for the confirmation."

"You would risk your life to come here to save me, someone who has hurt you over and over? And you still tell me you care for me?"

"I know. I'm a total dork."

He blinked. Hard. "You are a gift I did nothing to deserve."

I felt a big hot tear slip down my cheek. "What?"

"Are you finished with your little speech?"

I nodded.

"Very good. Because now you will listen to me." He shifted in his seat, his hands still locked behind him. "You are too young, much too naïve, and more than your share of . . . *goofy*. This is all true. And tonight after all I said to you, and didn't say, I believed that I had lost you forever. You and Quinn . . . I know he cares for you. I know you care for him. I knew it was the right decision. But I wasn't prepared for the knife I felt cut through my heart at the thought of him with you. Him and not me."

He paused. My heart was thudding madly in my chest.

"This is wrong. You and me," he continued. "Logically I know this. But I cannot help but wish it were different. That we lived in a different world. That I could ensure your safety both from the outside world and from me. I thought, when I bit you, that you would finally come to your senses. Finally see me for the monster that I had tried to hide from you by distancing myself at every opportunity. But when you didn't seem to care . . . when your sense of self-preservation seemed to stop in your dealings with me, I knew that I had to take harsh measures to ensure your safety. Even if it meant hurting you."

He blinked again. "I underestimated your tenacity. Your stubbornness. Now to hear from Nicolai that you would willingly put your life at risk in order to help me, whether or not I ever knew . . . " He swallowed. "And when you were still there, open to me, caring for me even knowing of my deep flaws, I knew there was only one answer. I had to leave. It would hurt you, once again, but once I removed my presence from your life, I assumed you would thrive. And yet, here you are. Risking your life to save someone who has brought you nothing but pain."

"No, Thierry, that's not true."

"Sarah, I am a very private man. I always have been. But your presence in my life has shone light into my darkness."

"Is that a bad thing?"

"I thought so. But now I'm not so sure. You are so open. So willing to give yourself over to that which may bring you pain. I don't understand. I thought I could control it. But when I witnessed you with Quinn the other day, in his embrace, I lost all decorum. It drove me mad with jealousy. Made me make rash decisions. And earlier tonight that jealousy blinded me and drove me into the night and into the clutches of Janie."

"She's gone now."

"No one has ever rescued me before, do you know that?"

"Veronique did."

"A very long time ago and for her own purposes. And ever since she plucked me from the heap of burning corpses there has been a part of me that wished that she hadn't. For centuries I have wished that death would take me, to let me rest."

I pressed my lips together, trying not to cry. Well, trying not to blubber, anyhow. It was a little late for the not crying.

"And then I met you," he said, capturing my gaze. "In my darkest hour. When I felt there was nothing left to live for. I knew I'd found an angel who'd come to save me."

"An angel?"

"Not literally, of course. You are far from angelic sometimes, Sarah."

I frowned at him.

A smile tugged at his lips. "I had spent centuries with Veronique and had come to care for her in my own way, but she never touched my heart. In fact, I had begun to doubt that I even had one. But a few days with you and you . . . you saved me. Over and over again, and you probably never even realized it. With your words, with your touch—with simply *you*. And I had never been so afraid in my entire life. For I know who I am. What I am.

And the thought of becoming close with someone, after so very long, was too much for me to bear. So I tried to push you away."

"What are you trying to say, Thierry?"

"What I'm trying to say is that I . . . " His throat worked. "I adore you, Sarah. Every day that you're in my life. Despite my brain telling me to push you away, to save you from yourself, my heart cannot help but be self-ish. The thought fills me with fear, that I may hurt you, that you may be hurt by others, but I can't be silent any longer. I . . . I love you, Sarah. I do. Please, never doubt that."

Holy shit.

"You *love* me?" I blinked. In shock. "Really?"

"You sound surprised."

"Well, I'm surprised. Yeah, I am."

"You didn't think me capable of love?"

"Actually, no. No offense."

He shifted in the chair, looking a little uncomfortable with his admission. "None taken. So now what—?"

I threw my arms around him and cut off his words with a kiss, ignoring my tears, as they'd become tears of happiness. Thierry loved me. *Me*. How in the hell did that happen?

"I love you, too," I whispered into his ear. "But I'm pretty sure you already know that, don't you?"

I let go of him, finally, and leaned back. His eyes were dark.

"So you forgive me?" he asked.

"No. But I think I will eventually. You're not leaving for France anymore, right?"

He studied me for a moment. "I suppose any trips I have planned can wait."

"Good answer."

He smiled. "I won't be much good to you tied to this chair, you know."

"Oh, I wouldn't be so sure about that." I kissed him again and felt his response, his lips parting as the kiss deepened. After a moment, I leaned back again. "I'm *so* keeping the handcuffs. Just try not to struggle too much, because they do pinch."

He raised an eyebrow. "Indeed."

"Yes, *indeed*." I beamed at him. "So we're together. You're not going to go all cold and distant on me again, are you?"

"But I do cold and distant so well."

"You really do. It's a gift."

"If you wish to be with me, I don't wish to argue."

"And you love me."

He smiled. "Yes, I love you, Sarah Dearly."

"Then everything is perfect."

My heart swelled almost enough to burst. So I said nothing else, and instead hugged him tightly, my mouth meeting his in another kiss that left nothing unsaid, with nothing restrained. I knew nothing could ruin this moment. It was perfect. My fractured fairy tale come to life.

His cell phone rang and I leaned back, reached into his inner jacket pocket to pull it out, and held the call display up for him to see.

He raised an eyebrow at me. "It's my wife."

I grimaced. Well, maybe things weren't *that* perfect.

"Don't answer it," he said.

"I wasn't planning to."

I saw motion off to the right. George and Quinn were coming toward us, limping slightly and rubbing their heads.

"What in the hell happened?" Quinn asked.

"My brain feels like it's going to explode," George said. "And not in a good way."

"You both got shot with garlic darts," I told them.

George sniffed his shirt. "That would explain why I smell like a Caesar salad."

"Janie," Quinn growled. "Where is that bitch now?"

I shrugged. "Gone."

His jaw tensed. "She's damn lucky. If I ever get my hands on her she'll be very sorry."

"So," George said. "Were asses kicked?"

"Sort of," I said. "Turned out that Gideon wasn't all that interested in me after all. It was all Nicolai. He was nuts. Wanted to kill me in front of Thierry."

"Gideon Chase," Quinn repeated, "is still interested. I'm sure of it. He's no good."

"There's a newsflash."

"Where's Nicolai now?" Quinn asked.

I nodded over at the stain. "He exited stage left. Permanently."

Quinn eyed me and Thierry. "So are you two—?"

I nodded.

He looked away. "Good. Then I guess there's nothing left to do around here." He leaned over and picked up the key that Janie had left behind. "I assume this belongs to you?"

I took the key from him and worked on Thierry's handcuffs for a moment before they snapped open.

Then I checked my watch. "You know, the party's probably still going on."

"We must leave immediately," George said. "Cake would be greatly appreciated. Unless there's anything else you'd like to do to almost get us killed, Sarah? Is there?"

I shook my head. "No, this should about do it for tonight."

"Hallelujah."

When we got back to Haven, nobody had even noticed that we'd been gone. Which was good, though it was also a little bit disappointing to realize we were not the life of the party. We decided not to fill anybody in on what had transpired in the past couple of hours. At least not yet.

Thierry had definitely sold the club. That couldn't be changed. But it was okay. No club meant he would do something different. We'd do something different. Or nothing at all. It didn't matter, as long as we did it together.

Starting with my moving in with him. George had told me in no uncertain terms that while he did enjoy my company on a temporary basis, we were not going to be roommates forever. So I'd decided to move in with Thierry. He didn't exactly know this yet, but he couldn't possibly have a problem with that, could he? Don't answer that.

I gave Amy the gold necklace as her birthday gift. She took one look at it, said thank you, and slid in into her pocket instead of putting it on. It was really ugly, and she was more of a platinum kind of girl. I felt certain that whatever it was would be safely kept locked away in her jewelry box from that day forward and never worn in public. Passing the buck? Maybe a little bit. I knew where to find it if I ever needed it, though I couldn't imagine why I would.

Quinn seemed to make his peace with me and Thierry being together. I don't think he liked it, but peace had been made. I introduced him to Barkley the werewolf at the party, and the two kind of hit it off. Since Quinn had an itch to get out of the country—possibly to get as far away from me as possible, imagine that—he'd volunteered to drive Barkley (who was apparently deathly afraid of airplanes) down to Arizona to rejoin his werewolf pack. They'd split gas money. I was going to miss them. Both of them. Although those 3:00 A.M. trips out to take Barkley for a walk I wouldn't miss. Quinn was a little less high maintenance that way.

I did wonder if this Gideon Chase guy I'd been hearing so much about was really interested in me. It wouldn't be long before the truth that I wasn't anything all that special got to him, right? Then he'd find something else to interest him. At least I hoped so. He didn't sound like the kind of guy I ever wanted a face-to-face meeting with. Thinking about that would keep me up at night worrying. And I had enough things to worry about.

For example, my ten-year high school reunion was coming up very soon. Thierry insists that I leave my old life behind, but I wonder if he'd mind if I went to it, just for old time's sake. Maybe he could come too. I'd use the opportunity to introduce him to my parents as my much, much older, married vampire boyfriend who turns into a blood-crazed monster when he gets a taste of the red stuff. And that I was crazy in love with him. Oh, and that by the way, I was a vampire, too. They'd be happy for me, right?

Time would have to tell on that one.

But I'd face all of that after the party.

Thierry approached me and slid an arm around my waist to draw me closer to him. Still not wearing the party hat. Also, not a big fan of dance music, strangely enough.

"You know, Sarah," he said, "there are a great many problems we still have to resolve. The life of a vampire is not easy, and seems to grow more difficult every day."

I traced a hand across his chest to find that his heart was beating as fast as mine was.

"You sweet talker, you. Let's just face our problems one at a time. Together." I stood up on my tiptoes to kiss him. A kiss he returned with a passion that curled my toes. "But do you think we can worry about it tomorrow?"

He smiled wide enough that I caught a glimpse of his fangs. "Yes, Sarah. Tomorrow."

And it sounded like a promise.

Acknowledgments

Thank you to my editor Melanie Murray and my agent Jim McCarthy. What would I do without you two fabulous people?

Congratulations to the fabulous WRITE-ONS! who wrote and finished their fabulous books while I wrote F&F: Deborah Beckers, Kate Cannon, Fanney, Heather Harper, Mel Hiers, Kayla Hill, Alyssa Hurzeler, J. Madden, May, Yolanda Sfetsos, and Bonnie Staring.

Thank you also to Tim Hortons. Without your large double-doubles, I don't know if I'd want to carry on.

Turn the page for a sneak peek at the next novel in
the Immortality Bites series, *Lady & The Vamp*

Chapter 1

It was none of his business, but that never stopped him before.

Quinn watched from the shadows as the two hunters approached, moving stealthfully through the dark parking lot of the roadside restaurant, until they had their prey cornered. He wanted to ignore what he was seeing, turn away and head back to the car, but that wasn't going to happen.

He approached silently from behind the hunters.

"Need any help?" he asked.

They spun around to face him. One was large with thick forearms and a scuff of beard that looked to be there more from laziness than fashion sense. The other was younger, thinner, with round glasses that magnified his eyes to twice their size. A rather unlikely dynamic duo at first glance.

"Get lost," the large one said.

Quinn shrugged. "I can take a hint. No problem."

He turned away.

Forget it, he told himself. *Just walk away. You've got more important things to think about.*

But then he turned and glanced at the pair of vampires who'd just been trapped in the Burger King parking lot near the garbage Dumpster—a male and female who could have been anywhere from 20 to 200 years old in his opinion. You just couldn't tell about that sort of thing. They looked back at him with wide, terrified eyes.

"Please, help us," the female pleaded.

She was cute. Small and blond. Looked like a college student out on a date with her dark haired, wide-eyed boyfriend who was bravely shielding her from the hunters with his own body. Almost couldn't see the fangs unless you were looking for them.

"Help a vampire?" Quinn said with a laugh. "Why would I want to do a crazy thing like that?"

"Hey—" the younger hunter moved the wooden stake to his other hand. "I think I know you. Don't I? You're Roger Quinn's kid, Michael. Yeah, we met a couple years back. Toasted a nest of vamps up in St. Louis."

Quinn turned to the guy and tried to see the face behind those large glasses. He didn't look familiar. Then again, he'd drunk a lot when he was in St. Louis. Bad month and a half. Beer helped. "Sure. Good to see you again."

"Yeah, you too, man." He scratched absently at his leg with the stake. The vampires, who now clutched at each other for support, eyed the deadly sharp weapon with trepidation. The hunter turned to his friend. "Quinn here's one of the best hunters I've ever seen. Got a nose for vamps. Can smell them in any corner they try to hide."

Quinn waved his hand. "Aw, you're just saying that."

"I'm Joe, remember? This here's my buddy Stuart. Listen, you can totally help us out. These are our first two tonight. I figure they were lying in wait for victims coming out of the restaurant." He poked the male vampire in the chest as his magnified eyes narrowed. "That what you're doing? Looking for a little snack, you bloodsucking freak?"

The vampire set his jaw and tried to look brave. It wasn't working very well.

"Well, you know vamps." Quinn eyed the restaurant as a car that had just gone through the drive-thru left through the far exit to merge back into the highway. "Evil to the core."

"You live around here?"

He shook his head. "Just passing through town. Stopped for a bite."

"Hey," the larger hunter spoke up. He was frowning. "You're Michael Quinn?"

"That's right."

"Please," the female vampire's voice shook. "We're not evil. We just wanted some dinner."

"Yeah," Stuart snarled. "From unassuming victims. Their blood."

"No, a chocolate milkshake." She shivered. "I don't need any blood right now."

The other licked his lips nervously. "I got Chicken Fries. With dip. Just leave us alone."

"Bloodsucking freak," Stuart snapped. "Vampires don't eat solid food."

"Some of us do," the female offered.

"Shut up." Then he turned back to Quinn. "I feel like

I've heard something about you recently. I'm just trying to figure out what it is."

Quinn crossed his arms and tried to ignore the pleading look the female vampire was giving him. "Oh yeah? Something important?"

"I feel like it was. But what was it?" He scratched his chin.

"Well," Quinn began. "You may have heard that I've recently retired from hunting vampires."

Stuart nodded. "Yeah, that sounds right. But there was something else." His brow furrowed, and then his gaze shot up. "Wait a minute. I remember. You . . . you're a—"

Quinn punched him in the face. "Bloodsucking freak?"

The hunter howled and covered his nose that had started to gush blood.

Joe tensed and raised his stake. Quinn turned and kicked him in the stomach. He staggered backward and banged his head on the Dumpster, knocking him immediately unconscious. The stake clattered to the ground.

Stuart looked up, holding his nose.

Quinn flashed fangs at him. "I've also lost a lot of friends recently. For some reason they're not speaking to me anymore. I wonder why?"

The vampires huddled together, frozen in place, watching with wide eyes.

Stuart rushed Quinn. Quinn grabbed the stake out of his hand and then flipped the hunter over his hip.

Quinn crouched down to press the stake against his neck. "Like I said, I'm just passing through town. I strongly suggest you do the same."

The hunter gurgled.

"Doesn't feel so good, does it? I've had a change of heart recently about killing vampires. Why don't I let you guess why that is?"

"Don't kill me!" he begged.

Quinn pulled the stake away. "The next time you're out hunting, just remember one of the bloodsucking freaks let you live. Got it?"

The hunter nodded, holding a shaky hand to his neck, fear naked in his eyes.

"Now take your little bespectacled buddy and get the hell out of here."

Joe was beginning to regain consciousness. Stuart grabbed his shirt and the two of them staggered away. Quickly.

Very quickly.

Quinn watched them run.

Amateurs. Could spot them from a mile away.

"Holy shit, Quinn," a voice said from his right. He looked over. Matthew Barkley had just emerged from inside of the restaurant carrying a large bag filled with fast food. Quinn breathed in and with his newly heightened vampire's senses could immediately tell it was two Whoppers with cheese and a large—no, an *extra* large—fries. The smell of solid food made him feel a little queasy. Some vamps could still eat solid food. Unfortunately, he wasn't one of them. "I thought you were going to wait in the car."

"I needed to stretch my legs."

"Were those hunters?"

"They were trying to be."

"You just kicked their asses?"

Quinn shrugged.

"Nice." Barkley nodded. "Good to see you're not a big fan of your old buddies. I guess that makes total sense."

The vampires approached timidly.

"Thank you so much for saving us," the female said. "We didn't know what to do. How can we ever thank you?"

Quinn didn't look at them. "You can start by staying the hell away from me."

"But we—"

"Go away," Quinn snarled.

They glanced at each other, and then turned and ran in the opposite direction from the hunters.

Barkley had started to eat one of his Whoppers. He chewed thoughtfully before speaking. "And you don't like vamps either. That actually *doesn't* make sense. You're okay with werewolves, though, right?"

"Don't worry, I'm not going to run you off too."

"Good to know. You ready to leave, or what? We need to put in a couple hundred more miles before we can grab some sleep."

Quinn's heart was beating hard in his chest. He felt a little ill, actually. Cold and clammy. "I just need a minute. I'll be right back."

"I'll be in the car. Eating a great deal of food."

Quinn made his way to the public washroom in the restaurant to splash some cold water on his face. He clutched the side of the sink until his knuckles whitened.

Keep it together, he told himself.

Christ. Two months as a vampire now and it wasn't getting any easier. When was it going to get easier?

Soon. Very soon.

He touched his pocket to feel the reassuring outline of the letter and immediately felt his heartbeat come back down to the normal rate for a thirty-year-old freshly made vamp. *The letter*. The only thing from his father's many possessions that he'd cared about after the old man died.

The letter was going to lead him directly to his answer. Solve all of his problems.

He just had to be patient. Just a little while longer.

Nobody knew about it. Not one soul. His father had spent a good part of his adult life—the part that wasn't concerned with hunting down and killing vampires—in his search for the *Eye*. Quinn knew why he'd never been able to find it. It was because the timing was all wrong.

Now it was right. And the Eye was Quinn's.

Then none of this would matter anymore. He could fix this mess he'd gotten himself into once and for all.

He looked up into the mirror that reflected nothing but the washroom behind him. When he bared his teeth he couldn't even see the fangs he knew were there.

With one smash of his fist he shattered the mirror.

The door opened. A young kid in a Burger King uniform poked his head in. "Everything okay in here, mister?"

Quinn growled at him.

The kid gave an uneasy smile as he assessed the damage. "Never mind." The door closed.

Quinn took a deep breath and closed his tired eyes.

Not much longer and he wouldn't have to be a monster anymore.

Janie Parker was going to die.

Accepting it, she thought, *really is half the battle.*

Also drinking four vodka martinis for lunch before it's going to happen helps. A bit.

"He'll see you now," a voice said.

She nodded. Okay. Showtime.

She stood up from the sofa in the waiting area and walked the long hallway to her boss's office. The walls were lined with the photos of other employees. On the left side of the hallway were the stars. The people who'd never failed at a job. For them, the sky was the limit. They could have anything they wanted: money, power, influence.

Anything they wanted except the opportunity to quit. Ever.

Along the right side were the employees that had messed up a job. Failed on an assignment.

They hadn't needed to quit.

They would have had an appointment with the boss just like the one she was about to have. Then their photo would be moved from one side of the hallway to the other.

She had always known a place that had "burial options" on the application form had a few potential human resource issues.

Janie had had two meetings with her boss prior to this one. The first had been when her very ex-boyfriend had tricked her into taking his place at The Company (which was what the organization was known as to those unfortunate enough to know it even existed). He'd been able to trick her because she'd imagined herself in love with the good-looking creep. He'd been so convincing and charming that she'd signed the dotted line happily. A little less happily when she realized she had to sign in blood, but

still. He promised that they would work there together.
The jerk lied. He took off late one night when she was
fast asleep and she never saw him again. He'd managed
to beat the system.

Now she *was* the system.

The second time she'd had a meeting with her boss
had been a year ago when her previous partner screwed
up a job and tried to blame it on Janie. They'd both been
dragged in on the carpet where the boss had been very
calm in listening to their explanations before cleanly and
efficiently decapitating her partner right in front of her.

Janie swallowed hard. She'd liked her old partner.
Trusted her like she hadn't trusted anyone in years. It just
showed how people change when faced with owning up
to their failures. Not to mention having their heads
chopped off.

She didn't trust anybody anymore.

Since that unfortunate incident she'd been an exem-
plary employee. Doing everything she was told.
Whenever she was told. Wherever she was told. Gritting
her teeth over the unpleasant jobs. Since most of the jobs
she had to do were unpleasant she was afraid her teeth
were going to be ground down to nothing but stubs very
soon. But the image of her last partner's untimely death
haunted her. The Boss was nobody to mess with. Nobody
to let down.

And she'd done just that.

She'd very recently let a job slip through her fingers.
Just a regular retrieval of a magical piece of jewelry. She
didn't know what it was or what it did, only that her boss
wanted her to pick it up and bring it back to him.

She'd failed. Accidentally, on purpose. She was sick of

the bullshit. She knew there was only one way out of this job, and that's the route she was taking.

But now that the moment had arrived, she was shaking in her brand new Jimmy Choos.

"Get in here," the Boss growled from behind the slightly ajar door.

She painted on her best fake smile and pushed open the door. "Hey there, boss man. Good to see you. You look fantastic."

He didn't, but Janie knew she normally was a good enough liar to pull it off. He was a tiny little shrew of a man. Skinny and frail-looking, with hollow cheekbones. He reminded her a little of a live action Mr. Burns from *The Simpsons*. Only meaner. And older. And much less yellow.

"Save the compliments for your next life, Parker."

"Listen, boss, I can explain everything."

He waved his bony hand. "You can save that too. Come closer."

Janie swallowed, then commanded her feet to start moving. She wanted this. It would only hurt for a second. She hoped. After she was dead, she'd be free from this lonely, disappointing, horrific life once and for all. It was the best decision. Suicide by proxy.

She'd miss her new shoes, but that was about it.

It seemed like it took about two hours for her to reach his desk.

"I'm sorry," she heard herself squeak then mentally kicked herself. *Shut up*.

He stared at her with watery, pale grey eyes. His hand slipped down into the drawer on the right hand side of his black-as-pitch monster of a desk.

What was he reaching for? A gun? A knife? A vial of acid? A bowl of piranha?

She squeezed her eyes shut and braced herself for impact. Nothing happened.

"Take a look at this," the boss said.

She tentatively pried one eye open, and then the other and looked down. On the surface of the desk was a color drawing of a small crystal sphere almost completely enclosed by a spider web-like filigree of silver at the top of an ornate golden wand.

She forced the smile back to her face. "Is somebody thinking about going out as Harry Potter next Halloween? It's only January but I always say it's good to plan ahead. You will look adorable, I think."

He tapped the drawing. "I want this. And I want you to get it for me."

"You want me—" She paused. "But I thought I was here for—"

He shook his wrinkled head. "You're a failure, Parker. A disgusting waste of space. But I'm willing to give you one more chance. Retrieve the Eye for me and all is forgiven."

"With that kind of a build up, how can I possibly refuse?" She snatched the drawing off the desk and looked at it closer. "Why's it called the Eye?"

A grin twisted on his face. "You don't have to know anything more than what I will tell you to retrieve it. There is one who has a map to its location. It was foreseen just this morning. A vampire who wishes to use the Eye's power for his own gain. Follow the vampire and you will find the Eye. Bring it to me before Friday at the stroke of midnight. This is all I ask."

"Sounds simple enough. And if the vamp gives me any problems?"

"Kill him."

Janie took a deep breath and let it out slowly. "Is he evil?"

"Does it matter?"

She hesitated. *Don't mess this up, dumbass.* "Of course not."

"Then there is no problem." He leaned back in his huge black leather chair, his gaze still uncomfortably fixed on Janie. "The vampire drives with an acquaintance, a werewolf, en route to Arizona." He pushed a piece of paper toward her. "You will find them there tomorrow at noon."

She picked it up, glanced at the address, and then tucked it into her pocket along with the drawing. "Then I guess I'll be on my way." She turned her back.

"Parker."

She froze, then twisted around to face the man who had the starring role in most of her nightmares. "Uh huh?"

"In case you were thinking about failing again, just know to do so would displease me greatly."

"I understand."

"Do you?" That hand slipped down into the drawer again and he pulled out a photo, then placed it on the top of his desk. "Your own life may mean little to you, but should you disappoint me again there are other punishments I can think of."

Janie drew closer to the desk and looked down at the photo of a pretty blond woman and her heart nearly stopped. It was her younger sister Angela, who had disappeared five years ago just after her eighteenth birthday. She'd searched non-stop for over a year, but found no clues to where she'd gone. After that she'd convinced herself Angela was dead, just like the rest of her family.

Her eyes flicked up to meet the evil ones of her boss from hell.

"Where is she?" Her voice was barely a gasp.

He spread his hands. "Bring me the Eye and we will discuss the matter further. Fail me and she will take your punishment. And I promise you, I will not be merciful. Do you understand?"

Janie fought back the stinging tears that threatened to escape. Shit. She hadn't cried in years. Her lips thinned and she nodded at the bastard with one jerk of her head. "I understand."

"By Friday at midnight, or you will watch your sister die."

She grabbed the photo and jammed it into her pocket, then stormed out of the office, slamming the door behind her. She turned and braced herself against the door frame and tried to calm herself down.

Her little sister was alive. The idea thrilled her and filled her with so much dread she couldn't contain it. Her parents had died when she was just a teenager. Her brother had abandoned her to become a vampire hunter until he'd gotten himself killed a couple months ago. She'd thought she was all alone in the world. Sure as hell had felt like it. Maybe that's why she'd latched onto the loser who'd roped her into working for the Company to begin with.

The penalty for failure was huge. But the payoff was even bigger if she was successful. And how couldn't she be? It was just a regular retrieval. She was one of the best at that. She'd grab her current partner, Lenny, and the two of them would leave immediately.

She'd kill a hundred nasty vampires for the chance to find out where her sister was.

One little vampire wouldn't be any problem at all.

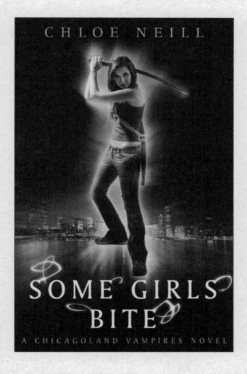

Michelle Rowen was born in Toronto, Ontario. As a child she decided that when she grew up she would become a flight attendant, a jewel thief, and a writer. One out of three ain't bad. She is a self-confessed bibliophile, the proud owner of an evil cat named Nikita, a Reality TV junkie, and has an unhealthy relationship with anything to do with *Buffy the Vampire Slayer*. She currently lives in Mississauga, Ontario.

Visit Michelle's website at www.michellerowen.com.